THE
WILD
FALL

THE WILD FALL

BY

KATHERINE SILVA

Strange Wilds Press

Copyright © 2023 by Katherine Silva

Print ISBN-13: 979-8-218-17503-0
Ebook ISBN-13: 979-8-218-17504-7

All rights reserved. No part of this book may be reproduced in any form or by any electronic or mechanical means including information storage and retrieval systems, without the permission in writing from the author, except by a reviewer, who may quote brief passages.

This book is a work of fiction. Anything that bears resemblance to real people, places, or events is coincidental and unintentional.

ADVANCE READERS COPY

Content warning: This book contains animal abuse, blood, bones, child death, cults, death, decapitation, depression, drugs, fire, gore, gun violence, hostages, kidnapping, murder, occult, profanity, PTSD, skeletons, suicide, violence.

Published by Strange Wilds Press

Kindle first edition: August 3rd, 2023
Print first edition: August 3rd, 2023

Cover design by Katherine Silva
www.katherinesilvaauthor.com
Strange Wilds Press Logo by MartaLeo

Cover photos courtesy of Pexels and Unsplash

"It is part of the nature of every definitive love that sooner or later it can reach the beloved only in infinity."- Rainer Maria Rilke

More books from Katherine Silva

<u>The Wild Oblivion</u>
THE WILD DARK
HALLOWED OBLIVION
ORCHARDS
DAN & ANDY'S SCARY-OKE HOLIDAY

<u>The Monstrum Chronicles</u>
VOX
AEQUITAS
MEMENTO MORI
ACQUOLINA

<u>Other Works</u>
THE COLLECTION
NIGHT TIME, DOTTED LINE

ONE

Liz

There was snow. There was always snow when I remembered Brody. The moment I let my eyes close, he was there with me. Flakes whisked over us in chaotic majesty, muting the streetlights over us as we drove, his warm fingers clutching mine. I didn't know where or when we were, only that we were together and this reality was impossible. Brody was long gone from my life.

A car horn honking made me open my eyes to slanted sun streaks on cracked pavement. The driver's seat of the Jeep was weathered and comfortable and I'd nearly drifted off to dreams while I waited. The sun was almost a myth now, departing toward the trees on the horizon. The line for supplies at the old Pontiac van had dwindled as it always did right before dusk. No one wanted to get caught out after dark: not here in this deserted town in the New England wilderness.

Climbing out of the Jeep, I crossed the street to become the last in line for the traveling supply wagon. Raheem's operation was known throughout the White Mountains. He was the only person willing to drive there from the government-run city of Gideon, formerly known as Boston. The wilderness was unpredictable to most of the people left. It could sneak up on you; it could kill you. Better to be safe in the confines of brick and mortar than risk death out here. Unless living out here was safer than in there...

Raheem closed a hard cooler in the backseat as I made myself known. "Was wondering when you were going to show yourself," he said, not turning to look at me. "You're cutting it kind of close."

I glanced toward the setting sun. "My list is short this time."

He finally turned to look at me and scratched at his scraggly beard. "You know the rules. What are you offering?"

I swung my pack off my back and unzipped the main pouch. Reaching in, I pulled out a loaf wrapped tightly in aluminum foil. "Zucchini bread."

His eyes danced. "Zucchini? You're shitting me."

GRCs like Gideon didn't have much farmland. Fruits and vegetables were scarce, sometimes only available if shipping routes were clear between cities. Since the Merging began ten years ago, most of the farmland in New England was now dominated by the Woods. There was no clearing it, no taking back any of the land for cultivation. And no one dared try.

"And," I pulled a Ziploc bag of brown powder out.

"No..." He stiffened in his seat. "Don't tell me that's chocolate..."

"Cocoa powder. We've been saving it."

Raheem reached for it.

I stepped back. "Your turn."

He scoffed and snapped open his glove box. As he rifled around inside, I listened to the sounds of evening as they unfurled around me. Crickets became a symphony amidst the blooming haze of night.

Raheem produced a rolled-up brown paper bag and handed it to me. "Antibiotics for a kidney infection, iodine, toothpaste, permethrin for the ticks... Stuff isn't cheap. Getting it nearly cost me the whole operation."

"And?"

He shook his head. "I don't think you're listening. You of all people should know what it would mean if I got locked up. You'd lose your only access to Gideon, to the only civility within a hundred miles. You wouldn't get medicine; you wouldn't get the information you need to keep surviving out here playing colonist like you do."

"That's what it feels like to be excluded, Raheem, or had you forgotten the way things used to be?"

His gaze narrowed. "Fuck you. You're excluded from Gideon because you chose to be; not because people were racist pricks."

I didn't say anything, choosing to stare at the ground rather than acknowledge his point. He and I both knew despite communities being forced to coexist in GRCs like one big happy family for the last several years, people still carried all their old prejudices; all their old hang-ups and distrusts. There would always be racists. There would always be bigots, misogynists, transphobes… And we would always see them pricking at communities like forgotten pins in sewn clothing.

"My point," Raheem said, clearing his throat, "was if I get thrown in detainment, you'll have to consider changing your lifestyle."

I hadn't chosen to avoid Gideon because of social differences. If any trackers knew who I was, they would put me in containment, locked in a lab to study. But Raheem didn't need to know that. In fact, the fewer people who knew, the better.

"Gretchen will be grateful for the meds," I answered, looking over everything in the bag. "It was looking bad without them. Thank you."

"Okay, then. It's your funeral."

I handed him the shopping list for next week. Raheem glanced it over quickly, his eyes intermittently peeking at the horizon. "Chickpeas?"

"For Nettie."

His eyes softened. "Anything for her. If she keeps making me bread, I'll keep bringing her all the random shit she needs." He read farther down the list. "Light bulbs, blah, blah, blah…Does that say 'condoms?'"

I rolled my eyes. "Ash has a sense of humor. Forget him."

Raheem nodded and turned over the engine in his van. A small jolt of panic raced through me with the sudden noise. I considered my return to the cabin. I needed to head back now.

Then, he said something else. "There's something I think you should know, too."

An owl called across the sky. "What?"

"I heard someone mention that guy you were looking for: Astor."

I let my pack thud to the ground as his words hit me. "Where? When?"

"The last camp I stopped at: about eight miles west of here. They said he stayed with them for a while. Left something there for a redhead named Elizabeth." He glanced me up and down. "Suppose she's probably you."

I'd given Raheem a fake name, not wanting my identity to be discovered. Again: it was safer keeping our interactions to the basics. The fact he now knew my name meant the report was probably true. I could barely believe it. I'd spent ten long years looking for Astor and had only heard whisperings of his whereabouts. It was hard to think he had been within eight miles of me and was already gone. "Do you know where he went?"

"I'm guessing it's in the note he left you. I was heading this way, so I brought it. It's in the bag I gave you with the meds."

I desperately uncurled the bag again and dove my hand in. Soon, I was staring at a tri-folded piece of notebook paper, dirtied, but scribbled on in pencil. "Thanks."

Raheem nodded. "I'll see you in a couple weeks. But not here."

I swallowed. "You saw?"

"The Woods are closer: too close. I won't do this spot again. I'll meet you in Onyx River?"

It was the name Astor had written on the paper he'd left me. In fact, it was the only thing on the paper at all. "Where is that?"

"On the Vermont border. The group Astor was staying with packed and moved there. Supposed to be self-sufficient, off the grid. Not like the GRCs. I suggest going there, too."

"The Vermont border is a day's journey from here. That's farther than we can afford to travel for supplies."

"Then maybe you should resettle there, too." He put the van in gear and stepped on the pedal. "Get home!"

The van rolled out of the town square and around a turn in the road. Dirt kicked up into clouds behind it.

The Jeep bumped over the washboard ripples of the mountain road as I drove. Each shake upped my anxiousness. We'd run out of time here. I knew it had been foolish to think this place would be a refuge for us because of some lingering nostalgia I had for it. But the feeling of home had sunken into my skin like warm oil over the months and then the years.

A long time ago, my family owned the cabin in Middlehitch, New Hampshire. We'd vacation there in the summer; whenever we could get away from the urban sprawl that was home. My dad used to tell a story about how his grandmother's family owned the cabin and vacationed there back at the turn of the century. His grandfather vacationed at one of the neighboring cabins. They met, wrote love letters back and forth to one another. This was where the Raleigh family tree began, bolstered by summer romance.

This is also where it ended.

THE WILD FALL

My last memories of this place as a child were of packing our car with our belongings which echoed with Dad's presence. Mom couldn't afford to keep the cabin itself. She sold it to someone; never found out who. They took it apart, insulated the walls, installed wiring and plumbing (it had neither when we used to visit). But the bones remained, the promise of hope spread like tendrils of light from its sunny walls. When I brought our group here three years ago, I let myself be blinded by it.

The Jeep hit a pothole and jarred me back into the present. I had to pay attention. I couldn't afford to crack a wheel axle on the old car, not now. We were lucky to have a working vehicle at all.

The crunching of pebbles and dirt abated as I came to the only paved section of the road running alongside the old hotel.

The Highhall Mountain House was an inn known for its preened golf courses, an unimpeded view of the White Mountains in all their glory, for luxury in a small-town quaint setting… Sometime around when the Merging happened, a fire broke out inside. The majority of the Highhall Mountain House burned and left a charred skeleton in its wake. I'd never been inside, but every time I'd driven by as a kid, I'd imagined exploring its long-carpeted corridors, riding in the old-fashioned cage elevator and peeking into all the off-limits places like a modern-day Eleanor.

Back to dirt road. We, me and the car, ascended again. I wanted to force myself to ignore what I knew was coming, wanted to keep my eyes fixed on the gnarly road ahead. But the field opened and my eyes drifted there.

The Woods were growing: ever morphing the land, chewing through the old cow pastures, fields of wildflowers, and eviscerating human civilization as we knew it. Six or seven oak trees used to pass off into the distance with a hand-built rock wall beside them. From there, a deciduous forest had rippled through the hills beyond. That wasn't visible now.

A swath of evergreens stood before me, shrouded by a darkness oozing from between the crowded tree trunks. Once, these forests had appeared like green portals amidst the New England winter, warming the areas subtly, inviting unsuspecting people into their jungles. As time went by, they lost their vibrancy and any allure they might have exuded.

The darkness from the Woods eventually faded and the pink sunset returned as I climbed higher. After another few minutes, I pulled the Jeep off the road into the driveway of a two-story, pale yellow cabin with a green metal roof and a wrap-around deck. I cut the engine and took a moment to listen to the dogs as they yipped in the barn next to me, the sounds of the perimeter fires crackling as Ash fed them more wood, the song of the crickets chirping from the blonde grass in our field…

I would miss this.

Climbing out of the car with my pack, I waved to Ash across the lawn as he lit the last signal fire, nodded to Gjon as he disappeared inside the barn to feed the dogs, and stepped on to the weather-beaten boards of the covered deck. Inside the house was warm harmony: the sounds of Richard plucking out a tune on his guitar, distant laughter from the kitchen, the smell of vine-ripened tomatoes stewing in a pot…

"*Liz.*"

Something touched my hand.

I flinched. Nothing but a lilting moth, attracted by the solar lights as they popped on around me. I shoved my hand into the cotton of my pocket. It wiped the feeling of contact from my mind, the idea it had been anything other than something real just now. I opened the screen door, and then the main one inside.

The front entry was a parade of dirt-covered boots, of tattered jackets, rucksacks and rain suits, crowded on hooks on the wall under the stairs. The boards creaked overhead. The door at the top of the steps opened and Gretchen appeared. She'd likely been waiting for me to come back.

I met her halfway up the stairs, my hand already in the bag rifling around for the antibiotics. "Here. One a day for the next five days at least. That should do the trick."

She grunted as she popped the cap and swallowed one. "Thank fuck. I was starting to think this was how I was going to die."

I smirked. "Don't be dramatic."

"Nah, you'd have dropped my ass at the front door to Gideon and sped off." The look in her eyes told me she was joking, but we both knew small infections were life-threatening out here. Things that could be solved with a trip to the hospital or doctor's office back in the day weren't easily remedied in a world without access to synthetic medicine. The herbs we stored and used worked for some things but there were injuries and ailments we couldn't cure without help.

I had hated hospitals. I'd spent too much time at them back in the day. A memory reached out to me like a hand on my shoulder: me standing under a pale light in a parking lot. Brody emerging from the emergency room doors with a bandage on his head. He'd fallen while we'd chased a perp through the woods. Got a concussion. All because he was trying to keep up with me...

"...And you aren't listening to a damn thing I'm saying, are you?"

"Sorry." I couldn't excuse the wandering mind: not today. After all, if I didn't allow myself to think about him today, when would I?

"Ash mentioned the Woods are closer. He's getting antsy. You know what he's like."

I raised my eyebrows. "We need to have a meeting. I need to talk to Hank first."

Gretchen seethed as she held her lower back and sat on the top step. "He's in the kitchen with Miss Thing. It's a wonder they're not having sex on the kitchen table with all the noise they've made. A girl's gotta sleep sometime..."

I cocked my head. "Least you could do is be happy for them."

She took a deep breath. "It's not me who has a problem with it."

People finding kindred spirits, others to connect with, was part of being human, a part of surviving the day-to-day grind the Woods had caused us ever since the Merging. Everyone in our party thrived on connection, on trusting each other as family and knew at any moment, someone could be stolen away. Some of us got even closer. And some of us didn't understand it. Hank's daughter, Evie, was one of the latter.

"Where is she?" I asked.

"Last I checked, she took Tempest for a walk to get out of the house."

I glanced at the boots and noticed hers weren't there, nor was her jacket.

"She knows the risks," Gretchen said, before I could get a word out. "She'll be back."

I knew Evie wouldn't delay. She'd seen first-hand what it was like to get caught out after dark, had experienced years of it as she grew up in this frightening new reality. Now, at sixteen, it was her normal. She'd officially lived the majority of her life in this; more than anyone else here.

"But, you'd better distract Hank before he finds out she left. He won't be as cavalier about it as we are."

I nodded before descending the steps and threading along the crowded hallway to the kitchen.

Hank was laughing as I emerged in the kitchen door, his body convulsing with the movement. He barely looked the same as when I met him ten years ago on my cabin's front porch in the woods. His hair was longer and a silvery black beard coated his chin and covered the scar on his upper lip. The crow's feet around his eyes had deepened, as well as the creases by his nose whenever he smiled. The soft clarity to his green eyes remained, a trait that made me focus when everything was spinning out of control around me. Hank was consistently my root to the earth.

"And I remembered looking at them and thinking, 'Okay. Not how I was imagining this would go…'" he said between chuckles.

"Sounds like you got the wrong impression, darling," Nettie said from her stance at the stove, a large grin pulling her lips apart. She was a little woman, barely five feet tall with dark hair pulled up in a kerchief. Steam pillowed the space above a pot of bubbling sauce as she stirred it methodically.

He reached out to her and somehow, blindly, she knew and took his hand, all the while keeping her attention on cooking the meal. He pressed his lips to her fingers.

I cleared my throat as I took a step into the kitchen.

Hank glanced at me. "You're back."

"There was a long line today. Word about Raheem is spreading." I looked to Nettie. "He about died when I gave him the zucchini bread, by the way."

Nettie smiled shyly. "I'll take that as a compliment."

"Give us a minute, Net." Hank followed me into the dark hallway. The sound of boiling water faded and was soon invaded by the haphazard strums from Richard in the living room. Outside, the dogs still barked. This was the closest we could come to quiet in our small home, the closest to privacy.

"How did it go?"

"We've got problems," I said. "Raheem isn't coming back to this area. The Woods have invaded too close for comfort. He told me the closest camp to us has also picked up and moved. We're the last ones to leave."

Hank took a deep breath. "I'd hoped we could ride it out another six months but not at the rate it's coming. It's moved another ten yards since Monday. Suppose that's just the way of the Woods now. If we're going to follow suit, we have to do it now. Otherwise, we're looking at a long, ugly winter."

Winter. The season seeped into my body like a long illness. The cold and the dark lasted a little longer every year, in spite of the temperate forests overtaking the region. The last thing I wanted was for us to be eking out our existence without enough supplies somewhere new.

In the other room, Richard cussed as a string twanged off key. The tension slightly lessened, we suppressed laughs.

"Any idea where he's setting up shop next month?" Hank asked.

"He mentioned a place called Onyx River. You heard of it?"

"Once or twice." He hummed. "Supposed to be off the grid. One of those towns ran on renewable energy when the Merging happened. Wind and solar back in the day. No idea how it's doing now, though."

"Seems like people think it's worth it."

"Does this mean you're ready to finally join a larger community?"

I gritted my teeth at the question. I avoided people because larger groups led to larger problems. More people to watch, more people to manage, more people to feed and shelter… We could barely feed our own group of eight people and three dogs.

But if I wanted to find Astor, I'd have to get comfortable with living with more people. We all would.

Some of us longed for more companionship. Some of us would have a harder time adjusting. Most of us spent the years avoiding GRCs because of the bigotry that thrived in several of them.

"I want to be sure it's the right move first," I reasoned. "I think we should scout it out first. A small team can leave tomorrow, see if it's worth it. If it's safe, we can head there."

Hank cocked his head.

I frowned. "What?"

"Seems strange you're suddenly okay with the idea, which isn't like you at all."

I rolled my eyes. "There's the Hank I know…"

"The rest of us have spent time in a GRC for one reason or another and you're the only one who has actively avoided them. As much as I'd like to think it's just an aspect of your sparkling personality, there has to be something in Onyx River that warrants you socializing with another community."

The words irritated me; mostly because they were true. Hank didn't know about Astor. He didn't know about the fact I'd been Attached back in the day: I had seen the ghost of my former partner and friend. But I didn't want to have this conversation here and now. Not when today was the day I couldn't escape Brody's memory no matter how hard I tried.

I pressed on. "I want Ash to come."

"Good, he's been—"

"Wigging out?"

"Well surmised. Who else?"

"You. I could use a social butterfly to help make friends."

He grinned. "I couldn't help you make friends even if you paid me."

"I want Gjon, too."

"You sure you don't want to have him stay behind? Gretchen's been kind of touch-and-go, and it wouldn't be bad to leave the only one with certified medical training here…"

"She can handle it for a day. She's got antibiotics. I'm nervous about what we might encounter out there and I don't want to get blindsided."

Hank nodded. "Fine. What about—"

The front door opened behind me. A silver and black German Shepherd slipped through, tongue lolling happily. Behind her strode Evie: a petite girl swathed in her father's raggedy park ranger jacket and topped by a wide-brimmed canvas Tilly hat. She looked at us, her eyes large at being caught in the act of returning.

"Speak of the devil," Hank muttered. "Where did you go, Eves?"

"Out," she said as she kicked off her leather hiking boots.

"Where?"

"Chill, Dad." She slid out of her jacket and joined Richard in the living room.

Hank watched her go with furrowed brows.

"You seem troubled, Pops," I said, yanking him out of his melancholy.

"She's been staying out later and later..." he said under his breath.

"I think she's a sixteen-year-old exerting some independence." I glanced over my shoulder at her as she slumped into a chair, the dog circling into a tired ball at her feet.

"It's not safe out there after dark."

"She knows."

Hank leaned against the wall and stroked his beard. "I want to trust her. But we don't talk much anymore. Guess I've become too much of an old man for her?"

"I know I was all over the place as a teenager. Bet you were, too."

"Not sure I'd choose the phrase 'all over the place'..."

"My point is she's growing up. Also: she's a young woman and there are things you'll have trouble talking about no matter how close you are. For instance..." I thumbed toward the kitchen. "She might feel like she's got a rival for your attention."

Hank stared at his boots. "Nettie's been with us for over two years. Our relationship isn't new either."

He was right. I wasn't the only one who recognized the spark between the two of them.

Nettie had lived on an off-grid farm, growing her own vegetables, catching fish from the river and existing in total seclusion. A bad storm destroyed her nets and killed most of her crops. She'd have starved if she hadn't left and gone into the nearest town looking for supplies. She was lucky Hank was there foraging at the same time.

Since she'd joined the group, our lives had been enriched by her knowledge of canning and preserving, the joy she found in cooking, and her ability to make whatever we were about to eat, no matter if it was the same thing several nights in a row, taste incredible.

It was also a comfort to see Hank happy. I had known him for so long as the man who protected everyone else, showed patience no matter how exhausted he was, mercy no matter how much vitriol was slung at him for being the one who stated the things others would leave unsaid. He deserved every good thing left in the world as far as I could see.

"And Evie is still a kid figuring things out. Expect her not to understand and expect she might have some strong feelings about it."

Hank stared at me through his eyelashes and hummed: his signature approval. "Suppose you're right."

"Dinner is ready!" Nettie called.

Ash and Gjon came through the door, the last breaths of day settling from them as we all gathered around the dining room table.

We ate Nettie's spaghetti and vegetarian meatballs, made from cauliflower, by the comfort of the waning light over the kitchen sink. Ash, a craftsman, had fashioned a bench from some old wood in the barn. Both he, Gretchen, and Richard sat on it slurping their noodles enthusiastically.

Mealtimes were story times, times of wistfulness when someone was allowed to reach into the recesses of their former life and offer the group a recollection of something they experienced before the Merging. Something funny. Something uplifting. Something beautiful. One-of-a-kind, once-in-a-lifetime things we would never experience again. We were allowed to pretend things weren't as fucked up as they actually were.

Tonight, it was Ash telling us the story of how he accidentally met some well-known actor while working in a music store. We got lost in his words, imagining the glossy acoustic guitars, the snap of the drums, the sultry, brassy saxophones… We always got lots of detail in these stories, particularly because Evie had only been six when the Merging happened. There was a lot about our bygone world she never got to experience.

Evie sat in an oversized camping chair, picking through her dinner and occasionally sneaking a meatball to Tempest when she thought no one was watching.

Gjon eyed her and chuckled before digging out a cauliflower meatball to toss to Tempest as well.

The dog wolfed everything down within seconds, her golden eyes pleading for more. She didn't seem to care they weren't made of real meat.

It felt like being at summer camp, an aura of tenderness and mirth and the comfort of being close to friends tinged with the sadness of being away from home and those you love.

Outside, the night sky was a cascade of stars, trillions of speckles blooming across a navy and purple-swirled blanket. I leaned back in my chair near the window, my ears ever tuned to the darkness beyond. The signal fires at the edges of the property usually warded off any creatures, but there was always the chance one could get ballsy and sneak in closer.

And so, we weren't at ease during this seemingly typical dinner. Every single person knew what lurked beyond the light and every single one could be ready to run a moment's notice.

But it didn't happen. Not that evening anyway.

After dinner, we retired into the living room to drink our tea. Richard picked his guitar up and began strumming "Harvest Moon." His voice had a lower timbre than Neil Young's and his Scottish accent tweaked some of the words here and there. All in all, his version of the song was more upbeat, the kind of music the vibe called for that evening.

Hank knelt by Evie's chair, resting his head on her shoulder. They swayed back and forth in time with Richard's strumming.

I found my mind clouded with thoughts of Brody.

My friend. My love.

THE WILD FALL

It was August 3rd. If he was still alive, Brody would have turned fifty-eight.

He had died on a cold January day eleven years ago, bleeding from the throat on a sidewalk after being shot. The world stopped being normal that day.

The next November, he came back to me as a ghost when the Merging happened. Like most of the world, I thought I was going crazy, under the influence of some kind of hallucinogen or psychotic break. But it wasn't only me. Most of the world had succumbed to it.

With the ghosts came the Woods. With the Woods came the wolves.

Over time, I realized Brody wasn't the same person I knew and loved. He'd changed, become corrupted, to use a borrowed term. It became clear to me he would do anything to stay with me, to remember what it was like to be alive again. He even went as far as possessing my ex-fiancé, Josh.

So, I killed him.

I released his spirit for good.

Or at least, that's what I thought then.

When everyone had settled into bed for the night, I remained downstairs, watching the signal fires on the edges of the property dwindle. As long as we were all inside, asleep and quiet, we weren't a risk to the wolves who lingered in and around the Woods. But they weren't the only things creeping in the dark.

There was a figure, at the edge of the trees beside the road, a dark specter of the man I used to know. We'd stare at one another, each shielded by the night. This wasn't Brody though. This wasn't even the ghost attached to me I'd thought I'd vanquished. This was something far, far worse. He was something not even my nightmares could have conjured, because I didn't want to believe he'd become such a monster.

But there he was.

The thing that was Brody still haunted me.

TWO

I used to have nightmares and wake, remembering the shadow they left on me. Always sorrowful. Gruesome things. People I'd lost. Places I'd never see again. Experiences I'd never have again.

I didn't dream them anymore.

Instead, I dreamed of what life would have been like if Brody had never died. It is, by far, worse than anything I'd manufactured in my head before.

That night, I dreamed about us at the beach.

It was the end of summer. The tourists had returned to their houses in the city, leaving the white sand on the rocky coastline nearly empty. Pockets of people dawdled as the sun set. Two women played Frisbee. A boy made a sandcastle too close to the water and it was washed away with the incoming tide. Gulls cried and glided on the wuthering air.

Like most dreams, rational thoughts never occurred to me there. I didn't think about how we were openly together when he was technically still married, when acknowledging our relationship would have gotten one or both of us transferred or fired from our precinct. Nothing mattered except the sun and the water and how we were there together.

THE WILD FALL

He laid out our beach towels, planted the chairs in the sand. I read a book, though the words on the page were blurred. Brody lay on his back and soaked in the sun; his already olive complexion glistened. The white noise of the waves rolling in was our soundtrack. We walked and he held my hand, the slight grittiness of sand barely acknowledged between our fingers. The wet sand clung to my feet.

We were all alone. The sun was a sliver against the horizon. His gruff laughter unspooled mirth inside me I didn't think existed anymore.

Then, I awoke in the cabin. Evergreens rustled outside, Richard snored and Nettie talked in her sleep. The smell of dinner lingered, having filled the house only hours ago. My consciousness grasped a handful of sand from my dream; the grains slipped through my fingers with every passing second.

Soon, it was gone. Reality seeped in like a frost and filled all the warm, muddled parts of my head. Dawn stained the sky.

I got dressed, tied the laces on the long played-out running shoes, and stepped outside. The grass was speckled in early-morning dew. I went to the barn, and let the dogs out of their crates. They shook their bodies delightedly, eyes shining, waiting for our daily routine. When the sun came out, we ran. Even when didn't, we ran. They needed the exercise and I needed the ritual.

We waited until the light reached the dirt road and left. I breathed in the day: the expectation ahead, the charge of being alive, the comfort of the people I had around me. I breathed out the dreams; the night.

The dogs panted and galloped beside and ahead of me, the three of them acting as protectors as much as fitness partners. They would bark if something wasn't right, if danger was near.

"Always be moving forward" was a common mantra I chanted to myself when I could. The running was symbolic of this. I had to follow it or else it was too easy to get mired in the past, in mistakes, in memories… I did enough of that when the Merging happened.

Always be moving forward.

When we returned, I noticed a shape sitting outside the attic window, knees to chest, dark hair tangled over her shoulder. Evie thirsted for the light like I did, craved the moments she could capture it for herself. Her attention was fixed on something beyond the signal pyres at the edges of the property.

Once I got close enough to see through the trees, the dogs yipped frantically. We were both distracted by them. When I looked again, there was nothing there but golden grass and fluttering moths.

Perhaps Evie was only staring; lost in thought.

My caution bristled with the feeling of having just missed something. I took note and kept moving forward. The dogs were happy to be home and so was I. I took them all inside.

Evie

I watched a silhouette vanish into the mist that morning. This wasn't the first time I'd seen it.

Like every time before, I was frozen in place. It was a black shape, human-like but devoid of any features. It reminded me of caves in the mountains where we used to hike when I was younger. I'd see them saturating the fog with their smoky depth and wonder how deep they were.

I remembered the first morning I saw this figure. I'd woken earlier than usual, pulled from bed by the sounds of birdsong and a terrible dream that was more memory than I wanted to admit. I felt trapped and needed light, needed an escape. I was at the window to greet the rising sun and saw them there: darkness clinging to the remaining shadows.

Over time, I started going out onto the roof to greet them. They never got any closer or farther away. They stayed at the edge of the grass in the field like a sentry. That's how I became convinced it was someone

THE WILD FALL

I used to know, someone who had died. Only recently had I started to suspect it was someone more.

I crept from the attic, my nerves fluttering with intention. Everyone was gathered in the dining room for breakfast. Liz stood at the dining table over the road map while everyone else craned their necks to see where she was pointing. They were planning a supply run, though it felt soon considering Liz had finished a drop with Raheem yesterday. Maybe we were lower on supplies than I thought. I didn't care. She was distracting Dad. I didn't need him following me right now, not when I was already teetering on the brink of uncertainty about going out.

Tempest sauntered in from the kitchen, her ice-colored eyes glinting with the promise of adventure. I wanted her with me, not only for security but because she provided extra strength and was always reliable. I needed her this morning.

I stepped into my beat-up hiking boots, slipped Dad's old jacket on over my arms and we slid out the door. The morning light was inviting. It lessened my uneasiness and pushed me to the end of the deck. I focused on where I saw the figure disappear and gave chase.

Mosquitoes zinged in at us as we meandered the dirt road alongside the field, chasing the darkness as it receded downhill.

This was stupid. Dad would hate this if he knew what I was doing. My willingness to do it grew with the realization. Dad clung to my vulnerability, the idea of me as a child unable to defend herself against the things hunting us from the dark.

I looked back over my shoulder toward the house. No one had come out onto the front porch, no one looked from the windows.

I needed to know. I needed to do this.

Liz

Everyone was awake and present for breakfast, save for Evie who I assumed was still on the roof above. This was fine. We had to discuss our scouting mission. The quicker we did, the quicker we could plan and pack for it.

Breakfast was cubed zucchini, carrot, and cucumber slices for the pups; for us, boiled lentils and chopped tomatoes, sprinkled with homemade chili powder and salt. Richard grew the chilies himself. They hung in the rafters on twine, drying until they were grated and jarred. Sometimes, we got spices if Raheem had them, and when he could get them, it was the usual salt and pepper and the more random things like dill or adobo or nutmeg. We used whatever we could get and harvested whatever we grew to fill in the gaps.

Hank pulled out the atlas, a raggedy New Hampshire road map printed ten years ago that we had marked to hell. We'd crosshatched in areas where we knew the Woods had taken over, penciled in where we suspected nearby camps were so we could avoid them, detailed locations where we had checked for supplies…

This time, we flipped to a page that ran along the Vermont border and focused on the bolded town name of Onyx River. We hadn't gone that far out before, mostly because of the risk. We couldn't be too careful when heading out on a supply run. Fuel for the car was limited and there were few routes unimpacted by the Woods. It was rarely ever a straight trip to get wherever we intended to go. Getting caught out after dark included more risks.

Onyx River would normally have been a two-hour drive from our present location. Since we hadn't ventured in that direction before, we didn't know what obstacles could be in our way. We had to plan for the possibility we'd have to leave the car behind. We had to plan for the worst. This meant strategizing who would bring what, refining the packing list of supplies, going over everything with a fine-toothed comb…

I was barely aware of the sound of soft footfalls on the stairs, the quiet shuffling of boots and a jacket being collected in the entranceway and the front door squeaking open. Evie was going out and I was okay with that. I needed her uninvolved in this. After the conversation with Hank last night, I didn't want her thinking this was an opportunity for adventure. I needed her here, grounded and keeping an eye on things. I needed Hank unworried, at his most alert, and acting as my second set of eyes while we were gone. Maybe the separation would be good for the both of them.

Evie

They were places I'd been before, places I'd mapped out over years of daily walks with my best friend. I knew where each one led, how long each one was liable to take to hike and the fastest routes to get home from wherever I was. Today, I didn't feel at home on my trails as I usually did.

There was someone out here, a dark presence. I needed to know who they were, who they used to be. The fact they came every morning as if waiting for me, the fact they stayed until the sun forced them away made me hunger for a time when none of this was ever a thing. For normalcy. For my mom.

She had died trying to protect me ten years ago, killed by people who had stolen me away from her. Before, my mom had problems. She was an addict and often craved her time with pills and alcohol over time with me and Dad. We'd taken her to rehab so many times it became an extension of home.

And then, she made some good decisions. She tried to get clean. She tried to take care of me.

The Woods happened then. The ghosts came back to haunt the living. I'd never met anyone who was Attached, never knew anyone who had been haunted. But with these morning visits from this dark shape, I started to wonder if it was her, if maybe Mom had been searching for me this whole time and now had found me.

Tempest and I came to the end of the Oak Loop, named aptly because of the huge oak tree that marked its conclusion. There were no signs of the dark shape from earlier in the morning. Even the times when I'd come around a bend in the trail and thought perhaps I'd see her standing there, it was wilderness and chirping birds.

I looked at the age-old map on the pavilion nearby and at the markers for the next couple trails. I'd repainted these over the last several years. Liz had liked my initiative and had told me it could mean our survival someday, being able to use those trails as a means of escape or to hide.

We followed the dirt road back up the mountain toward home and the nearer we got, the more nervous I got about seeing the others. I didn't want to have to apologize for sneaking out, for investigating something that could have been a danger to the group. Even if it had been to satisfy my own curiosity. Even if it had been because I missed my mom.

"This was reconnaissance," I said aloud to Tempest, my boots crunching in the dirt. "We did our part to protect the group."

I took another step and my arm lurched back. The leash had extended to its maximum length. I glanced back from where we'd come. Tempest had stopped by the side of the road at the entrance to an old farm and was sniffing the driveway intensely. Her head jerked up, large ears pointed tall, and barked.

The shrillness of it made me jump a little. She smelled something, something that wasn't supposed to be there.

I walked back to her and cautiously hooked my fingers around her collar. "What is it, girl?"

A low growl rumbled from her throat. Her gaze was locked intently on the old house. The front door was open a crack.

Yesterday, when we'd walked down here to go to the river, that door was closed. No one from our camp would have gone inside for any reason; we'd cleared the house of supplies years ago.

Letting go of Tempest's collar hesitantly, I crouched and slung my backpack off. I zipped open the large compartment and pulled out a pistol.

Dad didn't know but I'd learned how to use a gun almost two years ago.

I'd asked Ash about it two summers back. He'd taken me to the pasture at the bottom of the road from our house and gave me one of our group's handguns. It was heavier than I was expecting and at first, getting my grip right on it was strange. Ash had shown me everything: how to dismantle it, how to load the magazine, how to turn the safety on and off. He'd ordered me never to aim it at anyone unless I was in danger and to never keep my finger on the trigger if I wasn't going to fire. I'd spent days shooting at glass jars while he used the table saw to cut pieces for new house siding nearby, the sound effectively helping to mask my practice shooting.

I didn't take a gun with me on my day-to-day walks but after this morning, I'd sneaked the one from under my mattress. While I had the inkling the dark shape was someone I knew, hoped it was someone I had loved, I didn't want to be wrong. Having the gun was a safe bet.

Slinging the bag back on, I unclipped Tempest from the leash and grabbed her collar with my hand once more. We carefully edged toward the house.

Tempest yanked against my hold and barked again, this time louder and more aggressively. I kept the gun pointed at the ground as we drew closer, my shoulders as rigid as hickory. There was a growing lump in my throat. Even if I'd wanted to scream, I wasn't sure I could get a sound out around it.

We reached the bottom of the steps. Tempest's growling hadn't ceased. It took everything I had to hold onto her, her body full tilt in the direction of the door.

"Who's in there?" I finally called out.

Maybe they'd identify themselves. Better to give them a chance before Tempest ripped them to shreds.

But no one answered.

"I have a gun," I declared strongly. "And my dog is going to tear you apart if you don't tell me who you are right now!"

Tempest snarled as if to further my point.

Still no answer. Not even the sound of movement.

"I'm coming in!" I yelled.

Tempest practically pulled me up the stairs and through the front door before I had a chance to steady myself.

Inside, the darkness drowned my senses. There was a musty smell coming from the room ahead of me. I was freezing, my arms and neck coated in goosebumps before I knew it. My eyes tried to adjust to the limited light in the entranceway. I didn't understand why it was so dark. There was a full wall of glass in the living room at the end of the hall. That should have been letting in more than enough light.

I stepped forward and folded over something. I let go of Tempest's collar to catch myself before I fell. The gun slammed against the floor, the clap of sound like fireworks in the silent space. Tempest bounded off into the hall, her barks increasing in ferocity.

"Tempest!" I shouted, scrambling to my feet. I rounded the table I'd hit and ran after her. My heart thundered in my head as I burst out into the giant living room. I swirled around, searching for someone who didn't belong, pointing my gun at the walls and the faint shapes of white furniture in the darkness. Nothing jumped out, let alone moved. Tempest stood at the window snarling and scraping the glass with her claws.

I walked over to her and grabbed her collar again. "Jesus, you're going to get me into trouble someday…"

I followed her gaze.

THE WILD FALL

The Woods were less than ten feet from the house. Inside the frame of tall trees was a swath of deep green and black, brambles and evergreen bushes thicker than I'd ever seen. All the light from the sun was swallowed by the enormous wall of trees in front of us.

My bottom lip hung as I backed away from it, pulling Tempest along with me.

How the hell had it moved so close so fast? We'd lived here for four years, the Woods barely moving an inch and never presenting much of a worry, though we had always been vigilant in tracking them. This didn't make any sense. It was like it didn't know we were there until now. Like it was coming for us...

I tugged Tempest back from the window. We needed to get back and let the others know.

Tempest growled again and barked at the window as I pulled, glancing back to see how far away I was from the front door.

The front door.

That's what hadn't made sense.

It was open when we got here.

I turned back to the window. There was a person standing in front of it.

I screamed.

Tempest barked louder and jumped, tearing herself out of my grip. She launched at the body.

And went right through them.

My body jolted into action, my hand swinging the gun and taking aim at the thing's head. I squeezed the trigger and felt the weapon buck in my trembling grip. The window behind the thing splintered with the impact. Spiderweb cracks raced across the glass as the figure advanced, hands raised. It was like they were made of pure blackness and it was expanding to engulf me.

I turned and ran. Bumping into the walls in the hallway as though I couldn't control my own body, I raced for the front door. I blindly shoved the table out of the way as I threw myself into daylight. I lay there in the dirt for several seconds, waiting for something to barrel out after me, to land on me like a wolf and start biting me. When I finally had the courage to glance back, all I saw was the darkness.

My panic doubled. "Tempest!"

Her barks resonated from deep inside.

No, no, no, no. Not my dog. Please, not my dog.

I yelled her name again, fear streaming from my eyes and bubbling in my throat.

A silver and black shape emerged from the darkness as Tempest raced down the stairs and joined me at my side.

I grabbed hold of her and hugged her. Her heavy panting matched my own.

Not someone I knew. Not Mom.

It was something that wanted to kill us.

THREE

Liz

Vermont was unknown territory. I'd heard nothing about the conditions there from any people we'd inadvertently met on the road. Hank had gone to college in Vermont and talked about missing it often, though he remarked longing for how things were before, too. Knowing most of Vermont's population was evacuated during the first year after the Merging meant some of the outer-lying towns might be of some interest to us.

Once we'd packed the car, we said our goodbyes to the people staying behind to look after the house. After giving Nettie a kiss, Hank searched the house for Evie and a bit of the surrounding property before joining us back at the car with his head hanging.

"I'm sure she's okay—"

As the words left my mouth, I noticed Evie hurrying along the dirt road with Tempest racing at her side. She kept looking back over her shoulder as if something were following her.

Hank's face dropped. "Evie?"

We ran to the end of the driveway to meet her. I searched the road behind her for intruders, for some evidence of something wrong.

Nothing felt out of place. Insects buzzed. Crows cawed from a nearby tree.

Hank grabbed her, pulling her close to him. "What's wrong? What happened?"

"There was something in the cabin down the mountain. A black shape. It tried to kill us!"

The words prickled over my skin. I stared at the edge of the field where I'd seen Brody's shape last night.

"Eves, take a deep breath," Hank commanded. He looked over his shoulder. "Ash!"

Ash hustled over, his towering frame coming to a stop beside me. "What's going on?"

"Evie saw something. Could be a wolf, could be another person…"

Ash yelled back to the house: "Rich, grab my shotgun."

"You can't kill it," Evie rambled. "Bullets go right through it."

Hank narrowed his gaze. "What do you mean?"

I nodded to Gjon who had finished putting our best tracking dog in the car. "Grab Sanz. We'll go check it out."

I looked at Hank. "Take her inside. We'll be back in a few minutes."

Putting his hand on her back, Hank guided Evie back to the house.

Richard brought Ash's shotgun to him and put his hand on his arm. "Don't need to say it but I'll say it anyway: be careful."

Ash popped the gun open to check the shells and closed it. "Always am."

Gjon retrieved Sanz from the car. The rusty-colored Irish Setter loped to meet us at the end of the driveway and the three of us and the dog set off toward the Rivera farm.

Evie

Dad walked me inside, Nettie and Richard right behind him. I slumped into the armchair in the living room. I couldn't stop shaking. Every time I closed my eyes, I imagined the shadow looming closer and closer.

Dad knelt in front of me, putting his hands on mine. "Take some deep breaths. In and out."

I followed his lead, inhaling through my nose, exhaling through my mouth. It was a method he'd taught me years ago when we would have to hide, have to run, have to stay quiet to stay alive. Within moments, the trembling subsided. I looked around the small room. I felt safe, secure.

Nettie walked in from the kitchen with a mug full of water and handed it to me. I gulped it.

Dad unzipped the main pouch of my bag and looked inside, his brows furrowing. He pulled out the handgun and emptied the magazine.

"I've known how to shoot for a while," I said before he could get a word out. "Ash taught me."

Dad looked over his shoulder at Richard.

Richard shrugged. "Don't look at me: that big idjit makes stupid decisions without me all the time."

"You know it's dangerous. You know the risks. Hell, I don't like using a gun at all," Dad said under his breath.

I rolled my eyes. "Yeah, it's a necessary evil. Blah, blah, blah…"

"Hey, you could have gotten hurt. Or you could have accidentally shot Tempest. These things are not toys."

The words made a heat rise inside my face. "The fact you think I consider them toys is offensive, Dad. I'm not six anymore. And you're not always going to be around to protect me."

Dad's face changed. The worry shifted into doubt. "That's not the point. You were running around with this behind my back. Did you think I wasn't going to find out?"

"It did take you two years, Hank," Gretchen said, leaning back in her seat on the couch.

"I don't need the side commentary, Gretch."

"You wouldn't have let me use it even if I had told you about it sooner," I said, my tone unhinged. "You'd have kept it locked up until I was your age."

Dad frowned. "That's not fair."

"Hank," Nettie said calmly, setting her hand on his shoulder.

The movement only stoked the fire inside me. The realization that creature I'd followed all morning wasn't my mom hit me with new clarity. I glared at her hand.

"He's worried about you," she said, her voice soft and plaintive. "I'm sure he doesn't think you can't take care of yourself."

"No," Dad growled. "That's exactly right. I don't think she can. This whole thing this morning proves it."

Gretchen and Richard looked back and forth between themselves and said nothing.

I wanted to be anywhere but sitting there, roasting under Dad's interrogation, taking sympathy from a woman he still barely knew. I stood and side-stepped him. "Whatever. I'm so over this shit."

"Watch your language," he said.

Nettie's hand curled further over his shoulder with the words.

I turned back to him. "Shit, fuck, damn, piss, cocksucker, motherfucker!"

Dad stared at me wide-eyed.

A small proud smile grew on Richard's face. Gretchen had one eyebrow arched at me.

"I've listened to everyone say them my whole life. Even you, Dad." I turned around and headed toward the stairs. "I knew them all by the time I was ten."

"Evie, don't—"

"Hank, stop it," Nettie said.

"Oh." I turned back around as I reached the third step. "And I don't need you sticking up for me. You're not my mom. I can handle myself."

That shut her up. She blinked as if I'd slapped her.

Dad's cheeks burned.

I continued to the second floor and slammed the door behind me.

Liz

The farmhouse had belonged to Nate and Josie Rivera, back when my family used to own the cabin down the road. Whenever we visited, we would usually stop by the Riveras' house to see the livestock: play with the goats and feed the sheep. I remembered helping Josie wash her garden vegetables in their farmhouse sink and the close warmth of their small kitchen.

When we got here four years ago, there was no sign of the Riveras. The animals were long gone, and the house had been renovated into a ranch-style home with an open-concept floor plan, tall glass windows, and an ugly chandelier. Whoever bought it from them must not have lived there all the time; they weren't there when this shit went down.

As we approached, it was clear it had changed even more. The front door was wide open, the dark interior glaring back out at us. Armed with the shotgun, Ash was the first to enter, with me following him to shine a flashlight and Gjon behind us, Sanz on a leash.

A furniture craftsman by trade, Ash was barrel-chested and Black, sporting a full beard, a clean-shaven head and full-sleeve tattooed arms. Ash also looked a lot meaner than he truly was. He had been vegetarian up until the world went to hell. His favorite singer was Nina Simone, and on a perfect day before the Merging, he could be found drinking grapefruit rosé and listening to a book on tape from Oprah's Book Club. Ash was usually one of the first people awake in the morning checking the perimeter for any intrusions, the first person to welcome you home from a scout if he wasn't on it, and the first person to jump to another's defense.

He was also the first person to throw himself into a fight if need be, which had caused some issues with other smaller groups we'd traded with the past few years. Ash was instinctively suspicious of anyone we came across and rightfully so; you never knew who you could trust these days. Naturally, I'd wanted him to come with us to check out the house. If we ran into any trouble, he was our intimidation and our chance to ward off any problems.

Negotiating through the entryway to the main living area brought us face to face with the tall glass windows in the living room and what lay beyond it: the Woods. It was worse than I'd thought. They were moving even faster than we had charted over the past week. We needed to get to Onyx River and check it out before we lost our buffer time to pack.

"Liz," Gjon said, pointing to the window. The crack spread across it was new and I recognized the point of impact: a bullet. Evie did have a gun and she had shot the window.

I gave Ash a side-eye. "Why do I get the feeling you knew about this?"

He glanced between me and the window. "She's not a little kid anymore. I figured it was important for her to learn."

"I agree. But Hank's going to be pissed. You should have thought about that before you went ahead and did it."

"Yeah, yeah," Ash grumbled.

"Can't wait until we're all in the same car together for five hours," Gjon said under his breath.

I swept the light around the room, searching the dark corners for any moving shapes. Nothing. The balloon of anxiety in me deflated. "Let's go."

We left the farmhouse, closing the door behind us, and marched back to the house. Ash walked ahead, his head bowed, no doubt already thinking of how to apologize to Hank.

Gjon and I walked side by side. He took off his baseball cap to reveal his short salt-and-pepper hair and scratched at the back of his neck. Of all the people who had joined our small caravan, Gjon was the only one besides Hank who I felt most at ease with. He reminded me at times of Brody; sometimes too much.

Brody always had a solid head on his shoulders while I would let loose with fire and brimstone. He kept me grounded, his little bits of wisdom like cooling dunks of water to my psyche. That was back when everything kind of made sense.

Thinking about my old friend only made the pain much closer and harder to escape.

"Interesting start to the day," Gjon said, breaking me out of my cloud of memories.

"Yup," I sighed. "Every day is interesting with a teenager, I suppose."

He chuckled. "How's the leg? Saw you went out running this morning."

"Gets better every day." It was a lie. Years ago, when I'd finally gotten back to my home city of Flintland in Maine, I'd let my guard down and had been shot by a tracking group, looking for Attached people. Since then, my leg had good and bad days. The scar tissue was a persistent problem. Some days, I could run for miles and feel fine. Others, I'd wake and my thigh would throb like I'd been hit with a nail-covered baseball bat.

Gjon was the closest thing our group had to a doctor and had been trying to provide treatment as best he could. He had been a veterinary technician and his love and care for our group's dogs whispered of his life from before.

I knew he knew my lie, too, so I wasn't surprised when he smiled and rubbed this beard with his thumb and forefinger, as if he were a professor in deep pensive deliberation about quantum physics or antimatter.

"I like it," I said.

When he frowned, I mirrored his beard stroking.

He chuckled. "It's been a long time since I've had a beard. Not sure if I like it yet or not."

"I get it."

For years, he was the most clean-shaven man in our group and seemed to prefer that look. The facial hair made him look older, more worn and torn by the world. The small crook in his previously broken nose was more defined, the bags beneath his dark-brown eyes deeper, especially when he frowned, which he was doing right then.

"Why did you want me to come along on the scout?" he asked. "To Onyx River?"

Because I'd feel safer with you there, I wanted to say. Instead, I stared at the ground. "Your input. Whatever new location we end up in, we'll need to make sure we have access to clean water and medical supplies, also a big enough space for the dogs to roam. I don't want to make any mistakes with where we move our people. Your opinion is crucial to our group's survival."

His chest swelled. "Fine, but don't think I don't know the real reason."

"What's that?"

"You can't get enough of my stimulating conversation."

I blew a raspberry and laughed, the first real laugh I'd had in what felt like weeks. "Get the fuck out of here."

Back at the house, Hank fumed. He tucked the gun he'd found in Evie's bag into his own holster. When Ash tried to apologize for his teaching her how to shoot, all Hank could do was shake his head and say, "Not right now. We'll have this talk once we get back from the scout."

We piled into the car, Hank in the driver's seat, me in the front passenger's seat and Gjon and Ash in the back with Sanz. I glanced at the second floor and noticed Evie sitting on the roof where I'd caught her that morning. I waved and she didn't.

Our Jeep rumbled out of the driveway and onto the road.

Hank kept his eyes focused on the road but the tenseness in his shoulders told me he was itching to look back at the house one last time, back at Evie. "I know she's mad she doesn't get more of a say with us."

I cocked my head. "Then we should include her more in the future."

Hank glanced at me. "I'm not going to be able to keep her out of danger for much longer, am I?"

"She needs to become an adult eventually, Hank."

FOUR

Liz

Even though it was the first day of fall, the temperature soared into the eighties. Despite this, we kept the windows closed and blasted the A/C instead. Were we going somewhere close, we might have put them down. But we were heading into towns we had no pulse on and anything could have been there. Or anyone. Better to be safe than sorry.

Most of the trip was by car, thankfully, though the roads were often blocked with obstacles. When the world had gone to shit, a lot of people had taken their cars and fled south toward the promise of government-run communities and medical aid to try and explain why they were seeing their dead loved ones, among other things. As was expected, there were several people who stayed put, several who resorted to rioting and looting supplies and then holed up in their basements, waiting for the world to end.

Our first car-stopping obstacle was along a small cut-off road intersecting Routes 16 and 302. There was a car sitting squarely on the train track crossing. Hank pulled the Jeep back and put it in park before we all climbed out. I watched our surroundings, my handgun hot in my sweaty grip by my side. Gjon went around to open the driver's side door of the car on the tracks and stopped.

"Dead guy?" Ash asked from the back of the car.

"Yeah," Gjon answered hesitantly, taking a step back and waving his hand in front of his face.

"Figured as much."

Ash joined Gjon at the front of the car. "Hoo wee," he muttered, popping open the door. "That's a ripe one." Ash grabbed hold of the body by the shirt inside and gave it a tug.

"Seatbelt," Gjon reminded him.

"Yup. Had to be a safe motherfucker when he decided to kill himself." Ash clicked off the belt and gave the body another heave. He tossed it onto the tracks with a soft, wet thump. A cloud of flies burst out after it and both Gjon and Ash gave them space to disperse, coughing.

Hank walked over to the trunk of the car. "He tried to kill himself by train?"

I scoffed. "Too bad trains aren't exactly running anymore."

"What can I say?" Ash yelled back to me. "Had to be some lucky dumb people that made it through all this, I suppose."

"Looks like he got tired of waiting," Gjon added, reaching into the car and pulling out a handgun. He handed it to Ash.

Ash ejected the magazine. "One bullet missing." He clicked it back in and stuffed the gun into the small of his back.

Gjon climbed into the driver's seat and twisted the keys in the ignition. Nothing happened. "Battery is dead."

"Alright then, throw it in neutral," Ash said, joining Hank at the back of the car.

I scanned the surrounding area. The brush was close on both sides of the road. If it were it nighttime, I would have expected an ambush. But the sky was bright and clear and the wolves that roamed near the Woods wouldn't come out in direct sunlight. Nor would any gang of people looking to loot us for supplies.

Ash and Hank leaned against the bumper of the car and Gjon called back, "Okay!"

They shoved the car the rest of the way across the tracks, Gjon turning the wheel to guide it to the grass. Once they were done, we loaded up and drove on. I didn't look at the body on the tracks as we passed. Too many people had died. I didn't need to add another face to the growing catalog in my brain.

We drove along Route 302 for a solid hour before needing to refuel. The Jeep didn't run on gasoline but on ammonia. Most of the gas that had sat in vehicles for the last ten years had lost its viability and was practically useless. Between the three of them, Ash, Richard, and Hank had modified the fuel injector years ago to take ammonia after researching alternative fuel options. We had to refuel more frequently, but at least we could find our fuel in most grocery or hardware stores.

The road was wide, empty, and open. It almost seemed like a normal summer day, except for the lack of traffic. Ash rolled down his window in the back and let his hand ride the air current. Gjon allowed Sanz to climb into the backseat and stick her head out his window for a while. I watched her rust-colored fur billowing in the wind, her tongue flapping in the wind joyfully. For an hour, we were allowed to forget our circumstances.

We met an armada of abandoned vehicles around the turn off to Route 116. Ash had explained this was where military trucks had collected citizens for transport to larger communities south of us. The cars were left behind, making it virtually impossible to keep going that route. Shortly after, we found our next roadblock: one we couldn't get our car around. A large tree had fallen into the roadway. Various spindly branches stuck out like needles all over, keeping us from even climbing over it. The only way past it was on foot, cutting around through the forest for a moment.

Hank parked the Jeep off the road with enough room for us to turn around when we came back through. Then, we grabbed our respective packs, took the car keys, and climbed out to continue the rest of the journey on foot.

It was only about a minute of being in the forest before we were back out on the opposite side of the tree. But for us, those seconds were full of fear and the unknown. On the road again, we walked for close to four hours. The only times we rested were when the road opened on either side and we could see for miles around us. No one could sneak up on us.

The sun began to burn a more intense orange by the time I heard rushing water. Soon enough, signs for Onyx River appeared along the roadside, two miles, then a mile, then a half-mile. We'd depleted most of our water stores walking in the intense heat. As I'd suspected, we wouldn't be making it back to our cabin until probably tomorrow night. We were further behind schedule than I'd hoped.

Crossing the bridge into Onyx River was like entering a ghost town. We took a moment to fill our water bladders and canteens and let Sanz drink for a while at the river's edge before continuing. Gjon led with Sanz on leash, while Hank, Ash, and I brought up the rear with our weapons ready.

Ash had pulled the shotgun off his back and had given the handgun he'd found in the car to Gjon.

Hank carried Evie's gun, his expression uncomfortable.

"What do you know about Onyx River?" Gjon said, as we approached the first house, a white two-story Cape with black shutters.

"Onyx River was one of the first cities to be evacuated by the military on their sweep of New England nine years ago," Hank volunteered. "When they got here, they found a ghost town. All one hundred and eleven residents had disappeared."

Gjon flashed me a look. "Great. Twilight Zone here we come."

I rolled my eyes. "They vanished?"

"Well, it was a year before the army got their shit together to evacuate the rest of the Northeast. Maybe everyone got the hell out here before they came," Hank said.

It was possible. The U.S. military was compromised when the Merging happened: members of the presidential cabinet defected, several high-ranking officials unable to perform their duties. As it turns out, when your dead loved ones start appearing to the majority of the population but not all of it, the ones who can't see anything start to assume the rest are insane.

Those in the minority finally rose to power following a coup that overruled the president and vice president. The American people didn't get wind of that change in power for almost another three months. I didn't hear about it until a year after it had happened.

"What else did you find out?"

"Wasn't much in our books, but here's an article in an old *Vermont Magazine*." Hank dug into his bag and retrieved a folded-back magazine which he handed to me. "Onyx River not only has a continually flowing resource of fresh water, it also is one of the only towns to be run entirely on renewable energy. There's an orchard on the eastern side of town with a colonial house attached. That was a focal point in the story they ran. One of those wedding venues with a hunting lodge. That house is large enough for us and there's plenty of room for the dogs to run."

I flipped to the page. The house was immense. Probably could have housed an entire football team comfortably.

Gjon looked as though someone had kissed him. The excitement in his face was barely contained.

I looked around. "When Raheem mentioned the other groups were headed here, I had assumed we'd see someone…anyone."

The streets were silent. The houses stood quietly behind their leaf-covered lawns, the sun casting long thin shadows across them from the trees in the front yards, the bird baths, the tire swings…

Hank nodded. "It seems barren."

"Maybe they disappeared just like the townspeople," Gjon jested, though some of the enthusiasm started to drain from his face.

"Don't fucking joke about that shit," Ash grumbled. "Makes me uncomfortable."

"We should check out some of these houses for supplies," I answered, nodding toward the two-story Cape. "We'll probably need to split up."

Everyone gave me uneasy glances. Hank's was the most unnerving. "I'm not sure that's the best idea."

"Then making sure this place is safe will take days…maybe even a week. We don't have enough supplies and we don't know how fast the Woods are going to close in on our cabin back home. Time isn't on our side." I traversed the overgrown brick walkway toward the front door of the house.

Behind me, I heard Ash say, "She has a strong point." The sound of his boots followed me. "I'll cover you."

I glanced over my shoulder at Gjon and Hank. "You guys take the next house. That way we won't stray far from one another."

I didn't wait for Hank's approval before I opened the front door and crept into the entryway. Ash followed, keeping his back to the opposite wall so we faced each other.

The door had opened into the living room, the space vacant of human life. There were still bowls and spoons sitting on the coffee table in front of the television. A set of stairs scaled to the second floor next to Ash and a hall led to unknown rooms behind the fireplace in the living room. Steeling ourselves, we carefully entered the room, our shoes sounding cavernous on the pristine laminate floor.

The hallway led to a spacious white kitchen and a secondary living area with a back porch exit. Despite the urge to check the cabinets then, we both continued through the rest of the house, carefully peering into the last few rooms: a bathroom, the master bedroom, and upstairs, a children's bedroom and half-bath.

The weirdest thing was how unlived-in this place felt. No personal items left behind. No photos. No clothing or toys. It was as if someone had come in and scrubbed it of any history it may have once had.

The basement was the last area to confirm and both of us stood in front of its door with trepidation.

"You wanna…" Ash started and then motioned twisting a doorknob with his hand.

"Not particularly," I answered.

"Well…"

We stood there for a few more seconds in silence.

Ash finally spoke: "I got an idea." He reached out toward the doorknob and twisted the lock.

I smiled. "I can live with that."

Ash grinned. "Sometimes the best move isn't with might but with smarts."

We spent a good five minutes searching cupboards. Most of the perishables had been taken, probably with the family who had vacated the place at the beginning of this whole mess. The refrigerator was filled with spoiled food and the stench of it made me sick to my stomach upon opening the door. Ash packed the one box of rice and canned tomatoes he found in his bag and we left to go to the next house.

Hank, Gjon, and Sanz were gone when we got back out front. The door to the house next door was open.

As Ash and I crossed the street to a gray split-level, I heard the twinkling of a leash and turned to see Gjon and Hank exit the house. Hank gave me a thumbs-up and they continued on to the next home.

"I'm hoping this one has some chocolate in it," Ash said as we climbed the stairs to the front door. "None of the powdered crap. I want a bar of the good stuff."

He wasn't wrong. It had been several months since anyone at home had had chocolate. The last time we'd found a can of cocoa powder, Nettie had baked brownies. They didn't have eggs or butter, but they'd all been eaten in a single sitting.

"Okay," I said as we readied to enter. "Let's pray there's chocolate."

The afternoon dipped into night. Clearing houses and rummaging for supplies was the secret to making time pass quickly. Not wanting to get caught out after dark, we made a decision to go back to one of the first houses we had cleared, the split level, and stay there for the night. We were anxious as we flicked the first switch to try the power. Lights came on and we all breathed a sigh of relief. Somehow, even after ten years, the combination of hydro-power, wind turbines, and solar had kept electricity running. I had fully expected us to need to visit the power plant, and perhaps we still would, out of an abundance of caution.

Hank got ready to put a couple pots of rice and beans on the stove. The faucets, though reluctant to at first, dribbled water. This particular house must have had a well. After a few moments, the well pump warmed and the water flowed more freely. Hank filled each pot and put it on the electric stove top. He flipped on both burners and within moments, the coils reddened.

I slumped into a chair at the kitchen table, slinging my pack to the floor beside me.

Hank took the seat across from me, running a hand through his mussed hair.

Ash, unable to relax, had gone to check the rooms in the house one more time.

Gjon pulled a plastic tub of cubed cooked sweet potato and carrots from his bag and set it on the floor for Sanz, who slurped it noisily. The rest of us watched her, our own stomachs growling as the rice and beans bubbled away.

"It feels so strange," I said, looking around us. The prospect of having a home with running water and electricity was staggering. We had a small diesel generator at our cabin which ran the refrigerator, stove, and a few lights. But it was nothing compared to what this town would offer us.

Ash appeared in the kitchen door, his eyes bright and smile growing. "You think that's great, you oughta come see this."

We followed Ash out of the kitchen and down a hall to the bathroom. He walked over to the bathtub and turned the faucet. Water poured in and after a few moments, steam followed. He chuckled. "Any of you interested in a bath?"

"Hot water," Hank said slowly, almost as if he'd forgotten what it was.

"Seems like the water heater is okay, too," Gjon added.

"I checked downstairs," Ash said. "A lot of the equipment is new. Water pump, furnace, water heater... Like it's never been used."

"We'll have to check the farmhouse and make sure the equipment is in good shape, too." I thought about the large house Hank had mentioned upon our arrival. I wished we'd had a chance to get there today, but caution was important. We couldn't dive into this until we were sure there were no threats. Not being able to see the Woods put me on edge much more.

"If it isn't, this might not be a bad place to bring our people," Hank said, glancing at me out of the corner of his eye. "It's smaller than the cabin but at least we have running water and the potential for a working furnace here."

"One step at a time," I told him, an equal reminder for myself as it was for him. "We need more of the lay of the land before we can call this good."

We returned to the kitchen and waited on our food. Between the four of us, it wasn't much and we finished in a fraction of the time it took to cook. Ash took the couch in the living room, while Gjon and Sanz climbed the stairs to the second bedroom and slept there. Hank and I took the master bedroom.

Both of us climbed onto the bed in our clothes and lay side by side staring at the ceiling. I'd turned the lights in the house off, my paranoia waging a war with my happiness at finally having light. We didn't know who else was nearby. We had to preserve caution above all else.

"So," I said. "What do you think?"

Hank let a soft breath out through his nose. "It seems too good to be true that anything should be working this well after ten years of sitting."

"I agree."

"But," he added, turning to look at me. "This could be the miracle we need."

"I know after the last move you thought we should have joined a GRC."

He didn't say anything.

"But the numbers of people, the strain of resources… all the things that were difficult about our world before are shoved into an even smaller space in those communities. Not to mention my notoriety."

Hank chuckled. "Are there wanted posters of you out there somewhere, you think?"

"I kind of hope so."

We both laughed.

"Anyway, I'm glad you gave me a chance to set it right. We have a good thing going here. And you wouldn't have met Nettie if we hadn't done this."

Hank grinned. "I'm thinking of asking her to marry me."

My eyes widened.

"I've been having these dreams. They're so real. She's wearing a white dress: short, like knee-length. There's this light coming in behind her. She's so beautiful."

I wasn't sure what to say. "Wow, Hank."

"Don't tell anyone yet," Hank quickly added. "I need to talk with Evie about it first. You understand why."

I did. Hank had told me about Evie's outburst. She didn't want anyone mothering her. I still remembered her real mother, Melissa, dying at the bottom of her own stairs, a knife sticking out of her chest. She'd fought to protect her daughter and had died trying. It was clear Evie hadn't let that go. Though I hadn't been there when Hank had broken the news to her, I'd seen the repercussions of it over the years. This was going to be a hard pill for her to swallow.

I nodded.

Within a moment, I heard Ash call out from the living room, "Did I hear something about marrying somebody?"

From upstairs, Gjon answered, "I heard it, too."

We both glanced at the hot air vent which connected our room with the upstairs one.

I couldn't help but giggle. Living in silence, listening to every sound that could potentially be danger, had made us all incredibly adept at hearing. Trying to tell a secret in a place so quiet was almost like declaring something on a bullhorn.

"Don't say anything," Hank repeated, louder this time.

We all broke into laughter.

FIVE

Evie

That night, while Richard, Gretchen, and Nettie sat in the living room by the fire, I stayed upstairs. The realization the Woods were moving closer had dropped a blanket of caution over the entire house. Gretchen wasn't laughing and Richard wasn't playing his guitar and Nettie wasn't slurping her tea loudly. They sat there, murmuring to one another, probably because they didn't want me to hear what they were saying. It didn't matter. I knew what they were talking about anyway. They were worrying about when the scouting party was going to get back, whether or not we had a safe place to move to and could get out before the Woods shut us in. They were worried we might have to leave before they returned.

I fed the dogs in the barn per Gjon's instructions. As I crated Tempest for the night, I gave her an extra treat. I didn't want her to be away from me, not when the darkness had nearly sunk its claws into both of us today. Gjon kept them in the barn because it was with the rest of our supplies. They were there to guard them, just as they were there to guard us. The moment they barked, you could hear them and assume something was wrong.

I tucked myself into bed before anyone else came up and stared into the rafters in the dark. At least I had the space to myself for a time.

I thought about Mom. I couldn't remember much, my memories of who she was and the world as it used to be faded every year I was stuck in this strange reality we found ourselves in. Sometimes, it was little things. I'd remembered a year when I got a giraffe-themed Valentine from her, the cartoonish animal's eyes heart-shaped and the speech bubble declaring "I love you from my head to my hooves!"

I remembered the smell of her when she stopped taking care of herself, choosing the pills over a hot shower several days in a row. The vomit on the toilet seat when I'd gone to use the bathroom once and hadn't been sure what it was.

I remembered the day she painted my bedroom pink, like the color of the sunset from my favorite book she used to read to me so I could fall asleep.

When she used to sing songs by The Eagles to me when I felt sick. When...

A sound woke me. I sat up on my bed, not even realizing I'd fallen asleep. My heart hammered as I took in the darkness around me. No movements, nothing out of the ordinary. Gretchen and Nettie were asleep nearby. I strained to listen in the darkness.

The dogs were barking.

I reached over to the bed nearest me and gave Gretchen a small nudge. Her deep-brown eyes opened and took me in. "What's wrong?"

I didn't say anything. I let the barking seep into the surrounding silence. She threw off her blankets. She reached to the top of the bookcase and grabbed the emergency rifle stored there. The adults left it loaded, even though they told me it wasn't. They couldn't afford to be scrabbling for rounds if something happened.

Gretchen woke Nettie, who rose more immediately, her eyes huge and panic-filled.

The three of us carefully approached the window and nudged the curtains aside.

A thick mist had overtaken the front lawn like a soup. We couldn't see anything, not even the signal fires at the edges of the property.

"Fucking shit fuck," Gretchen whispered, pulling the curtain closed again. "Maybe we can see something from downstairs."

"The wolves respond to movement, don't they?" Nettie said, staying where she was. "We should stay where we are."

The thought of those wolf-like creatures from the Woods being anywhere near us filled me with instant dread. I hadn't seen any in almost four years; I wasn't eager to see them again.

"We don't even know if that's what the dogs are barking at," Gretchen said, calmly. "And even if it was, they would go away with all of that noise."

I thought of Tempest, stuck in her crate, howling as a large monster towered over her. "We need to save the dogs," I declared.

"Let's find Richard." Gretchen walked to the top of the stairs. "I think he crashed in the living room last night."

Gretchen led us down the stairs, keeping the rifle aimed at the floor. Each step creaked as we descended and my muscles tightened with each little noise we made. At the bottom, we opened the door into the dark first floor of the house. We swept left toward the living room.

I couldn't take my eyes off the windows that looked out from the front of the house. I kept thinking I'd see something emerge from the mist.

Gretchen stopped as she passed through the door into the living room. "Shit."

"What?" I asked.

"He's not here."

The dogs' barking in the background only grew louder with the realization.

"Where would he go?" Nettie asked, fright lacing her voice.

"Maybe he heard it before we did. He could have gone to the barn to check on the dogs first."

Gretchen walked over to the couch and crouched, her arm reaching under it. "Yeah. He must have. The rifle is gone."

Nettie shook her head. "Why wouldn't he have woken us first?".

Gretchen rolled her eyes. "Because he's a brave dumbass."

We returned to the front hall and gathered around the front door. It was strange having the moon out in such clarity, lighting our yard and the fog to the point where I thought we should be able to see everything. The mist was mere feet from our fire pit in the front yard, barely concealing it. Anything could have been inside the haze and it was clear from our lack of movement no one wanted to take the first step outside.

I grabbed the handle on the door finally, and twisted it until the latch bolt popped free of the frame. I pulled the door open into the house and the cool air stung me. I didn't have my socks or boots on and I'd left my jacket upstairs. I don't know what I'd been thinking. If we needed to run, all I had were the clothes on my back.

We pushed open the screen door, the spring yawning the wider it was pushed. We stepped out one by one. Gretchen nodded to me to start down the length of the deck toward the barn, Nettie behind me, while she took the rear, aiming the rifle at the fog beside us. I tried to move carefully, and zigzagged around where I knew boards were loose and made noise.

Nettie didn't do the same. It felt like she hit every single one, the creaks peeling into the air alongside the dogs' incessant barking.

Gretchen did the same behind her.

I reached the end of the deck and descended the steps into the dewy grass. My feet were freezing and the chill consumed my entire body within moments.

"Keep going," Gretchen whispered.

I made my way toward the driveway, my head on a swivel looking from the fog to the barn and back again. What if there was a wolf in the barn? What if it had already gotten Richard?

I stumbled on a small hump in the earth and nearly fell. Nettie grabbed my arm and delicately let me go once I'd righted myself. We reached the driveway, the grass giving way to dirt and small stones which stabbed my feet. I barely noticed the pain, my entire being concentrating on what we were going to find inside the barn.

At the barn door, I glanced back at Nettie and Gretchen. I don't think I'd ever seen Nettie so full of terror. Gretchen maintained a level of calm somehow, her attention to the fog behind us. I knew she would whip around at a moment's notice once we were inside and had the door closed behind us. "Let's go," she said, as if she could tell what I was thinking.

I lifted the latch and pushed open the barn door.

I wasn't expecting the lights to be on inside. The barking was so much louder, it hurt my head to be so close to it. We all filed in and Gretchen yanked the door shut behind her. I took in the small space quickly. The dogs were still in their cages.

I rushed to Tempest's cage and opened it quickly. She rushed out, whining, and curled around my legs, her gaze pointed at the farthest corner of the room. The punch of dog urine hit my nose. She'd peed her bed. Otto, our pit bull, faced that direction as well, snarling and baying.

Gretchen aimed the rifle there and we all stopped in place, as if waiting for something to emerge. But there was nothing there, only a stack of chests where we kept tents, tarps, sleeping bags and other camping supplies in case of an emergency. There was no room for anything to hide there and no corner dark enough for something to conceal itself.

Still, the dogs reacted as if there was something we couldn't see.

I lowered myself toward Tempest and scrubbed her ears. "It's okay," I soothed, trying to rub the hackles around the back of her neck. "There's no one here."

Gradually, the barking died. Nettie and Gretchen each checked over Otto, and then, we inspected our supplies. It looked like nothing had been tampered with, nothing opened or stolen from. We gathered in the middle of the room after we were done.

"I don't understand," Nettie said. "Why were they so upset?"

Gretchen shook her head. "Maybe they were reacting to something outside."

We looked at the corner again, the one the dogs had been so agitated about. It was the closest one to the road and to the forest behind us. What if the Woods were closing in from that direction, too?

The thought sent a ripple up my back. I hadn't hiked there for a few days now.

"We still don't know where Richard went," Gretchen added, picking up the rifle from where she'd set it.

"What should we do?" Nettie asked.

"The dogs should stay inside," I said.

Both of them looked at me.

"They've peed in their crates. I don't know about you, but I don't want to clean that tonight."

Gretchen nodded and took a deep breath. "Yup. Okay."

We leashed the dogs. I held Tempest while Nettie got Otto. Gretchen held onto the rifle and we made our way to the exit.

The door opened before we could get there.

"Hold it right there or I'll fucking shoot!" Gretchen yelled, steadying the rifle.

Nettie and I hit the floor with the dogs, grabbing onto them as we dropped.

"Easy, easy," Richard's voice called as a raised hand appeared through the crack in the door.

Gretchen lowered the gun. Nettie and I heaved in sighs of relief from the floor. I couldn't be sure but I thought Nettie might have been crying.

Richard eased into the barn, eventually dropping his hands. "The fook, Gretch…"

"Where the hell have you been?" she shouted at him.

"I was walking the property line," he said, holding the rifle in his hands. "The dogs were barking up a storm. I thought we might have an intruder."

I thought back to the Riveras' house yesterday, to the shadowy figure that had tried to kill Tempest and me. What if it was one of those things? What if it had been the same one?

"You wandered out into the fog on your own?" Nettie said, standing. Otto licked at her hand but Nettie didn't seem to notice. "Are you stupid?"

"I didn't think—"

"That's right," Gretchen interrupted him. "You didn't think, did you?"

"Can we go back inside?" I said. I didn't want to be in the barn anymore. Not while the thing might have still been around in the darkness.

Everyone nodded and we stepped outside. Richard took Otto's leash from Nettie and we all walked back to the house. I'm not sure why, but the fog didn't seem as thick as it had before. I could almost see the flickering of the signal fires at the edges of the property now.

Back inside, I took Tempest into the bathroom and gave her a quick scrub to wash the urine from her fur. Then, we went back to the bedroom while the others gathered in the kitchen. I barely heard Gretchen telling

Richard "he almost got his white ass killed" before I closed the door on them.

Back upstairs, sleep evaded me. Tempest seemed to have lost most of her fight and circled into a ball on the rug by my bed. I remained at the window, watching the mist fade from the lawn back toward the field. Tomorrow, as soon as it was light, I'd take Tempest up the mountain and see if the Woods were coming at us from that direction. If they were, then we were screwed.

SIX

Liz

At sunrise the next morning, we packed and headed through town toward MacCoughlin Orchards, the site of the colonial house and a farmstead that was large enough for our group of eight people and three canine companions. We'd found the town's Chamber of Commerce the day before, which still had a cartoonish town map of all the places potential tourists could visit in Onyx River. The orchard was outside of town proper, close to the wind turbines which helped power the whole grid.

It was a half-hour walk before we could see the large wooden sign for MacCoughlin Orchards at the end of a long dirt road. Nearby the large wind turbines spun against a backdrop of churning gray clouds.

"Don't like the look of that," Ash said.

"There's blue behind it," Gjon said. "Probably a quick storm."

Sanz cocked her head and let out a soft groan.

"We'll sweep the farm and hopefully, it'll be over by the time we need to leave," I answered.

Hank and the others gave nods of approval.

THE WILD FALL

The dirt road was only a five-minute walk. In a turnaround at the end stood the grandiose MacCoughlin colonial, a yellow three-story masterpiece with black shutters and a widow's walk on top.

The house wasn't as beautiful as it had appeared in the dated magazine. The yard was tossed with downed branches and piles of leaves from years of storms and no clean up. Small saplings had sprouted all over the once pristine front yard. The brick walkway to the front door was covered over with moss and grass, mostly hiding it. The red barn, paint stripped and weather beaten, sat dark and empty nearby. The orchard was full of twisted green trees, but it was hard to tell if any of them still bore fruit.

It didn't look like anyone was living out here anymore. But we had to be sure.

We took the house first. It was pristine inside, as though preserved from the last ten years of this horrible nightmarish world somehow. The only damage we found was a broken window where a branch had come down outside.

It didn't feel real: being here. The red-carpeted stairs led to an open second-story hallway, dust-coated mahogany floors, and immaculate bedrooms painted in pastel colors. The kitchen was still well-stocked with non-perishables, although the refrigerator and pantry also stank with refuse of old vegetables and fruits that had moldered for so long.

There was a long, covered front porch lined with rattan chairs whose cushions had blown away in past years' storms. Crispy leaves were piled around them in places, and the wood was warped and paint flecked around the edges.

Our sweep of the barn was less encouraging. The horse stalls contained bones and rotting hay. None of us could say anything as we pushed our way through it as quickly as possible. People had left in such a hurry they had left some animals behind…not even setting them free to fend for themselves.

Gjon balled his fists the farther we went. "Fucking people," he growled and Sanz rumbled as if in agreement.

I let Ash and Hank continue toward the other side of the barn while I hung back with Gjon. "I'm sorry we found this," I said.

Gjon sighed. "Don't be. It's not your fault other people were assholes."

"Once we bring our group back here, we'll get this cleaned out. This might be a good location for our supplies and growing armory."

He nodded. "You've made a decision, then?"

I nodded. "It's not only my decision. I want everyone to be comfortable with this before we take steps."

"Well, barring this," Gjon waved at the barn around him. "I don't have any disputes. Moving somewhere with plenty of room and working electricity is huge. I'm not sure we can afford to say no to it."

We caught up with Ash and Hank outside and continued our tour of the grounds toward the apple orchard. It was more crowded than it should have been, probably because new trees had seeded and started to grow in amongst the older ones. They'd reached maturity years ago and now all fought for the same sunlight and nutrients from the soil. The closest trees to us seemed to still be alive and bearing fruit, though branches desperately needed to be trimmed back. Farther into the trees, we noticed worms burrowed into the apples, their white spindly webs covering several branches.

"Codling moths," Ash said. "I'll bet the owners of this orchard kept some spray to protect the trees every season."

"Is this something we can treat?" I asked.

"Probably not this season. We should harvest what we can from the trees back there and then at the end of the season, make sure we rake and dispose of all the fallen apples. The bugs will use those to overwinter in. We'll have to do some serious cleanup in the spring, but it'll be worth it."

Ash had spent much of his time reading about gardening, fruit trees, and how to care for them during our four-year span at the cabin. He and Richard had originally planned to grow apple trees there, but weren't able to find any saplings or seeds to plant.

We walked back to the dirt road where we'd entered the farm and looked over the MacCoughlin estate. Hank, who had been taking photos on his digital camera for reference, snapped one more of the entire place.

"So, what do you guys think?"

"It's going to be some work," Ash said. "But this place is fucking rad."

Hank scoffed. "We'll need to concentrate on winterizing it once we get everyone here. That and collecting supplies."

I agreed and turned to the only one who hadn't said anything. "Gjon?"

"The river is close by. Not as close as at our current location, but we can manage. I noticed a pharmacy and a veterinary clinic in town. Both are important. They'll have medications and tools we'll need for ourselves and the dogs."

I turned to Ash. "Didn't you say this place was also a hunting lodge?"

He nodded. "There were plenty of rifles and ammunition inside. Since the Woods haven't encroached here, we might be able to find a small population of deer or even a moose…"

"You mean ones that haven't been wiped out by ticks, right?"

Ticks had become prevalent since the world went to hell. There was nothing to kill them off, nothing to stop them from decimating the moose population. It had been many years since I'd seen one of those gentle giants and I wasn't sure I ever would again. But I still liked to think I might…

"So, we're agreed?"

Everyone nodded.

"Right. Let's get going."

The sky had cleared of the storm clouds while we'd been evaluating the farm. Clear pale blue surrounded us, and the sun struck like a beacon on the rise.

"How's our time looking?" I asked Hank, although I had a vague idea of where we were.

"It's about ten." He glanced at the sky, perching a hand on his brow to shield his eyes. "If we can make it back to the car in the same amount of time it took us to get here, we should have a chance to get back to the cabin before dark. We're on schedule."

"Good."

This was going to be the best option for us. We were going to make this place home.

Evie

The morning light brought relief and new trepidations combined. Tempest had stayed by my side all night. I encouraged her to keep resting while I changed into a different set of clothes; a black t-shirt with a logo for some band, and a pair of khaki hiking pants. As I went downstairs, I heard Tempest stand and the jingle of her collar as she followed me.

There wasn't too much different from an everyday morning when I opened the door to the first floor. Both Nettie and Gretchen were in the kitchen, drinking their morning coffee. I plopped myself in a seat across the table from Gretchen and Nettie served me a plate of potato hash. Tempest got a breakfast of quinoa with chunks of Spam. Otto had already finished his and lay on the wooden floor, his big eyes watching me eat forkful after forkful of food.

Gretchen finally spoke. "I think we're going to need to do a scout of our own today."

Nettie stopped scrubbing dishes in the sink and frowned. "We shouldn't go out looking for trouble. Not until the others come back."

"We might not have the luxury of that much time, Nettie," Gretchen said. "The mist that rolled in last night was hardly natural and there was something stalking the property that got the dogs worked up. We need to do our due diligence and make sure this is a safe place for our crew to come back to."

"I want to help," I said. "I know this mountain like the back of my hand. Tempest and I can go to the Birch Trail and see what's going on there."

Nettie set down the plate she was cleaning and approached the table. "I'm not sure that's a good idea..."

I rolled my eyes. "Of course, you wouldn't."

"Hank worries about you," she protested.

My tone got sharper. "Then let him. I'm not going to sit here and wash dishes while I could be helping."

"Enough." Gretchen put a hand to her head. "Nettie, Evie has a point. She's old enough to look after herself and needs to get used to doing it. Evie, everything everyone does here helps our cause. Just because she's not putting herself in harm's way, doesn't mean Nettie isn't sacrificing energy and time for us. You wouldn't have had breakfast to stuff your face with this morning if she didn't make it for us. Don't be so ungrateful."

The words stung but I was pleased by the idea I was getting to do something I'd rarely been entrusted with doing before. Going farther up the mountain had been my goal for today, a chance to make sure we weren't surrounded by the Woods on all sides.

"What are we talkin' about?" Richard said, as he closed the screen door behind him in the entryway and joined us in the kitchen.

Gretchen filled him in.

"I'm not sure we need to go to those lengths," he said, accepting a cup of coffee from Nettie. "We should be getting our supplies together and ready to go for when the others get back. No doubt, they'll want to get a start on that soon. We'll need to be ready to move when those Woods reach the edge of the property."

"That's why we're taking the precautions, Rich," Gretchen emphasized. "Liz is going to want to know where the Woods are when she gets back. She's going to want an idea of how much time we have left before we need to leave."

"That's not something you can quantify," he reasoned. "The Woods down the mountain seem to be coming at us at an unprecedented pace right now. Who knows where they'll be tomorrow morning?"

Gretchen crossed her arms. "So, you're going to tell me what happened last night doesn't have you the least bit concerned or curious?"

"Of course, I'm concerned. But it doesn't mean I want to run headlong into danger just so I can know how close it is to me."

"You didn't seem to be afraid of that last night," Gretchen retorted. "Running off into the fog like a trouble-finding magnet."

Richard closed his eyes and grunted. "I was checking the perimeter! I was armed!"

I slid out of my chair and made for the front door. "I'm going to check the mountain," I called back. Tempest's claws scratched on the floor as she followed me.

"Evie, wait."

I pushed out onto the porch and into the morning light. It flowed across me like a warm blanket and put me at ease once more. For now, I felt like this was my mountain again, my refuge from the awfulness of the world. It probably wouldn't seem so the farther I walked, but this strengthened my confidence enough that I was ready for whatever came my way, even if it was the shadow again.

"Evie," Nettie said, appearing on the other side of the screen door. Gretchen and Richard's argument continued in the background.

I turned around hesitantly. "What?"

THE WILD FALL

"I'm sorry you think I don't trust your capability. I do. I think you're incredibly brave for volunteering to do this. I'm only trying to keep you safe. So is your father. It's all out of love."

The words had started to make me feel better but the last sentence made my shoulders bristle. "I'm not helpless. You and my dad might be together, but that does not make us one big happy family."

Nettie's posture stiffened with my words. Without saying anything, she nodded and walked back into the kitchen.

I let out a long tense breath and proceeded to the road with Tempest to climb the trails up the mountain.

SEVEN

Liz

We were three hours into our walk back when I noticed the silence. It had happened gradually, which is why I didn't catch on until it was too late. There had been the distant sound of chirping birds, along with a slightly cool gust of wind. The guys were having a disagreement behind me about which of their favorite eighties bands was the best: Depeche Mode, Metallica, or New Order.

I raised a fist, a signal they all recognized to mean "shut up."

Standing there on the open road, surrounded by sudden silence in the middle of the day felt silly. The birds had gone silent. The wind had died. Worst of all those clouds we thought we'd left far behind were gathering ahead of us.

Sanz growled behind me. I glanced back over my shoulder at her. She was turned toward the field on our right and the forest behind it. It was dark inside, as though the light couldn't penetrate it.

Hank approached, keeping his voice low. "We should move, now."

"Let's go," I gestured, never letting my sights leave the tree line.

We quickened our pace, which was difficult with all the new weight we carried. Our backpacks were flush with canned goods, apples, medical supplies, and water. We hadn't found any fuel, but I was starting to feel better about that; we didn't need the extra weight now.

Sanz, who toted a small pack filled with some veterinary tools and medicine, was now also keeping the woods in her vision fully, jaunting along almost sideways as Gjon held her leash.

"I don't like this. I don't like this," Ash chanted as he upped his pace to a steady jog.

We stayed running on and off for a solid twenty minutes. The backpack straps on my shoulders chafed and I was overheating in my flannel jacket. As we moved away from the field and trees slowly filled in the sides of the road, I noticed our sun being covered by those menacing storm clouds. We were walking right into a growing darkness.

"We're not far off, now," I said. I'm not sure if I was trying to comfort them or myself. I'd marked the car on our GPS; it was less than an hour away, closer if we sped up.

"Not sure we should keep going," Hank said. "We should find shelter."

I didn't stop. "It's a bit farther."

We kept pace. Another ten minutes passed. Rain speckled the road in front of us. The first icy drops were like being yanked out of a possession. I had focused so hard on moving forward I almost forgot how much space we still had to travel. We were still thirty minutes out and the sun was blocked now. Noises sprung up on our right, the depth in the forest growing and growing. Bushes thrashed deep inside. The ominous cracking of sticks ahead of and behind us sent my heart thumping.

Sanz had gone into full aggressive stance, her hackles raised and teeth bared. She barked at the thicket and Gjon had to pull her along to get her to keep moving.

"We have a plan?" Ash asked, his shirt turning dark with each raindrop.

I stared ahead at the road. Going any farther was suicide. As much as I wanted to get back to our car, there was a real possibility it wasn't there anymore. The Woods could move in on a whim and did so randomly. We would have to find a way around. We had to make a break for it.

"Into the field," I said, gesturing to our left. There was a large corn field there with a barn beyond it.

We fled the road, skirting an embankment, and climbed over a wooden fence. There was still an old tin sign posted there that read KEEP OUT. I took Sanz's leash while Gjon hopped the fence. I glanced at the road and felt my oxygen leave me. The trees were moving forward, the darkness following. The sound was like the earth breaking apart, my ears hurting it was so loud.

"RUN!" I yelled at the top of my lungs.

I turned and fled into the corn. The stalks blanketed my vision on all sides, the leaves scratching and scraping at my neck and hands as I blazed my own path through them. Every time I'd break out into a new row, I'd look from side to side. I noticed Ash's foot disappearing into the next row and Gjon emerging next to me as I plunged into the next one.

Sanz yanked at the leash ahead of me and I let myself be pulled. My arm felt as though it was going to fall off.

The earth-shattering cacophony grew louder. A growing chill behind me snatched at me. I pushed my legs harder; faster. My lungs burned and screamed for air.

I burst into the next row. There. I'd seen an arm. I don't know whose.

Into the next row. More dry leaves hit my cheeks. One caught me in the eye.

The roof of the barn bobbed into view ahead of me.

Sanz yanked me out into tall grass, momentum never faltering. I glanced around me even as we came to another wooden fence. Sanz scooted under and kept going. I hit the fence dead on and my grip faltered on her leash.

Someone grabbed me under my arms and hauled me from where I'd fallen. I saw Hank's eyes briefly as I stumbled over the wooden fence and turned to help him. My hands closed around his wrists as he put his boot on the fence plank. Behind him, the world was a blur of flying grass. Like being caught inside of a tornado, I couldn't tell which way we'd come from.

I pulled and Hank and I tumbled onto the grass. I scrambled to my feet, my boots slipping in the muddy earth and ran for the barn.

Gjon reached the door and yanked on it. It wasn't opening. It was locked.

Ash ran in from the right and kicked the door. It cracked under the sudden force and caved in. Both ran inside.

At the door, I turned around, hoping to see Sanz somewhere in the ensuing pandemonium. She stood close to the fence, barking at the approaching chaos. Hank had gone to grab her.

"Hank!" I shouted.

It was almost on top of him.

Hank lugged Sanz into his arms as she wildly protested, still snarling and barking.

He wasn't going to make it.

I ran toward him.

Hank shouted something at me, something I couldn't hear over the grinding earth and insane wind.

And then, he was gone.

"No!" I stopped in my tracks, my legs wobbly and out of my control.

One moment, he had been there. The next, his body had vanished into the cloud of greenery.

Sanz tumbled to the ground a few feet in front of me, rolling end over end with a whimper of shock.

I started for her.

An arm closed around my chest. I fought it, but it was stronger than I was. It pulled me back into the barn and slammed the door closed in front of us.

I collapsed against the floor as the sound of the earth screaming tore over the barn. I bit into my arm to keep my cries from letting loose, to keep my soul intact. My fingers had wrapped around someone's hand. They gripped onto mine as hard as I held onto theirs.

Make it stop! Make it stop!

I could hardly hear myself think.

After what could have been seconds or minutes, the sound faded. The silence returned in full force. I lifted my head and rubbed at my eyes, trying to clear them. The barn floor was coated in dust and it all had gotten in my eyes and my lungs. When I finally was able to see, I noticed Ash crouched over me. My arm was bleeding from where I'd bit it. Gjon's hand still clutched mine. We all crouched together and held each other, our breaths hitched with tears: tremulous, and heavy.

"You held me back," I said, not staring at Ash but knowing my words were directed at him. "I could have saved them."

"We would have lost you, too," he answered.

I was the first to wipe my eyes and stand. I gathered my gun from where it had fallen and checked to make sure it hadn't jammed. I took a long deep breath. "Get your weapons out; we're going in after them."

"That's a fucking bad idea," Ash said.

"I'm not asking," I snapped.

Gjon had already pulled out his handgun. "They could still be alive," he added.

"We know what's in there and it isn't fucking unicorns," Ash growled. "We need to get out of here and get back to the car."

"They were only a few feet from the barn. Probably still are," I said. "We make sure they're okay and we go."

I didn't wait for Ash to say anything before I moved to the barn door. "Ready?"

Gjon nodded, wiping a stray tear from his face.

Ash rolled his eyes. "Fucking A."

Gunshots erupted from outside.

"Hank!"

We all rushed out into an alien world.

The vast cornfield had been replaced with a myriad of tall moss-coated trunks, whose tops stretched into a tangled maze of black branches blocking out the light. The forest floor was a mess of brambles, short bristling bushes, and dead leaves. The air was heavier, the warmth of summer replaced by a noxious wet heat that made me long for air conditioning. Nearly five feet out in the direction of the road, everything was masked by an impermeable fog.

These weren't the Woods I'd remembered. When I'd looked for Brody's soul all those years ago, the forest had been greener, more alive somehow. This reminded me of one of the many graveyards we'd passed getting our supplies in Middehitch. It felt like this purgatory was darker, chillier and more treacherous.

A scream echoed into the trees.

"Hank!" My feet jump-started me as I ran into the mist in the direction of his call.

I couldn't see where I was going. The whole ground had changed; roots had gathered, rocks had emerged through the soil. My boots caught on them continuously and nearly sent me sprawling. The guys' footsteps behind me made me double my speed.

Sliding down a small hill, I saw Hank backed against a tree trunk, holding his handgun out and pulling the trigger. The chamber clinked each time. Empty. The haunted look in his eyes slowed me, made me wary to get any closer. Had his gun still been loaded, he might have fired in our direction from the noise we made.

"Hank!" I called, tentatively. "Are you alright?"

He threw out a hand. "Liz! Don't—"

Something monstrous emerged from the darkness behind him, its jagged teeth closing on his shoulder. Hank screamed as blood surged across his chest.

"Fucking hell!" Ash yelled, raising his shotgun.

I aimed my own handgun at the creature and I fired.

The wolf's face exploded with blood. It let go of Hank and leapt into the space between him and us, crouching for an attack.

I kept firing, my hands like iron as every bullet hit home, my fury hotter and wilder than an spewing volcano.

Despite each hit, each burst of blood and fur from its frame, the wolf appeared unfazed. As I finished the magazine and Gjon finished his soon after, the thing only shook off the damage as if it was an inconvenience. It snarled, its golden eyes searing into mine as it readied to spring.

Ash's shotgun exploded and one of the creature's eyes popped. The wolf collapsed, a massive chunk blown out of the side of its head. I wasn't sure but I thought I could see its brain, something pink, jelly like and awful squirming inside. The wolf scrabbled to its feet and fled, vanishing into the mist.

"Hank!" I ran to him.

Six deep puncture wounds spread across his chest and shoulder and poured dark blood across his jacket. Rasping, he set his eyes on mine. "You shouldn't have come."

The words brought me back to the last time I'd been in these Woods with Brody. When I'd followed him to try and save him from the wolf and whatever fate had awaited him at the Monolith. He'd said the same thing to me: "You shouldn't have come here."

"We're going to get you home, okay?" I looked over my shoulder. "Gjon! Get over here!"

THE WILD FALL

Gjon dropped to his knees beside me, swinging his pack off and tearing fabric from something inside. "Hold this against his shoulder."

I pushed the cloth against the blood-soaked olive canvas but it only covered three of the puncture wounds. "I need more!"

Hank inhaled at the pressure, wheezing. Blood was already dribbling from his lips.

"Hey, hey." I wiped it away. "Look at me. This is not it. Evie is waiting for you at home and you still need to marry Nettie."

Hank said something but his words were too faint.

"I can't hear you," I leaned closer.

"I...saw him."

I shook my head. "Saw who?"

Gjon pressed more cloth against Hank's shoulder.

"Can we carry him?" I asked.

Gjon shook his head. "His lung is pierced."

Hank coughed. Blood spattered my face and got in my eye.

"I saw him." He coughed again. "Brody."

My neck tensed. I didn't understand. I put both hands on his face. "What do you mean? Hank?"

His eyes unfocused. He breathed in.

I waited for him to breathe out.

He never did.

"Hank..." His name fell from my lips. I couldn't move. I couldn't make myself take my hands away from him. Hank: my right hand. My most trusted friend...

Gjon let his hands slip from Hank's wound and fell back on his butt. "God..." he whispered.

"Damn it!" Ash shouted from behind us, kicking a tree stump.

I racked my brain trying to understand what Hank had meant. He'd seen Brody? How?

Brody was dead. Not only was he dead but I'd killed his ghost. The only thing that was left of him was the black shape that haunted our lawn every night. Was that what Hank had meant? Even then, how would he have known who that was? I'd never told him about Brody...

Gjon put a hand on my arm. "We need to leave before the wolf gets its second wind."

I took a shuddering breath and swallowed hard. I closed Hank's eyes and stood. I didn't want to leave his body here, not in this horrible place with these horrible things. But, there was no way we could take him with us. We would have to find an alternate route back to the car, one that would take much longer now since the Woods were in our way.

Gjon zipped his bag and swung it onto his back. After taking a quick moment to reload our weapons, we started back toward the barn. Our ears on alert, we traversed the terrain much quicker this time, remembering where holes and rocks were.

We reached the wooden fence that blocked off the cornfield from the barn. Gjon stopped and jerked his head to the left. "Listen. Do you hear that?"

"Less talk, more move!" Ash urged.

I craned my head in the direction Gjon was looking. A faint high-pitched squealing sound. No, not squealing. Whining.

Gjon clambered over the fence and pushed through the giant dark ferns, following the sound. "Sanzy? Here, girl."

I followed and with a grunt, I heard Ash give chase.

Gjon crouched and grabbed at something in the greenery. "Honey, I got you." He lifted the red dog from the ferns, fireman carrying her toward us.

"Is she okay?"

"Can't tell. We need to get her out of here into the light."

"Finally, yes. I'll lead," Ash said, aiming the shotgun ahead of us and following the small path through the trees toward the barn. We passed it by. The mammoth-sized building seemed so out of place. We trudged toward the faint light where we knew the border to the Woods and our world lay.

Gjon spoke to Sanz softly as he cautiously carried her over the various obstacles in our way. She whined and yipped, her normally wise eyes wet and fearful.

The further we got to the border, the more I thought about Hank. The more I imagined grabbing his hands and pulling him over the fence. I thought about us lying side by side in the bed last night together, laughing. I thought about walking in on him and Nettie in the kitchen the other day, all the times I'd watched them hold each other and kiss. I thought about Evie and her anger..

She'd never gotten the chance to say goodbye.

She was never going to see her father again.

As the tears streamed down my cheeks and the muscles in my jaw hardened, I realized we could finally see the border. The field on the other side was as flat and green as all the other ones we had passed by in the last couple days. We were due west of the road and hopefully our still-intact car.

A roar chased through the trees behind us somewhere. Ash and I quickly climbed through the weeds and bushes, holding them aside for Gjon as he carried Sanz out to safety. Then, we followed and were again bathed in sunshine.

We kept going, moving a good half mile away from the Woods before we dropped our bags and Gjon checked over Sanz. Ash walked to a random point in the field and took off his baseball cap. He stayed there for a long time. He shouted some. Swore a lot.

I sat in the grass, checking myself over for ticks, anything to keep my mind occupied. I found seven, two burrowed. I quickly pulled them out with a spoon and tossed them. I rubbed my hands through my hair and shut my eyes.

Hank was there behind closed lids. Those unearthly green eyes of his and his gentle voice. What the hell was I going to say to Evie? To Nettie?

I twisted a blade of grass in my fingers until it was a tight whip. Then, I started on another. And another. After about ten minutes and half a dozen grass whips, I abandoned my self-punishment and went to check on Gjon and Sanz. "Is she going to make it?"

Gjon nodded. "I think she broke one of her legs. I wrapped it to keep it immobile but I won't be able to do surgery until we get her back home." The muscles in Gjon's neck were strained, tears slipping from his eyes. "There was nothing I could do for Hank."

I grabbed his hand and held it hard, my fingers almost hurting with the effort. "It's not your fault. Hank didn't even want us to go in after him. At least we kept him from losing his soul…"

My mind got lost in a sea of mental images about what could have happened if we hadn't gotten there in time. How Hank would have become a husk, his body purged of the only thing that made Hank Hank. And then he would have changed, become something much worse…

Gjon squeezed my hand back. "Liz?"

I nodded and let the thoughts sink back beneath the waves in my mind. "Let's go."

He nodded and I helped him heft Sanz over one of his shoulders. I whistled to Ash, who rejoined us. "What are we going to do, Liz?" he asked once we were together.

Hank's words slid into my mind again. He'd seen Brody. In the Woods. Brody's soul was there. If Brody's was there, maybe Hank's was, too?

"We stick to the plan," I said, forcing my hopeful thoughts to drown in practicality. "We get back home. We gather everything. We move to Onyx River."

"We'll have to find an alternate route now," Ash said. "We need to be cautious we don't get ourselves in this kind of situation again. I'm not sure it's worth the risk right now."

"Then we'll find a safe fucking road," I growled. "We have to keep moving forward. Survival is ahead of us, not behind us."

Ash put his hands up as if to surrender.

We set out toward home.

EIGHT

Evie

Tempest and I spent the day roaming the mountain behind the cabin. We stuck to the more open trails initially, the ones with more sunlight. Ever since yesterday, I grew nervous we'd come across something on the trails we wouldn't want to find: another one of those shadow monsters. Within a few hours, it became clear to me there wasn't anything lurking in the trees here. The forest seemed normal, no dark depths to get lost in and no wolves prowling.

I spent a few more hours navigating some of the trails I was less familiar with. We couldn't be too careful . While I walked, I reminisced.

I remembered the night five years ago when we had let our guard down. The Woods had been within sight of our home. We had holed up in the school in Cardend. It had seemed strange living in a place I'd mostly hated in my childhood.

I remembered getting picked on by Ronnie Cole in first grade. He'd throw paper balls at me and sometimes put small sticks in my hair when we went out for recess. He lived with his parents in the most rundown house in the neighborhood. His older brother had lost most of his teeth.

THE WILD FALL

His dad worked as an individual contractor, a handyman who did odd jobs for whoever offered him the right price. They had holes in their walls covered in blue tarps and the yard was scattered with rusted car parts, old and faded plastic toys, and a broken swing set.

The same week this whole nightmare began, the same week my mom died, Ronnie had pushed me at recess and I'd cut my knee. I remembered the blurry school hallway through my tears as I limped to the nurse's office with the teacher's aid, Ms. Evelyn. The brightly colored posters on the walls reminding students to wash their hands and not to bully others and to say please and thank you…

I grew up after the Merging roaming those halls with the lights off, and always felt a little like I'd get in trouble for doing it. That maybe the cantankerous old librarian who used to work there and had done so for decades might wander out and yell at me for making too much noise.

When I turned eleven, everyone had thrown me a birthday celebration. They'd found some Little Debbie Zebra Cakes and created a massive birthday cake from them by forming a small circle and stacking them in layers. It was beautiful and every bit of the child inside of me felt as if I was sparkling with the love in the room. Ash had even found candles on one of our last scouts, stuck eleven in a circle on the outer ring of the cake and lit them.

Gretchen had given me a knife, with my dad's consent. It was high quality carbon with a small switch that helped flip the knife out and had a blue handle. We practiced together for a time until it became like second nature to me. I kept it on me all the time now.

Dad, Liz, Ash, and Gretchen were all there. Back then, there was Katrina, a former teacher who drew me a beautiful colorful birthday card, Darnell, Gretchen's husband, Alari, a professional gymnast, and Sully, an old man who reminded me of my grandpa, Shane. Always picking a fight. Never happy. He was nice on my birthday though. He gave me a ring that had once belonged to his late wife. It was a golden band with a small swirl engraved. Nothing fancy. I kept it on a necklace as it was too big for my fingers.

It was early morning when I got woken. I heard the sound of someone screaming, someone close by. Dad told me to stay where I was, lying under a tent we'd erected in my old classroom. I remembered staying still and worrying how loud my breathing was. My neck started to hurt from the position I was in but I didn't dare move or make a sound. When the door to the classroom opened again, I closed my eyes and burrowed into the sleeping bag further.

"Evie." My dad's voice, firm and even. "We need to leave, now."

He helped me out of my sleeping bag. Liz was there, helping him pack our things. I grabbed my unicorn backpack with my few treasured belongings. My stuffed zebra, Anthony, was rolled into my sleeping bag and tied hurriedly with an elastic cord. I wanted nothing more than to have him safe in my bag though.

More screams echoed in the halls outside. I recognized one of them and my stomach twisted in knots. "That's Sully!" I yelled.

Both my dad and Liz shushed me. We sat in the darkness for minutes, listening. That was the worst memory of that day: hearing my friends die. I don't remember how many times each of them screamed or for how long. All I knew was we were doing nothing to help them, nothing as their souls were ripped from their bodies, and I felt hollow.

Eventually, Liz and Dad decided it was time to go. Dad held my hand while Liz took the lead, holding her gun and hefting my sleeping bag under one arm. Dad had the rest of our gear strapped onto his back. He looked like an abominable snowman in the darkness, towering over me, dressed in his puffy warm jacket.

The hallways were clear. As we made our way to the front of the school, we passed by Katrina, lying prone in the middle of the hall. Her throat was slashed open, her right arm mangled to the point where

THE WILD FALL

I could see bone in the ravaged skin and muscle. Bloody paw prints streaked the black and white checker-tiled halls in front of us.

Whatever had killed Katrina had gone in this direction.

Dad told me to stay behind him and to close my eyes, but I had already seen it and I couldn't look away.

We rounded a bend with two corridors branching off on either side of us. The front of the building was another several paces ahead of us but outside it seemed darker. I didn't want to go out there.

Noise from the hall on our left made us all stop and clamber to the nearest wall for protection. All I could see was the backside of Dad's backpack and my old sneakers with a hole in the toe. We listened as footfalls ran toward the front hall. Two figures appeared around the bend: Gretchen and Darnell. Darnell was leaning on Gretchen heavily and I noticed there was a large cut running down his leg. Blood streaked the hall behind them.

"Daddy?" I said.

Gretchen and Darnell saw us and we joined together. Dad put his hand against the side of my head and for some reason, having it there reminded me he was real, and he would keep me safe.

"Two came in," Gretchen was saying, stumbling over her words. "Sully distracted them so we could get out. I haven't seen Ash or Alari but Katrina I think went—"

"We already saw her," I blurted out.

Everyone shared a knowing look.

As the adults conferred on what to do, I thought I heard a noise from behind us and turned around. The hall was dark but from around the corner I couldn't see came a kind of shuffling noise.

I pulled at Dad's hand. "Someone's coming."

Everyone turned in that direction and Gretchen suggested we go into the administrative office on our right. We ducked inside and closed the doors on either end. Ducked behind the visitor waiting chairs, we watched through the glass as something appeared around the corner.

The wolf was bigger than I'd imagined it would be, its back as high as the middle shelf on some of the trophy cases lining the hall. Its hair was black, like the pipe cleaners I used to use for projects in art a long time ago. The worst part about it was its face: a mouth of tiny pointed teeth and large, swirling golden eyes shining like a full moon.

All I wanted to do was to go back to bed. All I wanted to do was wake and have all this be a nightmare. I started shaking all over and couldn't hold back the urge to pee my pants. They were soaked within seconds. I felt my dad's hand on my head again; his attempt to shield my eyes so I wouldn't see.

A burst of crackling and light exploded on our right as a flare was thrown. The wolf reared back in surprise, roaring. It retreated into the darkness of the hallway where Gretchen and Darnell had appeared from. Moments later, Alari and Ash appeared at the front hall. Gretchen tapped the window to let them know we were inside and we carefully all filed out into the open.

I couldn't keep my eyes off the hall where the wolf had gone. "It's going to come back!" I whined, my voice bubbling with tears. "I want to go home."

Home wasn't a real place; it was a concept. I didn't care where home was as long as it was safe and full of sunshine. I couldn't explain to anyone at the time but it was what I had meant, what I had longed for and thought I'd found here at the cabin. Instead, Liz crouched to my level and pulled me into a protective hug. "Nothing is going to happen to you. We'll keep you safe."

Ash had sniffed the air. "Someone pee?"

I wanted to cry more. I hadn't peed my pants since I was a little kid.

"We need to leave before one of those things smells that," he added, keeping his gun pointed at the hall where the wolf had fled.

THE WILD FALL

We backed toward the entrance and the set of push-through doors there. Half our group was concentrated on what was ahead of us and half on what was behind. Dad was pointed forward and I was hysterical at this point, blindly holding his hand and following along. He'd had to put me down, the weight on his back and me in his arms too much for him to carry. We had kept the front doors chained shut for our protection. The wolves had broken through one of the windows in the old teacher's lounge, windows Ash had argued needed to be boarded.

As Gretchen fished for the key to unlock our front door, I heard Alari shift position and say, "Get it open, now!"

Everyone's weapons raised. Gretchen's keys jingled as she unlocked the door. I heard something scraping on tile inside behind us and the shakes took over my body again. Screams erupted all around me. I was whisked off my feet and we were running.

Liz's red hair was blurred by my tears as she ran with me in her arms Dad, Gretchen and Darnell were behind us. Dad was unclipping the pack from around his waist as he ran when I saw him get pulled back. I screamed for him.

Darnell threw himself at Dad, grabbing his hands, while Gretchen fired at the wolf masked in the fog behind us. Liz didn't stop; she kept running, carrying me farther away from Dad and concealing everything behind us in the fog.

Alari ran past us back toward the gunshots. Ash appeared and took me from Liz. "I got her, I got her!" They ran with me. I screamed for my dad.

We emerged through the fog into a place that seemed more real, more like the city we had known. It was still night, and the air was so cold, our breaths streamed from us like ghosts.

I was sobbing, my pants sopping wet. Ash and Liz ran to one of the nearby buildings, an old Italian restaurant. They slammed the door open and quickly fled behind the counter. Ash put me on the ground and quickly grabbed a folded tablecloth from nearby to drape around my shoulders. "Stay here, hun," he said.

They both went to the door to stand watch.

My dad and Gretchen eventually appeared. Gretchen was crying harder than I was.

We never saw Alari or Darnell again.

I returned to the house around mid-afternoon, the sun casting an orange pall over the fields and the house. I gave Tempest some water from our reserves and sat on the front porch. The group wasn't back yet. They had gone a way's out, probably had to abandon the car somewhere to walk. That happened a lot when scouting missions went out. I couldn't imagine a world of people leaving their cars wherever they felt like it.

I heard in the GRCs no one owned cars. People walked where they needed to go or took public transportation buses. Cars were liabilities. If people could leave whenever they wanted, it made the safety of the GRCs moot. We still didn't know how they dealt with Woods intrusions; or if they dealt with them. I hated to admit but I had started to wonder if us being in one of those places did make some sense. No more running from the Woods, no more scouting missions to find food, fresh meat… It sounded like these places still operated like regular towns once did, only in smaller more militant capacities.

But Liz had argued they weren't safe. She'd been quick to tell me they segregated people based on their ability to see ghosts or not. The ones who could were sent to get tested on, as if they were some kind of disease that needed to be cured. Those people were the Attached: people who had a ghost following them around and only that person could see them. While I hadn't thought at the time anyone in our group could be one of the Attached, I now wondered if I was. Seeing the dark shape yesterday had me second guessing everything I thought I knew about this Merged world.

Gretchen asked for an update on my trip to the mountain and I told her I'd found nothing out of place. She stood rigid, muscles flexed as if she was holding a breath in. She had kept her long black hair chopped short since that fateful day at the school. She told me Darnell had loved it more than she did. Now he was gone, she didn't want to think of it. She kept the sides of her head shaved, which I always thought looked so cool, but time consuming to maintain. "Ever heard of Grace Jones?" she asked me one day I caught her shaving it. I hadn't. "Coolest bitch alive," she'd said. "Did her hair like this a lot."

I had since taken to braiding my hair into a mohawk-like fashion. I'd seen a tutorial in an old magazine I'd grabbed on one of our scouts. I wore it like this today. It made me feel like I had some control, even when everything was spinning out of it.

Afternoon rolled into night. Signal fires were lit before the sun vanished. There was no fire pit tonight. Instead, we all sat on the deck in rocking and beach chairs anxiously waiting. I hadn't touched my rice and the bowl was now cold in my lap. Tempest and Otto waited with us on the porch, each lounging though their ears were perked and listening.

Minutes turned to hours.

The temperature plummeted. Richard and Nettie went inside with Otto. Tempest, Gretchen, and I remained. Nettie eventually brought us tea and though the mug was warm and welcome in my grasp, my throat had closed as the time had ticked by.

"Something went wrong," I finally said. "Something had to have gone wrong."

"If something went wrong, then Liz and your dad did the safe thing and rested somewhere for another night," Gretchen reasoned.

I wanted to believe her. This wasn't the first time the scouting crew hadn't come back on time and it probably wouldn't be the last. Liz was a master at reading the Woods. She'd keep them all safe.

"We should go inside." Gretchen stood. "We don't want a repeat of last night."

Tempest and I followed, and we locked the door for the night.

We all stayed in the living room that night. I took the couch while the others stretched out on sleeping bags on the floor. Lights off, listening to the others breathe, every terrible scary possibility of why the group was late played over in my mind. I imagined wolves surrounding the town of Onyx River and tearing them to pieces. I imagined their car plummeting into an icy river from a bridge. I imagined Dad calling my name one last time.

I awoke to a stream of sun blinding me. I nearly flung myself off the couch as I ran to the window to look.

No car. They still weren't home.

It was still early. Richard and Gretchen were still asleep on the floor, along with Otto who snored softly beside them. Nettie was in the kitchen making breakfast and coffee. Tempest had woken with my burst of energy and now sat expectantly beside me, head cocked as if waiting for some kind of speech.

I walked toward the kitchen, Tempest's paws tapping behind me.

Nettie had her earbuds in and was listening to something with a beat as she stirred at a pot on the stove. I entered the room and sat at the table. She glanced over and pulled a bud out of her ear. "Hey there. You want some coffee?"

I had waved off coffee for years, not understanding why something so bitter was so delicious to everyone else. This morning though, I accepted. She poured me a cup and set it in front of me with a small smile, as if everything I'd said to her was all water under the bridge.

"What are you listening to?" I asked.

THE WILD FALL

"Blondie," she said. "You ever heard of them?"

I shook my head.

She offered me the other earbud.

I shook my head again and took my first sip of coffee. The sourness of it made me pucker my lips.

"Here." Nettie dipped a spoon into some honey and then put it in my mug. "Give that a stir."

I did. "Why do you bother putting on makeup every day?"

Nettie looked at me. Part of her daily routine was red lipstick on her tiny lips and black eyeliner for her large eyes. She reminded me a little bit of a cartoon character.

"I do it because I like it," she said, stirring the pot on the stove. "It reminds me of a time when things were normal. Suppose it makes me feel more like myself."

"You don't do it because of Dad?" I had a faint memory of my dad and my mom dressing up for something, maybe a party. My mom had worn fake lashes and put on bright lipstick. The way my dad had looked at her made my insides melt.

"No," she chuckled. "Purely for myself."

I had always thought she was insecure, that she did this to try and make herself look prettier for my dad. No one else here needed or wanted to put on makeup. Certainly not Liz and I swore if Gretchen were forced to, she'd rather burn her face off.

But I had never considered the possibility this was merely routine; and it might make her feel good. Kind of like my runs with Tempest in the morning.

I took another sip of the coffee. Sweeter and surprisingly good.

She had her head cocked, waiting for my reaction.

I gave her a thumbs up. "It's like magic."

"Honey kind of is. Hundreds of bees getting together, pulling pollen from thousands of flowers all to make this sweet syrup." She was back to swaying back and forth with the beat of her music, which I could faintly hear. "I think Richard and Ash want to start beekeeping once we get to the new farm," she said. "Can you imagine having this at our fingertips all the time?"

I couldn't. But having access to little luxuries like this would be heavenly.

The crunch of tires on dirt in the driveway made me bolt from my seat. I ran to the nearest window, Nettie behind me. The Jeep was settling into place in front of the barn, the frame still rocking from driving over a large pothole.

I ran to the living room. Tempest barked in the kitchen.

Gretchen was already on her feet and Richard rose when I came in. "They're back!" I exclaimed. My entire body was flooded with relief.

I yanked open the front door and we all spilled out onto the deck as the others climbed out of the car. Liz was the first one I saw and even as I ran toward her, I slowed taking in the sight of her. Her clothes were slashed with mud and something else, something darker. Her eyes had a hollowness to them, and when they looked at me, it felt as though I was looking right through her. I'd only seen her eyes like that one other time: after we'd escaped the school.

Ash and Gjon exited the car next, both as dirty and panged with exhaustion as Liz. Gjon rushed to the trunk and opened it. He lifted out Sanz, who practically became a puddle in his arms.

My view was blocked by Gretchen and Richard who rushed in. "What happened to her?"

"Her leg is broken," Gjon was saying. "I'll need to operate."

"I'll help," Gretchen said.

Ash and Richard were hugging and kissing. Ash's eyes met mine for only a moment before he looked away again.

I raised my voice. "Dad?"

I hadn't seen him get out of the car yet.

I moved around Ash and Richard so I could see better, but the car was empty. I glanced around. Somehow, I'd missed him in the commotion?

Spinning. He wasn't there. I didn't see him.

Someone caught my hand and carefully spun me back around. Liz stood before me. Hollowed. Tears sparking the corners of her eyes. "Evie…"

"No!" The terror I'd fought to keep at bay all night long lashed out and grabbed me. I couldn't feel my face for a few seconds and blindly wondered if I'd lost all feeling in my body, too.

"He didn't make it," she finished saying.

I tried to pull away. "I don't want to hear it. Don't tell me."

I heard a sob behind me. I looked over my shoulder to see Nettie, sitting on the porch steps, a hand over her mouth, her eyeliner bleeding. Richard ran to her.

I was on the ground. The dirt was soft underneath, almost welcoming. I wanted to be part of it in those moments, to not be human and feel this way. I wanted to be part of the earth.

Ash was kneeling over me, holding my hand. The tears burst from me like an exploded dam, surging. My voice made these strange sounds, strained, animalistic wails barely resembling the words I tried to say. All I could see in my head was my dad. All I could picture was his face and the feeling of his strong arms hugging me a couple mornings ago. I could still taste the unpleasantness of our fight the morning he left. I never got to say goodbye. I never got to say I was sorry.

Liz didn't move toward me. Didn't do anything. I couldn't read her face through the mask of tears but I got a sense she'd expected this. She hadn't wanted to come back here because of this.

"You let him die!" I screamed at her as I started to get up. "Why?"

Ash held me to him, his large arms encasing me gently. I lost all my strength, all my will to move and slumped into grief.

THREE MONTHS LATER

NINE

Liz

Snow was on the horizon. It was hard to remember a time when I used to love it, when I thought it was beautiful and the scenery around it was enhanced by its majesty. Those were also the times where we had running water, electricity, heaters, and common conveniences. I had lived ten years in a world without many of those luxuries. The generator at our old cabin had powered a handful of lights, the fridge, and kept any electronics we might need charged. Our stove had been gas. Our water was pulled from a well. We bathed in the cold river of the creek or boiled water on the stove for weekly sponge baths.

Moving to Onyx River had been life changing. For the first time in a decade, I took a hot shower. I slept in a bed in my own room with plush blankets in a house with a working electric furnace. I was not as worried about the long New England winter ahead of us. I knew there were fewer things we'd need to worry about because of Onyx River's natural power sources.

In spite of this, I didn't feel safe and I didn't feel secure.

I was considering leaving it all behind.

THE WILD FALL

I sat in my room on my bed watching the clouds accumulate on the horizon. It was mid-afternoon. I'd taken a break from raking leaves in the front yard to make tea, something we always had in great supply. I'd brought a cup to Nettie, who had accepted it and then closed the door to her room once more.

None of us were the same after Hank's death. Nettie had lost her openness, her sweetness. Things Hank had brought out in her that we had all assumed were dominant traits, were now gone. She cooked the meals in the morning and evening, cleaned inside and read a lot about canning, harvesting, and preparing various foods. If asked to help out with a group activity, she did so without offering any conversation or opinion. She was always the first to turn in in the evening.

Likewise, Evie had also tucked into herself deeper. Her anger had bloomed like a large flower in the three months that had passed. She spent more time away from the farm than anyone, often choosing to stay in town overnight…which was something that always unnerved the rest of us, particularly me. When she did return, we fought. I was starting to wonder if she even cared if she lived or died anymore.

Oddly enough, it wasn't too far off from how I felt.

Hank's words before his death had stayed with me and I ruminated on them more and more as the time passed. He'd seen Brody.

Every time I thought back to the horrible day ten years ago, the day I pulled the trigger and watched him in Josh's body fall across the floor, I felt a small piece of me die.

Ghosts had roamed the earth since the Woods had appeared, attached to certain people and not to others. Brody had been attached to me, before I killed him. In part, I'd done it to end his suffering. Another part was because he had become something terrible, and had done things I knew the real Brody, the one I remembered and loved, would never have done. I'd heard it told if an Attached person killed their own ghost, they would be set free.

That, as it turns out, was a lie.

At night, he'd come. As he had come every night for the last ten years. The thing that was Brody would stand in the darkness outside and watch the house, or whatever building I was in and wait. I never made a move to go to him and he never made a move to go to me. We stayed in this weird stalemate, watching the other. Deep inside, I knew he was no longer anyone I recognized. He'd been transformed.

I worried about Evie being out in the darkness with him.

I'd spent a long time wondering about some of the things I'd seen in the Woods while I'd been searching for Brody back then. The purgatory realm had had strange buildings I hadn't been able to understand, hellish and frightening architecture. Screams had erupted from those places as if they were prisons. Did souls eventually go there? And when they did, what happened to them? Was that where Hank was?

A knock on my door pulled me out of my thoughts. Richard opened the door a moment later. "Gjon and Ash are back. Looks like they had some luck."

I nodded and rose from the bed. My mind was on fire with thoughts of days passed and my body ached to move. I followed Richard around the hall, our boots clomping on the dark stained wood to the staircase, passed the cream-colored walls with the huge landscape paintings of the English countryside. Nettie's door was ajar; she must have already gone to the kitchen to meet the hunting party.

We descended the white-painted stairs into the main foyer and turned to follow the hallway toward the kitchen. There, at the rear entry, I could hear Ash and Gjon murmuring about something.

Sanz emerged from the kitchen door, still a slight limp in her hind leg as she sauntered past us with a low woof. Gjon had been able to save her leg but at the expense of her being able to run. She was still a phenomenal tracker. Gjon had brought her on the hunting party for pure nostalgia. Otto had started training as a sporting dog to fill her spot.

I turned the corner into the kitchen and everyone's eyes lifted. Nettie, who had been flipping through some books for recipes, went back to searching. Ash held a dead turkey by the legs and grinned. "A few weeks late for Thanksgiving, I guess," he said, holding it higher for me to see.

I smiled. "That's a big Tom."

"There was a small flock out at the edge of the field surprisingly close to the windmills," Gjon said. "They're probably roosting in the trees on the edge of the forest there."

"Good," I answered. "Hopefully they stay there a while so we can do this some more."

"Well, I'm going to go butcher this sucker." Ash turned and headed toward the shed behind the house. It had been a slaughtering, meat processing location in the old days when this had been a functioning farm and hunting location. We'd have enough room there to hang up to ten deer, if we were lucky, and keep them cold in the ensuing months.

Gjon shrugged off his canvas jacket and hung it nearby. "I'll get some fires going."

I nodded approval and walked with him to the living room. While we did have a furnace, we tried to refrain from using it as much as possible. With access to dry wood, we opted for fires in the fireplaces. There were three in the house: the upstairs hallway, the living room, and the kitchen. Nettie had already lit the kitchen fire and had a large pot of boiling water hanging over it. It almost felt medieval, like having a cauldron set over flame to brew potions, but I appreciated the versatility of it, too.

The living room was green, cozy, and easily one of my favorite rooms in the entire house. It had quickly become the gathering place for meetings, dinner, and general get-togethers. The fireplace was framed by two white couches with speckled pillows and a giant beige ottoman. Several other pine and oatmeal-colored chairs spotted the room.

Gjon knelt in front of the fire and moved the screen out of the way. "Yard looks good," he said as he grabbed some newspaper and began tearing at it. "Must have been a lot of work."

"Makes me miss leaf blowers," I answered, sitting on the ottoman behind him. "Of course, it would have gone faster if Evie had come back to help. Nothing like the energy of a pissed-off teenager."

He shrugged and began twisting the newspaper. "She's off again?"

I nodded. "We probably won't see her tonight." I stared at my hands in my lap.

Gjon turned and put a hand on mine gently. "You need to stop doing this, Liz. It's not your fault."

"Mmm," I hummed, cracking a smile. "It is."

He closed his hand around mine and held it a moment. "We had to watch Hank die. It was awful. But it does not mean you or me or anyone else failed to save him. We were all there."

Thinking about it made me set my teeth. "If I could have gotten to him outside the barn before the Woods got him…"

"Hypotheticals are a waste of time." Gjon tossed the newspaper into the fireplace. He turned and held my hand with both of his. His touch was warm and it helped me surface from the lake of melancholy I found myself in. "We have to move on. And we have to help Evie and Nettie move on in time."

He was right. As much as I wished I could have done something, changing the past was impossible. We had all lost people we cared about here. There was a chance we'd lose more. As much as I wanted to be prepared for that, I couldn't be. I could lose any of them at any moment.

Gjon returned to building the fire.

I cleared my throat, eager to change the conversation. "I thought maybe I might take Sanz with me on my run tomorrow morning, if that's okay."

He smiled. "She would love it. It would be good for her to help with rebuilding those muscles. Don't expect her to keep up with you."

"I'm not running any marathons. I'll go easy on her."

Gjon layered the larger logs on top of the kindling and tinder and struck a match. The paper poofed in a plume of flame and quickly traveled back. The heat was a welcome rush to my chilled skin. He wiped his hands on his jeans and stood. "One down, one to go."

I followed him upstairs to the next fireplace. I had other things I could have been doing, should have been doing. I should have gone to check on the progress of the indoor conservatory Richard was working on. He'd found a ton of grow lights at the hardware store in Onyx River and had put a number of them in a disused office on the first floor, one that got a good amount of daylight until the sun swung around in the afternoon. Our tomatoes, potatoes, squash, zucchini, and green beans had been uprooted from our garden back at the cabin. There wasn't an outdoor greenhouse to keep them in here yet, so for this winter, we'd opted to make sure they stayed inside where it was warm and we could monitor them daily. Everything but the green beans seemed to be doing okay.

Gretchen had gone to check on the town's solar panels. I had wondered at first if it was a cover so she could hunt down where Evie was, but I'd let her go, knowing the solar panels were a legitimately important asset to keep tabs on.

Unlike me, Gretchen had kept a close relationship with Evie since the news of Hank's death. While I only seemed to fuel Evie's anger, Gretchen harnessed it, taking Evie with her on routine scouts to check over the property and take care of some of the more mundane chores. If I asked, there was usually dissension.

When we reached the top of the stairs, Gjon glanced back at me for a moment as though he was thinking the same thing I was. "You've got more on your mind, don't you?"

I sighed. "I do. But I'll spare you." I turned to go downstairs.

His hand caught mine.

I looked into his dark eyes.

Softly, he drew me toward him and slid his other hand to my face. I closed my eyes as his fingers brushed across my cheek. The hand that had held my arm wrapped around me and embraced me. I closed my arms around his middle and breathed in his smell, the aroma of evergreens and gunpowder and sweat.

The first time Gjon had held me this way had been two months ago. We'd been alone sitting in the living room after dark, watching the fire burn into embers. I'd started crying. I didn't like to cry in front of other people. I felt weak, felt like I could be knocked over with a strong breeze. I didn't like feeling vulnerable. But I had remembered our last night at the cabin, gathered in the living room, Hank smiling and holding Evie and had lost my spine.

Gjon had held me and not said a word. I hadn't been embraced that way in a long time by someone and the feeling of it was as addictive as caffeine. I hadn't wanted it to end. The worst part about it was, with my eyes closed, it had almost felt like Brody was holding me again.

I let myself be carried away by it then, as I did now. I tilted my head back and my lips connected with his.

He nudged his lips further into mine. Our breaths came hot and fast, our hands searching each other's bodies blindly. Mine slid beneath the buttons of his shirt. I traced the shape of his shoulders and abs with my fingers. He cupped a hand around the small of my back while the other worked under my shirt and caressed my ribcage.

"We should…" I said in between kisses.

"…stop?" he asked.

"No." I led him toward my room and closed the door behind us. I stripped my shirt while he unbuttoned his. I worked at his belt while he kissed me and unclasped my bra. We fell onto the bed together, the plush comforter pillowing our landing. The taste of his mouth, the feeling of his strong but tender touch on me, dropped me further and further into a place and time away from everything that had become familiar. I wasn't me: not this person I'd become. I was as I remembered myself from before. I was me then. And he was then, too… We were together lost in time.

Darkness closed in around us. We lay in the bed together, my arms around him. I listened to him breathing, one of my fingers caressing the hair at one of his temples.

"That tickles a little bit," he said.

"I was admiring your gray," I answered. "It's distinctive."

He chuckled. "Okay. I think you're telling me I'm old."

"Hardly."

Gjon rolled over onto his back and glanced at me.

"What?"

"You're a tough nut to crack, Elizabeth."

I frowned. "Is that a sexual remark?"

He chuckled. "No. I mean, you keep your cards close to the vest. Makes it hard to tell what you're thinking sometimes."

I propped my chin with a fist as I considered his words. "I've always been a loner. I process things better that way."

He blinked. "It kills me sometimes."

I narrowed my gaze. "A bit of an overstatement, maybe?"

"You remind me of people I once knew before this crap started, people I really liked."

"Because you normally hate everyone," I joked.

He smiled. "These people I used to know were the kind who never knew how to give themselves a break. Never knew how to turn off the switch. They beat at a problem until they cracked it or it made them numb from trying. It was hard to watch the latter."

"I can't take a break," I said, sitting up in the bed a little. "When I do, things usually…" For lack of better words, I simulated an explosion with my hands.

"Then let someone else help so you can. It's not all up to you. Everyone's lives aren't in your hands alone."

I sat a little straighter. "Why do I feel as though this has turned into a lecture?"

He laid a hand on my chest and gently guided me back down. "I'm asking you to talk to me…if you want to. It hurts to see you take the blame for so many things that aren't your fault."

I didn't say anything. I couldn't tell him how I was feeling. I couldn't tell him up until an hour before, I was ready to charge headlong into those Woods in search of some answers. In search of Brody's ghost and perhaps, Hank's. That would feel like the opposite of moving on…of letting the past be the past.

Ash's voice rose from the bottom of the stairs. "Liz? Are you up there?"

I grabbed the sheet to pull it over me.

Gjon's reaction was the total opposite; he stayed as still as possible. He may have even held his breath.

"Yeah! I'm here," I yelled back, quickly climbing out of bed and picking up my clothes from the floor.

"You haven't seen Gjon have you?" he called. "I had a question about Otto's hunting training."

I flipped on the bedside light. Gjon was mouthing, "Who me?" and I almost wanted to laugh Instead, I cleared my throat and answered, "No. Check the barn."

"I already did, but…okay," Ash gave in.

THE WILD FALL

After a moment of silence and when I was satisfied he was gone, I finished putting on my top and the rest of my gear.

Gjon followed suit. He sat back on the bed while I stood at the door.

"I think maybe I should go first. You follow in five minutes," I said.

He crossed his arms. "Sounds like a good plan."

I shook my head, opened the door and left.

TEN

Evie

I had spent most of my day in the adult bookstore, Bottoms Up, of Onyx River. I'd noticed it on our drive into town three months ago. Ash commented on it to Richard and both had giggled like little girls. When I asked Gretchen about it, she mentioned I should check it out on my own, that if I had any questions, I should ask her…and only her. At first, I didn't understand what the term "adult bookstore" even meant. I felt like most bookstores had to have adult content: how-to books, autobiographies, books about ancient history and trains and the Bible and all that crap.

On a couple of scouts into town to gather supplies and tools, I'd thought about sneaking over to take a look. But Liz kept her sights on me like a hawk, making sure I never wandered off, making sure I wasn't getting in trouble. Even if she didn't speak, her stare pissed me off more than anything. I'd shouted at her that morning that her protecting wouldn't compensate for her letting my dad die. I left before she could come up with any kind of a response. It only cemented in my mind she felt guilty and she must have been responsible because of that guilt.

THE WILD FALL

Tempest and I followed the sun-drenched roads into town, the steady swooping of the wind turbines behind us growing fainter and fainter as we left the farm behind. It was a good thirty-minute walk before I saw the tops of the buildings in town and another five before the line of shops with red awnings appeared. There were still packaged candy bars from ten years ago sitting on the shelves of the old Joseph's convenience store. I grabbed a Snickers, one I remembered loving as a kid, and tore into it. The chocolate looked shriveled. When I tried to bite into it, I found it as hard as a rock. I threw it across the road in a huff and continued on.

The bookstore had been my destination in mind. As we neared it, my eyes caught on the tower to the church at the end of the block and curiosity pinched me.

My dad had never been religious and no one else in the group, save for Alari back in the day, had much of a thought about it. Alari used to take an old copy of the Bhagavad Gita to one of the classrooms that overlooked a courtyard in the school where we stayed and did her own version of a morning at church there. I'd followed once.

She'd pray to Vishnu for our group's preservation, for our protection. When I'd asked Dad about it, he'd told me people believed in a higher power because it gave them strength, it empowered them believing that everything and everyone's existence was in hands out of their control.

It scared me more than it fascinated me.

As we climbed the white stairs and pushed into the church doors, I lingered on that old fear.

Dad was gone. It didn't make sense to me why a God or Gods would choose to take him away? And why was it worth worshiping anything that ultimately had its own designs for our humanity? It was dumb.

It was dark inside, the entryway pungent with the stench of must and old incense. Tempest whined uneasily.

I dug into my pocket and produced my headlamp, pushing the button and letting the light shine around the crowded space. Ahead, I found doors to the main room, and pushed them open. Pale sunshine gushed through the windows and lightened the space. I turned off the headlamp and resumed my digging.

Stacks of chairs sat in a corner collecting dust along with programs from the last Sunday parishioners had gone there ten years ago. The only interesting thing in the room was the overcrowded cork board pinned to death with event fliers and sign-up sheets. Grief counseling, Alcoholics Anonymous, Men's breakfasts, knitting groups. In the corner toward the bottom, I could see children's faces peeking out from behind a flurry of papers. Something in their eyes spoke to me, and before I knew it, I was yanking papers down, pushpins raining down around me until I cleared the board and showed what lay underneath.

It was a class photo. Juniors, maybe seniors in high school, all gathered on a lawn in front of a one-story brick school, the one I recognized from outside of town. People had drawn hearts over students' faces, and I realized that a good number of the papers I'd pulled free had been left over programs from funerals, all with similar teenage faces smiling back.

A newspaper article half hanging off the board caught my attention. "Bus accident tragedy kills seventeen. Town broken by loss."

I stared in horror at the faces in the photo, my throat closing up the longer I looked. Even here, this place was steeped in darkness, in death…

I retreated from the church, and once out in the chilly air breathed anew. Tempest and I raced to the bookstore without looking back. .

Bottoms Up had a funny sign, the U in Up had a cleave in the middle and the B in Bottoms was turned on its side so the loops faced down. I opened the screen door and tried the front knob. It was locked.

THE WILD FALL

I scanned the road, eventually finding a rock the size of my hand by the old bridge that led across the river behind the town's small inn. I swung my arm back and threw it as hard as I could through the glass door. The rock banged off the window. Not even a scratch. I found a larger rock and lobbed it with both arms. This time, it went through.

Tempest watched everything with the faintest bit of interest, yawning when I was finally able to reach through the broken glass and unlock the door. We strolled inside, me carefully sweeping aside the glass with my shoe so she didn't cut her paws on it.

The inside of Bottoms Up seemed like more of a toy store than a bookshop. There were shelves for merchandise behind the counter and a glass display case in front with all kinds of random items: handcuffs, a leather whip, a ball with a strap attached to it. It wasn't until I found the first copy of The Secret Service on Her Majesty before I realized exactly what I'd gotten myself into.

I took everything in for hours. I looked at the photos in the dirty magazines, read about the top ten best sexual positions for you and your partner, even took out the pair of furry handcuffs just to feel them. So, this was sex. This was something I had been almost oblivious to my entire teenage years, even after learning about and dealing with my monthly visitor. My dad had told me when I fell in love with someone, he would explain more of it to me. Liz had been a little more cavalier. When I felt like it was the right time, I would know.

The entire thing seemed pointless to me. I had only seen kids my age a few times in my life. There had been families passing through who had stayed down the mountain from us in one of the old ski resorts when we were at the cabin. I never got to spend time with them, but I'd seen boys and girls hanging out in the pastures or on the golf courses, seeming lost and confused. It had been probably three years since I'd seen the last one.

I was never going to find anyone unless I joined one of the larger GRCs. People didn't roam out here for survival in tiny groups like us anymore. They had all realized it was pointless by now. It was only a faster way for people you loved to die.

Around mid-afternoon, when I got tired of reading and trying to figure out why anyone would waste their time on this stuff, I noticed it had started to get dark. I'd forgotten how little light there was in winter afternoons. I could probably have made it back to the farm before it was dark, but the sting of Liz's and my argument that morning was still sharp and sent me into a cascade of angry imaginings whenever I thought about it. I decided to stay in the group's emergency house, the one my Dad had spent his last night in before he'd died.

It was a split level, painted gray with white trim. All the appliances in the house were new and it could house everyone in an emergency if needed. Granted, it would be a little bit like being stuffed back in the cabin again, but it was an idea I didn't mind much. There had been little wrong to me about sharing small space with so many people…it had brought us closer. Now, in that large farmhouse, I felt farther from everyone than I ever had.

First thing I did was check the cellar to find the footlocker we'd stored with some essentials. I opened the chest to find an empty box of oatmeal staring back at me. I'd had oatmeal every night I stayed here… which had been a lot of nights. I'd known I was depleting the stores in our emergency box and should eventually refill it but had always put off until the next day, and then put it off again.

Fuck. I climbed back upstairs empty-handed.

Tempest whined while I sat at the kitchen table. "I'm sorry, girl," I murmured.

She licked her lips and settled on the floor, her eyes like puddles of hurt.

THE WILD FALL

There had been nights when neither of us had eaten. It had been a long time, but back in the day before we'd found the house in Middlehitch, I remembered trying to fall asleep in our tent in the cold, my stomach panging fiercely every time I rolled over. I whined then. I had cried until Dad shushed me and sang me back to sleep to the tune of "Desperado."

Thinking about him chilled my blood. I stood from the table and shook out my hands. This wasn't like then. I wasn't helpless and he was gone. We didn't have to sit here and be uncomfortable all night long.

I glanced outside into the darkness. Several of the streetlights in town popped on after dark, dotting the road into town intermittently. The feed store wasn't too far away. We could walk and find food there. It wouldn't have been the first time I'd eaten dog food in my life: wouldn't be the last. The small market was closer to home than I liked, and too far to travel in the dark. Even then, our group had cleaned it out of whatever was left once we'd established ourselves at the house.

The thought of going out was polarizing, half exciting and half terrifying. We, as a group, had never ventured out after dark for any reason. I'd been taught from a young age the darkness held more danger than at any other time in the day and I needed to be indoors and secure for the night by the time the blackness fell.

I'd had nightmares of all the things lurking in the darkness that could lash out and pull me in. The wolves, the Woods, strange men and women whose only desire was to harm… For the longest time, I was scared someone would materialize out of the darkness with arms like steel, haul me out of my sleeping bag and slip away with me into the cold night. It had happened before. On the night of the Merging, men had come to my mom's house and yanked me out of bed. They'd killed my mom when she tried to protect me. Liz had come to save me.

The thought made me grit my teeth again. Liz was the reason these safety precautions were in place, yet she hadn't followed them. Ash had mentioned to me my dad had tried to get them to go into shelter sooner before the Woods came too close to ignore the day he died. Liz had told them to keep going; she had ignored safety for recklessness. If anything, that should have made me want to bury under the covers of the bed in the next room even more, sleep the memories of Dad away. I'd done that on so many nights, inevitably thinking about what my dad's last thoughts were, whether or not he had forgiven me for our fight…

But tonight, I wanted to push the boundaries and see what lay beyond. So far, the darkness was only to be feared if the Woods were nearby and as far as I knew, there weren't any Woods within a twenty-mile radius of where we had decided to move to.

I slung on my pack and stepped over to the front door, my hand on the knob. "It'll be like walking to Annie's Diner," I said, remembering fondly the times my dad and I would go to do laundry and then traverse the town's sidewalks to our favorite eatery. I twisted the knob and pushed out.

The night opened in front of me. But it wasn't inherently scary, more it was a different version of the town I'd grown accustomed to. Just as quiet, just as empty, only darker. I stepped down the front steps to the cement walkway. Tempest followed, panting as though there was nothing more natural in the world than going on a nightly jaunt through the neighborhood.

I got to the end of the driveway where the first streetlight was and stood beneath its bright circle of light, cautiously scanning the street around me. Nothing seemed out of place.

"Last one to the feed store is a rotten egg," I taunted Tempest and broke out into a full run. I heard the jingling of her collar and watched her lightning body whip passed me as we dove into the darkness between each light.

Liz

THE WILD FALL

When I made it downstairs, Gretchen was coming in the door. "Hey," I greeted. My entire body buzzed with energy, and part of me was terrified she would notice. I was even more nervous Gjon would descend those stairs and betray us both. Gjon and I had been together for months now. Keeping it a secret had been more out of fear that others wouldn't understand, especially so soon after Hank's death. But I also realized my desire to leave for the Woods made announcing our relationship much stranger and contrary.

Gretchen closed the door and locked it behind her before setting her side arm on the table to the left of the door. "We've got a problem," she said, under her breath. I thought I had heard her wrong at first. The seriousness in her expression made the energy in me more frantic than ever.

"Is it the solar panels?" I asked, getting closer to her to keep our conversation quieter.

"No. It's something else."

Usually, Gretchen wasn't one to be so cryptic. I usually went to her first when I needed an opinion with a non-bullshit filter. She was keeping something now though and I wasn't sure I liked it.

I was practically bouncing on the balls of my feet. "Tell me."

"I want to call a meeting," she answered instead, which made me straighten. "After dinner, we can meet in here and discuss what we're going to do."

"Gretch…"

"Together," she intoned and walked farther into the house toward the kitchen.

Ash had butchered the turkey for dinner that night, which Nettie had prepared in pieces to advance the cooking time and so she could harvest the bones for a stock once we were done. Dinner was taking longer than usual to cook, though, and every second I spent waiting for Gretchen to drop her truth bomb, I imagined how bad it could be.

Had something happened to Evie? I doubted it almost as soon as I'd thought of it. Gretchen wouldn't dare keep something like that to herself for so long. I wondered if she had found other survivors living nearby. In the three months we'd spent here, there had been zero signs of activity in town or at the farm. Everyone operating the electrical grids was gone as well as the water treatment plant officials. Maybe a group had come in from the Vermont direction though…

Another hour passed. We all sat in the living room near the hearth, engaged in our own activities. Ash and Richard were engrossed in a conversation about beekeeping, Gretchen was checking over her GPS, and Gjon was tending the fire and occasionally catching my eye. I kept my gaze on Gretchen and the GPS. What was she calculating?

"Group meeting," I announced, almost catching myself off guard.

Everyone looked at me. Richard's glasses slid to the end of his nose. "Well, good thing we're all here."

"Someone get Nettie," Gretchen said, keeping her focus on me. "There's something I need to tell you all."

Ash retrieved Nettie.

Gjon furrowed his brows at me and I shrugged my shoulders back.

A few moments later, Ash and Nettie returned. "This can't take too long," she was saying. "The meat will be ready to come out any minute."

Once everyone was settled, Gretchen rose from her chair. "I went north toward the solar panels this morning to check on them. Everything there seemed to be in order so I pushed a bit farther along Route 5 toward the Interstate. What I found instead was the Woods."

A chill raced through me. One of the things we had not done as a group on initial inspection of the property in Onyx River was scout outside of town to see what our exit options would be. Since our route along 302 had been overtaken by the Woods three months ago, we had detoured to Conway and had taken Route 112 (which eventually turned to 116) all the way in. It had been a longer drive but it bypassed the

Woods and that was all that mattered. Apparently, the northern route out of town was now blocked.

"We'll need to assign a bi-weekly check on it," I said, almost through a numb face. "We can't let them go unchecked, not with everyone's life at stake."

"It's still a way's out of town and judging from where the forward progression looks like it began, I'm willing to bet the farm is probably out of that one's path," Gretchen said.

"The whole point is you can't anticipate which 'path' these things take," Ash growled. "It doesn't follow rules."

Gretchen put up a hand, as if to block him. "We should take a group to 116 tomorrow and make sure we still have an exit there."

I nodded. "And the other routes south."

We broke again. Nettie returned to the kitchen, though I noticed she did so at rapid speed. Ash and Richard left as well, though I felt they did so because Gretchen and I were regarding each other in a "we need to have a conversation alone" kind of way.

Gjon made his exit too, giving me a small subtle rub on my elbow before leaving.

Gretchen noticed.

As soon as he was out of the room and it was the two of us, she said, "Been wondering when that was finally going to happen."

I frowned. "What?"

She smirked. "It's not like the rest of us didn't notice those looks you two have been giving each other the last couple months or so. It's good. He's good for you."

I shook my head. "Don't change the subject. Why didn't you tell me about the Woods when you walked in the door?"

Gretchen rolled her eyes. "Don't take it personally. I made this a group announcement because that's how we need to be handling decisions: as a group."

"You didn't think I was capable of that?"

"I didn't." Her posture had stiffened.

So had mine. "And why the fuck not?"

Gretchen rolled her shoulders back and took a deep breath. "Listen, these last three months have been a marathon for our group. We've been working non-stop to outfit this place as our new home, as a safe place for everyone, a place we can stay for years. We've ignored our old order of operations because we were all heartbroken and panicking."

I hated being called out for it, but I knew she was right. We would have done a much more detailed scout before deciding to move here. We should have gone another five miles outside of town to make sure there were no more people, that the Woods didn't close us off from an escape. That part didn't seem to matter as much though. The Woods had encroached on us more this year than any one before it, even the year we got trapped inside of it accidentally.

"You've been a de facto leader of this group for a long time, Liz," Gretchen continued. "And we've let you run it without being much help. It's time we stepped up and shared the responsibility. We need to all be on our guard and not be complacent about things anymore."

"It sounds like you're saying I'm responsible for making poor decisions."

"That's not it at all!" she yelled.

The ferocity of her response shocked but didn't sway me. "I made decisions that have saved this group time and time again. Decisions I've had to make when no one else would make them."

Gretchen waved her hands in the air. "It shouldn't be up to you. Don't you see what I'm trying to get at? It's unfair to put the responsibility on you. I'm saying we're not doing that anymore. This is not a bad thing. I don't know why you're acting as though it is."

Maybe because it was one of the last things tethering me to the group, the only other thing convincing me to stay. If I was in charge of their safety, if I was making sure they made it through, then I wouldn't feel the need to leave. But self-sufficient, in charge of themselves, I didn't need to be throwing myself at every problem every time as though I was their last line of defense. I could pay more attention to me. And right now, I wanted an answer for why this was happening. Why the Woods were slowly overtaking our world. Where the souls of my beloved friends and family had gone. I wanted to go into the Woods.

I didn't betray this though. Instead, I took a deep breath and let it out slowly, measuring the seconds that ticked by and told myself to relax. Turns out, I didn't need to.

Gretchen's stare had gone cold. "I know what you're thinking. It ain't worth it. Especially now you and James Harriot over there have started something. All that matters is the here and now. All that should matter is the future with people who are still alive." She turned and started out of the room. "But I can't make the decision for you. I only hope you'll start seeing things as they could be instead of how they are."

She left the room.

I sat on the sofa, curling my body onto it, and grabbed hold of one of the throw pillows there, something to chain myself to the present. Always be moving... No, plodding forward, surviving, making do with things as they were... It was my life for the last ten years. It was how I had envisioned the world needing to be. More and more, I'd started to believe there was something someone had to do to change things. It all started with going inside the Woods. The answers lay there.

I wasn't daft enough to think I was going to be the one to answer them alone. But hell, maybe I could make it farther than others could? Maybe I could make it back with more information than anyone had?

The fact most people had barricaded themselves into GRCs away from the Woods signified people weren't going to try and study it. They were adapting to live life in concentrated areas, in safe havens where the government would send its untrained privates into battle at a moment's notice, but they wouldn't know what they were fighting.

Then again, I could eke things out here. Gretchen was right; Gjon was good and this farm had been something I'd dreamed about for years. I'd pictured us living here harmoniously, the picture in my head like some stupid choreographed commercial; sitting around our large mahogany dinner table in the other room, laughing and eating our fill and feeling safe and whole and home.

But Hank had been in all of those thoughts and this place wasn't home without him.

ELEVEN

Evie

The feed store was a one-story ramshackle building at the edge of the town center across from the church. Our group had checked it out the first month we'd moved into town because we knew there could be necessary supplies.

Most of the bags of seeds were chewed through and depleted of their offerings by rodents. Richard had found some grow lights for our indoor garden and managed to salvage a few plants that had survived in the greenhouse through some minor miracle. Gjon had found some new leashes and harnesses for the dogs; ours were in rough shape. In the end, we'd declared the place picked through and hadn't had much of a reason to go back.

I had remembered seeing some canned dog food there. Though Gjon had told me it was long expired, I couldn't not try. We would both be miserable if we didn't find something and would probably be awake all night with growling stomachs. Besides, the number of preservatives in these things meant they were probably fine.

THE WILD FALL

The store emerged out of the darkness as we approached, following the streetlights through town. The light at the feed store was an ultra-bright beacon casting a weird green pallor over the parking lot in front. I dug my headlamp out of my bag, put it around my head and clicked it on. Tempest gave an encouraging whine beside me, tipping her head to avoid the bright light when I looked at her.

"Not too much longer, girl," I said, pulling open the shop door. A little bell tinkled at our entry.

Inside, the stench of moldy hay and bagged kibbles made me nearly go back outside for a fresh breath. It smelled a lot like the barn at our new home, before we'd gone in and cleaned it out. I breathed through my mouth as I continued inside, Tempest at my heels.

It was a small space with tall shelves that blocked most of my view on the right-hand side. Smaller shelves stood on the left, ones I could see over easily enough. They were crowded with packages of suet, dried out flower bulbs, bags of soil and mulch. I couldn't remember where the dog food was.

"Tempest, find the food," I said, pointing ahead.

She looked at me like I had a second head and moaned softly.

We moved through all the shelves on the left without finding any food and proceeded to the right side of the room. The long counter at the head of the store stood vacant, a doorway to the stockroom lined with a heavy blanket, maybe to keep some of the heat in back when this was a functioning business. I rounded the first corner and scanned the various hooks and bins: supplies for rabbits and smaller mammals. Small water bottles, bags of cedar chips, litter, and pellets. I rounded the corner to look at the next aisle.

Cans.

"Jackpot," I muttered, as I crouched to inspect the lowest shelf. There was a variety of different brands and flavors, all with pictures of a happy cartoon dog smiling at a dish of realistic meat cubes.

I slung my bag from my shoulder, unzipped it, and started packing in the cans.

Something clunked onto the floor on the other side of the shelf behind me. I stood and walked around to check and see if Tempest had bumped into something. She liked to explore and sometimes, that got her in trouble. I remembered back to a year ago when we had been going through a grocery store outside of Middlehitch and Tempest had knocked over a pyramid of stacked cranberry sauce on display for what would have been Thanksgiving years ago. It was like the sound of an earthquake, cans spilling all over the linoleum. Liz had been pissed; so had Dad.

The sudden thought of my dad tore open inside my gut. I tried to ignore the pain by looking around for Tempest or any fallen paraphernalia. A small can of cat food lay on the ground and a mouse scurried away into the shadows. Tempest had vanished.

"Tempest?" I called her name softly. "Come here!"

A low growl emanated from behind the blanket-covered door.

I stepped to my bag, retrieved my gun from inside, and zipped it back up. Hoisting it onto my shoulder, I called out once more for my dog. A shrill bark erupted from the back room.

Keeping my hands locked on the weapon, I skirted around the side of the counter and tentatively stood in front of the blanket. A cool rush of air rippled against it from the opposite side. Taking a deep breath, I swept the blanket out of my way.

A cloud of dust wafted into my face as I walked through. The stockroom was dark, vast, and colder than the storefront. It looked like the owners had added a warehouse on, large enough my footsteps echoed upon entry. I shivered as I waved the dust cloud from in front of me. My headlamp swept over tall metal shelves filled with boxes of parts for farming equipment and bags of extra mulch and potting soil. One bag had burst open and spilled dirt all across the cement floor in front of me. About twenty paces ahead of me, I could see the back door to the storage area was tied closed with a loose rope. The door banged against the frame with each gust of wind outside.

I followed the sound of Tempest's growling. It was coming from the back right corner of the storage room.

I cleared the metal shelves and noticed a forklift parked near a massive wall of stacked hay bales. I remembered the tower from when we had visited the feed store the first time. Had it not been moldy, I would have climbed to the top of it for a challenge. The stench reminded me to breathe through my mouth again, though most of my attention was on the darkness surrounding the pile and Tempest crouched in front of it.

Stepping beside her, I followed her gaze to the left between the hay bales and the wall, where the darkest section of the room lay. Tempest was crouched on the floor, a low warning growl thrumming from her.

I laid a hand on her shoulder blades. "Easy girl."

She gave a small rumbling woof in response.

"Hello?" I called out, keeping the gun leveled at the darkness.

Nothing stirred.

My vision adapted the longer I stood there. As it did, I began to see the outline of something curled there next to the hay beyond the edge of my light. It was slouched over unnaturally but I recognized what seemed to be legs…arms…

"Come out or I'll shoot," I warned. "Don't fucking…fuck with me!"

Still, nothing. I took one hand away from my gun and reached to touch the button on top of my headlight. My light brightened and stretched farther into the corner.

The body there must have died years ago. The skin looked as though it was melting off the person's face, revealing black tendrils of dried-up muscle on bone. The clothing hung off of it as though it had been draped on as an afterthought. I couldn't tell if it was a man or a woman.

I backed away, my stomach turning at the sight. I ran to the door, stumbling onto my knees as I threw up. I don't know how long I stayed there, trying to spit the last remnants from this morning's breakfast out of my mouth and the sour taste along with it. Tempest eventually came to my side and whined.

But I couldn't move. I had started to imagine what my dad's body would look like now, left to rot in the Woods these last three months. Would I even recognize it if I came across it? And where was his ghost? Why hadn't he come back like so many had done for so many other people?

A sharp bark brought me out of it. I had been crying, but couldn't remember for how long. I raised my head slowly.

An eye stared at me through the crack in the back door. My headlamp exploded against a black pupil and a twisted, human-like face. I threw myself away from it, shrieking. Whatever it was screamed in response and launched itself against the door furiously.

I ran, my boots slipping on the cement floor as I raced toward the front of the shop. Tempest's collar rang at my heels as I pushed through the blanket separating the storefront from the backroom. I vaulted the counter, a cup full of pens and box full of old candy splattering on the ground at my feet. I didn't stop.

The banging on the door seemed as loud behind me as it had when I was right there, staring into the creature's abysmal gaze. I slowed as I neared the front door. It was outside. I couldn't go out there.

With the realization came a horrifying sound: the back door battering open and claws scraping against the cement floor.

I barreled against the door, the bell jangling wildly as I stumbled out into the dirt driveway, Tempest nudging out around my legs before the door could close behind me. The ultra-white light over the door was like a shock to my system, almost blinding me. I spun for a moment, trying to get my bearings.

There! The streetlamp on the opposite side of the road. That was my way back into town. I plunged myself into the darkness, my lungs burning with effort and my throat on fire. My stomach bounced emptily inside me and my boots pounded the pavement unforgivingly. Behind me, I heard Tempest's steady panting and the click of her claws.

Then, the explosion of the shop door burst open followed by an ear-piercing scream plummeting through me like a knife.

The streetlamp ahead bounced into view. *So close! So close!*

I collapsed into the circle of light, the dog bolting in after me. I grabbed her collar to keep her from running through into the darkness beyond. With the blood rushing in my ears and my breath heaving, I couldn't tell where the thing was in the darkness. I quickly surveyed the feed store.

No one was there. The door was closed once more and all had gone silent again.

I crouched and held Tempest to me, tears of exhaustion rolling down my face.

Not a wolf. Definitely not a fucking wolf. My thoughts gyrated. What the hell was that thing? Why had it stopped chasing us?

I briefly recalled the scream I'd heard and the creature's reaction to my headlamp shining on it. Was it afraid of the light?

I scanned the darkness around us warily. The next streetlight was a good ten to fifteen yards away down the street. I had no idea where the thing had gone and I didn't feel comfortable venturing into the dark not knowing.

"We're in for a long night," I said, sitting on the sidewalk. Tempest sat, whining, and the night swallowed the sound.

Liz

I didn't sleep. Instead, I rolled around in the darkness, kicked my feet out, and tucked myself back in. I did the dance over and over again, unable to get comfortable. At some point, I dozed off and my dreams took me back to our old cabin. It was desolate now, our belongings gone, save for the furniture inside and the rocking chairs on the porch. Hank was sitting in one of them, staring into the field toward the golden grass and the looming Woods beyond it. I stood next to him and followed his gaze. I watched my father, long since passed, walking through the grass with his fishing gear, like when I was a child and we spent summers there. He seemed content. Hank seemed content. Everything seemed right despite the tormenting loss like an ache in my chest.

When I opened my eyes, I was in my bed again in the dark. But I wasn't alone.

The feeling was so familiar, a feeling I had felt numerous nights in the last ten years. I was never truly by myself at night. I could always look out my window and there he would be, Brody, his figure cloaked in the blackness. The point back then was I was inside and he was out there.

I turned over in bed and knew instinctively there was a figure in my bedroom that didn't belong. I snaked a hand under my pillow for the knife I always kept there, a kukri Ash had made back when we had forge capabilities. The kukri was a gift, he'd said, for saving his life, for adopting him into our group.

"Who's there?" I tempted the darkness.

It responded. "Don't tell me you don't remember." The voice was hoarse, as though the wind were speaking to me through a crack in the glass.

Goose flesh on my arms had risen, the hairs standing on end. "Remember what?" I whispered.

The darkness took shape, swirling into form as a figure surged forward from the shadows toward my bed. It stopped directly above where I lay, human-like arms braced on either side of it.

"ME!" It screamed.

I recognized the voice. The gravelly tone of it. The rage in it.

Brody.

My hand whipped the kukri out from beneath the pillow and I sliced it through the air. It slashed through the dark shape with no effort. I let go of it as iciness enclosed my hand. The kukri tumbled across the bed and I watched it fall to the floor on the other side.

As soon as I looked back at the dark force, it was gone. My room was empty again. The moon cast light in to reach me. I heaved and held my hand close to me, the cold and numb feeling beginning to subside.

Had I dreamed it?

A knock on the door startled me again. I forced the covers off of me and jumped to answer it.

Gjon stood there, a bat poised in his hands. Behind him, Gretchen emerged from her door with a gun and Ash from his and Richard's room with a hatchet. They stopped moving when they saw I was alright.

"You okay?" Gjon asked. "I heard you scream."

Had I? I didn't even remember making a sound. I nodded. "It's fine. A nightmare."

Ash returned to his room and closed the door wordlessly.

Gretchen kept her gaze in line with mine. "Your hand okay?" she asked.

I was still cradling it close to my body. I let it go and looked at it a moment. It seemed normal but somehow still felt cold. "Fine."

She nodded, exchanged a look with Gjon, and went back to bed.

As soon as her door was closed, Gjon gently took hold of my hand in his. "You're freezing."

"A bad dream," I said, as if saying it again could convince me that's all it was.

"Must have been, huh?" he murmured. The heat from his hands ebbed into mine. "Anything I can do?"

"Stay?" I opened the door wider.

"Alright." He came in and I closed the door behind him.

I picked my kukri up from the floor and set it on the bedside table.

He eyed it as we settled into the bed facing one another. Gjon wrapped his arm around my body, his other arm in an arc over my head. "You want to tell me what you dreamed about?"

"Ghosts," I said, not wanting to elaborate any further. I knew it wasn't just a ghost though. It was someone I had loved, someone I had been close to. Someone I had killed. Something that now haunted me.

"Sometimes, I dream about the people I lost," he said, catching me off guard. Gjon hadn't reminisced on his past much since I'd met him. Most of us avoided talking about who we'd left behind, mostly because it was too painful, and out of respect for one another. I hadn't told anyone about what I'd been through with Brody, though Hank had always suspected, even asked once. I'd told him small things, never enough so he could put the pieces together.

When Gjon didn't continue, I said, "Yeah?"

"There was this girl. I only went on one date with her but I was head over heels. The kind of person you get a good feeling about whenever you think of them. We went out to a restaurant, someplace neither one of us had ever gone. I liked her."

"She sounds like she was extraordinary," I added.

"I thought so." I could see his smile in the dark. "It's strange because whenever I try to remember her face, I can't seem to. But I dream about her like I'm there, like we're there together."

"I'm sorry," I said. The words felt numb but I knew too well the feelings he'd felt. The dreams I had about Brody that weren't memories, even though they felt so real. Ten years was a long time to hold onto grief.

"It was a long time ago." Gjon took a deep breath. "What's important is the here and now. The farm. Our people. The dogs. You."

A smile warmed my cheeks. I craned my neck forward and kissed him.

THE WILD FALL

"That was my nose, but you tried," he chuckled.
I gave him a small shove and our laughter lit up the dark.

TWELVE

Liz

Sunrise brought relief and trepidation all in one. Gretchen took Ash to go scout our exit on 116. Richard and I decided to take Otto and scout the remaining Routes 25 and 10, which were south of us. Gjon, Nettie, and Sanz stayed at the house to wait for Evie to return.

The path took us south toward the solar grid. Each flat panel glistened beneath the rising glow of the sun. We had spent several weekends here cleaning the surfaces of the panels as carefully and diligently as possible. They'd been encrusted with years of dirt and other debris. They worked better now, but still required upkeep and attention. We couldn't afford for them to get destroyed, not if we intended to live here the rest of our lives.

Otto was more apt to be found lounging around the farm on a normal day. Even in his laziness, he always had a curious expression on his face, and his bark was the shrillest and meanest of them all when provoked. He had once saved Richard's life while on a scout back when we were still in Middlehitch. A drifter was hiding out in the old sporting goods store in Gorham where they'd gone to look for camping supplies.

Before the drifter could do anything, Otto had attacked, bitten the man through his arm. The guy had been armed; heavily. He might have killed Richard and taken his pack and belongings had Otto not been there. Ever since then, the two had been close.

As for Richard, he liked to describe himself as a "sassy Scotsman." Once a renowned garden designer, foodie, and a well-known socialite in his home of the Hillsborough Township in New Jersey, he was on a holiday with friends TJ and Lottie, and his partner Webber, when the whole life-changing event happened.

Lottie started seeing an apparition of her dead aunt. Webber and the others decided to take her to the hospital while Richard stayed behind and called the local airports to book a flight home. All flights were grounded; all buses delayed until further notice. Transportation was halted while the government and local law enforcement tried to get a handle on the chaos. The others eventually came back hours later without Lottie. They stayed in the condo community for nearly six weeks, rationing supplies with fellow condo renters. When the food finally ran low, the group sent parties of two out to the local market. That was when they truly realized how fucked they were.

The entire time, Richard had stayed glued to his computer, his social media rife with posts of friends losing their minds with thoughts of seeing ghosts, others grieving for their afflicted loved ones, and the titanic and equally enigmatic updates from the government on how they were planning to deal with the situation.

While he tried to strategize plans for getting themselves out of this mess, the others, including Webber, were too fraught with terror and depression to want to listen to him. Most of them held out hope they'd see an army convoy sent for rescue. Some had already given up. One, a young woman in a neighboring condo, had slit her wrists in the tub during the third week in. Richard and Webber had found her while checking in after they hadn't seen her in a few days. He still got choked up to this day talking about it.

Eventually, the condo was faced with a new threat: the Woods. TJ was the one who first noticed them closing in. They had waved it off as fatigue and nonsense, the idea of being stuck inside messing with their heads. Being a photographer, Webber had wanted to get a closer look. He'd spent the last six weeks documenting each and every bowl of rice, every crying fit, every group meetup in hopes he'd someday be able to present it as a collection in a gallery, maybe even sell it to a magazine or news outlet documenting an insider's view of the collapse of human civilization. Richard hadn't seen him leave. But when he didn't come back, that was what finally broke his will.

Richard had gathered his belongings and told the others he was leaving. He invited them to come along. They told him he was suicidal, he didn't know what to expect outside, anything could happen to him out there. He'd taken the Jeep left by their deceased neighbor and fled. He never went back there, so he never knew exactly what had happened to the condo group. His best guess was the Woods had overtaken the area.

After spending several weeks drifting from place to place in the Jeep and siphoning gas here and there, Richard eventually found an abandoned bed and breakfast. Once a beloved place for tourists to visit during peak foliage season, the place had closed for the winter before the collapse. The only signs of life had been left by a caretaker, who was nowhere to be found. The kitchen was still stocked with non-perishables, there were fireplaces in most of the rooms, and there was a well on the property.

Richard stayed there for nearly five years. His gardening skills had allowed him to harvest from abandoned local farms and start hydroponic gardening. He'd used several rooms, all connected with one another to grow a variety of plants through the winter months and subsisted off of those and what mushrooms he could scavenge from the forest. On occasion, when he felt particularly brave, he'd venture out to search for canned protein.

It was on one of these trips he ran into Ash. The two had argued over a can of Spam. The rest was history.

Today as we walked the lonely road, I regarded Richard's short, wavy chestnut-blonde hair and the well-groomed beard that forested his upper lip and chin. In spite of his weight loss and his torn and stained down jacket, Richard always took care of his appearance. His hair never got long, his beard always pristine and his smile almost never vanished along with it. "You know," he always said, "once your looks go, then it's basically all over."

We left the solar panels behind, our boots and paws crunching in the sand and pebbles as we closed in on Route 25. I'd spent several months poring over what our escape routes were on our map of Onyx River. Route 25 branched off of Route 10, running almost parallel to 116 to the north. Route 25 was larger than 116, with more clearings and buildings along it. Gretchen had taken Evie to the edge of town on it once after doing a cleaning detail on the solar panels. They noticed an abandoned residence, but not one that seemed important enough to search for supplies at the time. I figured while we were out this way today, we might as well explore it. There was no use in not bringing something back if we were making the trip anyway.

The farther away we found ourselves from the solar panels and town, the smaller the fields became and more land was eaten by forest. Richard, who had been whistling a tune I wasn't familiar with, had stopped as we neared the lone home at a bend in the road ahead. The three-story green farmhouse still had a silver four-by-four pickup truck in the lot and a small trailer. The metal roof was rusted, the yard overgrown and scattered with toys for children and dogs alike. As we got closer, Otto seized an old red Kong and started chewing on it frantically. Richard tried to pull it away to no avail; Otto rarely surrendered things.

"Should we check the garage first?" Richard asked, nodding to a small structure on our left. The two garage doors were wind battered and paint chipped while the old basketball hoop mounted above had lost its net.

I shrugged. "Better to be safe."

Richard tried the door on the side: locked. I took Otto's leash while Richard used our crowbar to leverage open the door. The wood cracked when it eventually gave. We donned our headlamps and glanced inside. There was a workshop, complete with a table saw, lathes, drill presses, and a planer.

"Nice generator over here," Richard commented, poking his head from behind a tool bench.

"We've got no way to get it back."

"There is a truck still parked outside."

I glanced back out at it. "Those tires are as flat as hell." The truck had been sitting out in the elements for too long. They probably weren't any good to drive on after five years, let alone ten.

We left the garage and moved to the house. The front door was also locked; however, a quick search yielded a hide-a-key and we were able to get inside. The interior was like countless others I'd seen before: evidence of a quaint normal family, a hectic push to escape and the remnants of whatever was unimportant left behind.

Richard filed through the pantry. Otto settled on the kitchen floor and chewed on his toy as though nothing new were happening.

I found myself in the family room. There were dozens of pages of children's artwork on the table, drawn in crayon and colored pencil. I lifted the one on top and brought it closer to the light from the kitchen for a better look. It was a picture of a house, probably this one with a family of four. The stick figure was in the kitchen in front of a crude sink. The two children were in the living room, drawing or writing. It was hard to tell.

The last figure was in the basement. I couldn't tell what they were supposed to be doing.

"Hey," Richard called from the kitchen.

I dropped the piece of paper. Cold ran down my arms. "Yeah?"

"You should come and see this."

I returned to the kitchen. Richard had filled the entire dining table with non-perishables: cans of pureed tomato, sweet corn, butternut squash, boxes of mac n' cheese, and arrays of varied spice jars. "Goddamn. That's a lot more than I thought we'd find," I said.

"It gets weirder." Richard swished the curtain aside to the pantry. The shelves were still brimming with canned goods, boxes of rice, beans, and pasta, bags of flour, boxes of baking powder, soda, and corn starch. Aside from a couple boxes of rice chewed through by mice, there was enough food there to feed a family for several months.

I frowned. "It looks like they barely took anything…"

Richard glanced at me. "I don't think they did."

The chill returned to me. "Why do you say that?"

"Look at the sink. No dirty dishes. Family photos still on the fridge. There's even a bag of dog food in here."

"Maybe they didn't have time to grab anything," I said, despite knowing better.

"Did you search the rest of the house?" he asked.

I hadn't.

I cast a glance at the door nearby, the door where Otto had conveniently settled next to, the door that presumably led into the basement. "Fuck," I muttered.

"What?"

"I was looking at these pictures the kids drew in the other room . It was a little creepy. It shows one of the parents doing something in the basement."

Richard's face seemed to hollow even more at my words. "There was only one parent."

I nearly choked on the air I was breathing. "What?"

He pointed to the photos on the fridge. "Right there. Single dad. Two kids. No mother."

The photos were damning. And now I was paying closer attention, there was no evidence of a female presence in the house at all. In the bathroom, there was no second adult toothbrush, no makeup or bodywash, bleach-stained towels…

Who was in the basement in that drawing?

A ghost.

Had the kid let the ghost possess him? Had the family even left?

I stepped over to the basement door and silently twisted the knob. The door squealed open.

"Fucking shite," Richard cussed under his breath. "It had to be one of these houses." I wasn't sure Richard had ever encountered another Attached person after his friend, Lottie. His reaction wasn't too far off from mine though. These were the kinds of homes that made you want to stay curled in bed for a week and never go outside again.

A pungent odor floated from the basement, one that turned my stomach. Otto stopped gnawing on his toy and a low rumble surged from his throat.

I took a step.

Richard reached in front of me and closed the door.

I stared at him.

"Not today." He shook his head. "I can't."

THE WILD FALL

It took me less than a few seconds to agree. We packed our backpacks with the items Richard had pulled out onto the table and left. We locked the door behind us and took the key.

With more weight on our backs, I wanted to quickly check and make sure the rest of Route 25 was clear. After all, that was what we'd come out here to do. I left my pack sitting in the driveway and jogged to the end of the curve in the road where it straightened out again.

My heart sank. A quarter mile in front of me, the Woods lingered, the darkness eating into the perfect blue sky. The border seemed like water, transparent and still so black every cell of me felt it. Route 25 was blocked. There was no getting out of town this way. Worse was it seemed the Woods were stretching in from the south where Route 10 continued. If that way was also blocked, we were without an escape.

"Holy shit," Richard murmured from behind me.

I turned on my heel. "We need to get back. Now."

I picked up my pack and we started our long walk back to the farm. I hoped Gretchen had better news than we did.

Evie

After spending nearly an hour under one damn streetlight listening to the darkness and trying to discern shadows of violent monsters in its depths, I concluded I couldn't stay there all night. The temperature had dropped into the high twenties. I hadn't dressed for winter weather at all, a cotton sweatshirt under my dad's old green ranger jacket, black jeans, and my leather hiking boots. No hat, no gloves, no insulation.

I still had no idea where the monster from the feed store had disappeared off to. Logic said it was hiding in the darkness around us, waiting for its chance to attack. I knew though if I didn't get out of the cold, I could freeze. I had no choice but to brave the night back to town.

With Tempest by my side, we raced from streetlamp to streetlamp. Each time I entered the darkness, my heart leapt into my head, the beating the only thing I could hear. After what felt like the longest ten minutes of my life, we made it to town. The closest store was a yarn shop, one we barreled into and locked the door behind us. I turned all the lights on inside, which took a moment to pop on. I yanked down a few of the knitted blankets hanging on the walls and made a bed of sorts behind the counter. Exhausted and relieved, we both fell asleep.

I woke to sunlight peeling into our corner of the store through the large glass display windows. Judging from its height, it was about ten or eleven o'clock in the morning. I couldn't believe I'd slept in so late, especially after that night. Gathering my bag and waking Tempest, I unlocked the door and stepped out onto the sidewalk.

It was colder today, almost the same temperature as last night. I tucked my hands into the pockets of my dad's jacket and started down the road in the direction of the farm…and the feed store.

I had stayed out nights before, but I'd always come back before noon the next day. It had never stopped Liz or Gretchen from worrying but this had become ritual. Breaking that was going to start a complete shit show and that's not what I needed right now. I wasn't even sure how I was going to tell them about the thing that had attacked me last night. It hadn't been a wolf, which meant there was something else our group needed to be wary of now, something that didn't need the Woods nearby.

I walked fast, my breath puffing out into the late morning air, my fingers tingling even inside my pockets. Tempest kept pace, her large ears pointed and head taking in everything around us. Even in the sun and the quiet, it was as though both of us were waiting for everything to move all at once, from the trees to the stones in the rock wall alongside the park.

When the farm finally came into view, I breathed a small sigh of relief. All I could think of doing was getting inside, drinking a cup of tea, and taking a hot shower. As soon as we made it to the dirt driveway, I broke into a run. I all at once forgot about my fight with Liz yesterday and how she would react when I told her about the monster I'd seen. I wanted to be inside around other people. Safe.

Gjon emerged from the barn with Sanz as I slowed to a jog in the turnaround. Tempest loped over to greet her fellow canine friend.

"Evie? You okay?" Gjon asked, walking over to me. His brows were knit together, his eyes taking me in as if I were covered in human blood or something.

I opened my mouth to speak and felt my vocal cords strain. I hadn't been aware of it, but tears had begun to fill my eyes. I needed to get inside now. I couldn't do this, not in front of Gjon.

"I'm fine," I croaked. I moved toward the front porch. "Need a shower."

"You're sure?" he called after me.

The dogs growled as they chased each other in circles around him.

I threw my hand into the air with a thumbs up, knowing I couldn't say anything else or I'd start bawling.

I opened and closed the front door hurriedly, expecting to see Richard on the couch or Gretchen waiting on the stairs in expectation. But the front hall was empty. Even after I closed the door and waited for the inevitable tide of adults to check and see who was here, no one came. Where the hell was everyone?

I decided it didn't matter. I'd dodged a bullet and no one had seen me…yet. I climbed the stairs, my hand gliding along the banister around the curves in the hall until I reached the bathroom. I showered for a luxurious five minutes, letting the steam clear my head and the hot water beat against my body.

Somehow, in spite of it all, I had survived last night. I hated thinking maybe, somehow, my dad was still watching over me. Maybe, even if I couldn't see him, his ghost was here with me, making sure I stayed safe. I felt stupid for believing it, and at the same time, the thought of him still existing in some capacity made me feel more at ease. It also made me hate he was gone. It made me think about how much I missed him, how much I still needed him.

Even after the shower, my entire body felt weak, my nerves frayed and my psyche pitted with sadness once more. It hadn't been the first time I'd pinched myself and willed myself to wake from this nightmare. Like all the other times, it didn't do any good.

Somehow, I tore myself from the daze of the shower and went to my room to put on new clothes and get ready to face my inevitable doom at the hands of Liz downstairs. I brushed my hair and pulled it into a ponytail and then stared at myself in the mirror for a solid minute. I stared at my nose and my jaw and my ears… They looked like my dad's. What people saw in me that definitively showed we were related.

As I grew older, I respected his ways of harnessing the quiet to his advantage. He never escalated a situation even though I knew he had something to say. He would observe nature and rarely comment on its eccentricities and even its beauty, even though I could tell he was appreciating it in silence. I wish I'd gotten a chance to know more about what he was thinking. I wish I'd asked.

I had planned to go confront my mistakes and instead, I lay on my bed crying and circling the drain on wondering why he had to be gone. I fell asleep there.

I awoke to voices arguing in the hall downstairs. It took a moment to remember where I was and everything that had transpired. My stomach tied itself in knots as I listened to the upset voices. I recognized Gretchen and Liz as the main two, Ash chiming in occasionally, but couldn't tell what they were saying. Were they arguing about me? Gjon had seen me come home though. It wasn't about me. It had to be about something else.

Throwing the covers off, I peeled open my door and rounded the hallway to the stairs. The fire hadn't been lit in the upstairs hall and I shivered at the cold. There was no one in sight downstairs, which meant everyone was gathered in the living room off to the left. Everyone was trying to talk on top of one another. I hadn't seen everyone at each other's throats since the day I'd learned my dad had died.

Taking steps quickly, I hit the bottom floor and crossed into the living room. Everyone was still dressed as though they'd just arrived back from being out. All three dogs were present as well and Gjon was collecting their leashes to take them outside. Ash shook his head and muttered, "That's a dumb idea. That's such a dumb idea," while Richard rebutted with, "I think it's quite sensible."

Liz stood in front of the fireplace, a hand on her forehead and jaw set. I knew that look. She was upset, livid. She was about to lose it on someone.

Gretchen shouted something about not caring and not understanding when I walked in. Everyone's eyes landed on me.

"Hey," I said meekly, not sure what I was getting myself in the middle of. "What did I miss?"

Liz chuckled. Everyone looked at her, including me.

Gjon took the dogs outside. Before closing the door behind him, I heard him mutter, "God damn it, Liz."

I returned my attention to her. "Is something funny?"

"It depends." She shrugged. "Are you done with your latest tantrum? Because if you are ready to rejoin the adults, we have a serious situation on our hands."

"Liz, knock it off," Gretchen growled at her.

Normally that kind of baiting would have sent me over the edge. Liz wasn't one to start an argument with me; in fact, it was the other way around. But my fear of what kind of situation they were referring to was the only thing on my mind. Had they seen one of those monsters like I had?

I swallowed and asked, "What situation?"

"We're surrounded," Ash answered. "By the Woods. On all sides."

My stomach bottomed out. My knees buckled as I found the closest chair to slump into. "Fuck."

"Right?" Gretchen said.

"What are we going to do?" I barely felt my mouth forming the question, a numbness having settled over me.

"What we always do," Ash answered. "Gather what we can and make a break through these trees to the west. It'll be a hike…and we won't be able to take the car with us. We'll cross the Onyx River and eventually hit Route 5 in Vermont. From there, the town of Gregory is five miles, give or take, to the south."

"He's got it all figured out," Liz said, eyebrows perking.

"Sarcasm aside," Ash growled, "it's an incredibly risky move. We would be leaving behind a good deal of supplies and we don't know what's waiting for us on the other side of the river."

"Alternatively," Gretchen spoke, "we could stay here and wait until the Woods get closer. Our exit routes are blocked off but we're still several miles from any of those rifts. It's taken three months for them to close us in. There's a chance come springtime we might be in a better position to move. Weather won't be as harsh and we won't need to establish ourselves before a long cold snap again."

"And the Woods could overtake us in our sleep, again," Ash said. "We could put ourselves at risk waiting it out and hoping it doesn't come our way. Doesn't do us much good when this little town runs out of supplies and we need to scout out nearby towns, does it?"

I glanced back and forth at them. "Last time we ran too early, it cost us someone's life." I stared at Liz. "Let me guess: you're in favor of running again?"

Liz picked up a Nalgene full of water from the floor between her legs and took a long pull. "No. Call me crazy but I don't think leaving all this behind is the best idea."

Ash's face slackened. "Your idea is the most ludicrous of them all," he said.

Gretchen nodded. "Sure is."

I frowned. "What is it?"

Liz started to open her mouth but Ash interrupted her. "She wants to go into the Woods and try to find a way to stop it from moving in on us."

The sentence almost didn't register. I had to replay it in my head a couple more times before I fully understood. When I did, hot anger charged through my brain. "You want us to go in there and try to find a way to turn if off like a switch or something?"

"No," Gretchen said. "She wants to go in alone."

Liz's mouth straightened. "I've navigated these Woods before. There's something in there that can stop this…I've felt it for a long time. If I don't succeed, then you can all make the decision to either leave or stay. All I ask for is a reasonable amount of time before you make a decision."

"Except we lose you, you selfish tit!" Richard yelled, surprising everyone.

Ash cleared his throat. "We've lost too many people in those Woods—you've seen it enough to know, Liz."

"Tell me, Ash," Liz said, crossing her arms, "how long are we going to keep running from city to city like scared rats? Is this going to be the rest of our lives?"

"We could join a GRC," Richard suggested.

"And have the government ration your food, tell you which corner of what building to shit in, and submit you to random 'attached' skimming every month?" Gretchen shook her head. "Those places are like prisons. I was lucky to get out when I did."

I had nearly forgotten Gretchen and her husband had left a GRC due to the brutal racism and threats they'd received. It made me think twice about my latent desires to experience one of those places.

"When it comes to the safety of our own group, maybe it's not such a terrible option," Ash said.

"You didn't have someone threaten to hang you in your own front-yard tree," Gretchen snarled.

"No, but I did have someone tell me they'd 'shoot my gay ass' if I ever walked through their neighborhood again. Had someone try to rob me while going home from work one night. Had someone paint 'Faggot' on my car windshield."

No one said anything. The haunted look Gretchen and Ash shared could have shattered glass.

The door opened and Gjon reentered, all the dogs in tow. The noise broke the spell and almost everyone seemed to break from the tension. Gjon unclipped the animals from their leashes and they scampered off to different parts of the room. Tempest joined me at my chair. Her happy panting gave me back some of the courage I needed.

I cleared my throat. "I agree with Ash. I don't think we can afford to wait. I saw something last night in town."

Everyone's eyes flicked to me.

"What do you mean?" Liz asked.

I took a deep breath. "I went to the feed store."

"After dark?" Gretchen snapped.

"I was going to get food. I figured we were far enough away from the Woods we would be okay."

Liz shook her head. "That's not how it works. Plus, knowing what we know now, you could have been killed."

"But I wasn't!" I spat at her. "I can look after myself."

Liz squinted at me. "Clearly, you can't if you thought running into the dark in search of dog food was a smart idea. I'd hazard a guess you got lucky this time."

"Stop bickering!" Gretchen yelled. She turned to me. "What did you see?"

"Tempest found a dead body in the storeroom. There was something stalking us from outside. It broke down the door and chased us."

"A wolf?" Ash asked.

"No. Something else. Something that used to be human, I think."

Something shifted in Liz's gaze, some recognition that made me suspicious. Did Liz already know about whatever this monster was?

Before I could call her out on it, Gretchen asked another question. "How were you able to get away from this thing?"

"I think they're afraid of the light. I stayed under the streetlights."

Ash turned to Liz. "You willing to brave the Woods knowing that monster could be waiting inside with the wolves?"

She met his gaze. "Someone's got to try. Either way, we're fucked."

I felt my blood boiling with every clipped response she gave. Moreover, all I could think about was how she was probably doing this to get away from me, from her guilt over getting my dad killed. This was her way of abandoning the group like I'd assumed she would the last several months. It wasn't hard to see how disconnected she'd become.

Richard checked his watch. "Darkness will be coming within the hour. We need to prepare in case there are new dangers out there."

Gretchen nodded. "We should secure the windows on the first floor. Richard, Ash: help me get the shutters."

The group splintered. While the others left through the front door to attend to the windows, I watched Gjon and Liz exchange a look before he noticed I was still there, watching. He cleared his throat and stood. "I'll get the fire going upstairs."

Alone with each other, the anger and the heat filled the space around us. Liz turned and squatted in front of the fire, grabbing a stack of newspaper. She started tearing at it and twisting it. "You're being reckless, Evie," she said, not looking at me.

"Stop treating me like I'm helpless!" I burst, my anger spiking in my throat. "I don't need you to look out for me. I don't want you to. We both know how crap at it you are."

She glanced at me briefly before returning to her work. "I figured you'd be happy to see me leave. No more mothering. No more arguments."

"You being a coward doesn't make me happy. It pisses me off." I trembled, tears spilling down my face. "You don't care about anyone here but yourself. All you want to do is run away and hide and not face what you did!"

"Enough!"

The voice came from the adjoining room. I turned and noticed Nettie standing there, eyes watering, lip juddering, staring at me. "All you have done is blame everyone here for a mistake. For an accident."

"It wasn't an accident!" I yelled back, not even thinking before I spoke. My mind was a white, hot knife, my lungs searing. "She got Dad killed!"

"She made a mistake, Evie!" Nettie cried. "A stupid, human mistake. We all make them. You make them. I make them. Liz makes them. Hank made them. You know what else? Liz isn't responsible for the lives of everyone here. You repeatedly tell her. She wasn't responsible for your dad's life either. He made a choice to run back for Sanz. He made a choice to turn around even when he knew doing so was a risk. Hank made the choice, Evie."

My throat was tight, my muscles strained in my shoulders, in my arms, in my chest. I wasn't even sure I could breathe. I couldn't bring myself to look over at Liz and I could barely look back at Nettie, the woman I couldn't stand to think of being with my dad, who used to wear makeup, and used to dance while she cooked. Who I'd give anything to see happy again with Dad once more.

I fled the room, my footfalls pounding on the stairs as I ran. I heard the tapping of Tempest's paws as she followed me. I flew past Gjon who was striking the match to light his fire. He said my name as I blazed past him and into my room, Tempest slithering inside before I slammed it. I couldn't stop the flow of tears, couldn't stop the sobbing as it ransacked my body. I collapsed onto my bed and curled into a ball. Tempest leapt onto the bed and tucked herself in close to me, licking my arm.

After what felt like only moments, my door peeled open and someone sat on the bed next to me. I could smell the bouquet of our dinner and knew it was Nettie. I didn't dare move. I didn't want to look at her. I didn't want to see her sad face that mirrored mine so closely.

"Why did it have to be Dad? Why him? It's not fair," I choked out between sobs.

Her hand rested on my arm. After a moment, she answered, "No. It's not."

"How am I supposed to do this without him?" I said. "I need him."

Nettie's hand found mine and held it. "It's never the same after you lose a parent. I lost my mom when I turned twenty-one. Thought I was ready for what life could throw at me, thought I'd learned all I needed to. But I was wrong. Day after day, I'd encounter something I didn't understand, something I couldn't do on my own. I needed her.

"I learned to do a lot of things by myself. I broke up with my first long-time boyfriend. I learned how to apply for a loan. I graduated culinary school. I bought my first car. I cooked lobster. Each little thing I achieved, I would write down for her, so in some way she'd see each thing I did and that I loved her and missed her. And when this whole thing happened and she didn't return to me, I knew I'd made her proud. She didn't feel like she needed to come back to me. She didn't see I was in trouble. I'd grown up for her."

Nettie's hand stroked mine and I thought about Dad, watching me from some other place between worlds, watching each decision I made and path I took. Was he proud of me? Did he not come back because he knew I would be okay?

I wasn't sure what I believed.

The room had grown dark. After a few more moments, Nettie turned on the lamp on the table next to the bed. "I have to go back to making dinner. I can bring some to you if you'd like."

I shook my head and flipped over on the bed. The woman before me was not the same one I'd known for almost three years. She didn't wear makeup anymore. She didn't sing to her own music. All those things she told me she hadn't done because of my dad were a lie. I held her hand. "I'm sorry I was such a bitch to you for so long," I said. "I wish it hadn't taken this for me to see how much you and Dad loved each other. I'm sorry."

A tear slipped from one of her dark eyes along the side of her nose. "Me, too." She stood and took a deep breath. "You should talk to Liz when you're ready. I think she needs to know those Woods aren't the only answer for her." Then, she left, leaving the door open a crack.

THIRTEEN

Liz

I spent the night in the living room, keeping the fire going long after everyone had gone to sleep. I'd tried to lose consciousness for a long while, tossing and turning in my bed for hours before realizing it was never going to come. The fire had nearly burned down by the time I got downstairs to the living room. I took my time, moved as slowly as I could bear, in part because I didn't want to wake anyone and also because of what Evie had told us earlier. Something else was out there hunting, something that was more terrifying than the wolves.

While I had tried to forget the things I'd seen inside the Monolith in the Woods ten years ago, the images came screaming back to me in shotgun blasts of black and white. The twisted tunnels that took me deeper and deeper into the earth, the cells with the twisted, malformed prisoners and the faceless one that had attacked me as I'd escaped... They had been caged there for a reason.

Hank had seen them, too. He'd had told me about what had happened to him a month before I came to the White Mountains for my refuge all those years ago. Back when he used to be a forest ranger, he'd been sent into the mountains on a mission to find a group of lost hikers. It had been Halloween night and he'd hated to go, unable to spend the time with Evie.

On the exposed ridge, he'd encountered gruesome bodies, their figures twisted, faces cracked open at each orifice, bodies turned silvery and frozen. A wolf had done that to them. He hadn't known what they were at the time, didn't know he had encountered the first of what the Woods would wreak upon the world.

Worse, those bodies had vanished with the coming sun the next morning.

While we hadn't encountered any, we heard stories of sightings, things that were not wolves that had attacked settlements and camps. Things that were inhuman, silver, with contorted and grotesque limbs. Soulless things.

Was that what Evie had seen?

Some masochistic part of my personality longed to glance outside if only for a moment to glimpse one in the dark, slinking between the trees, a whisper in the shadows. Our new home, a place I had wanted to feel safer in, was no longer the picture of luck. The closed shutters on the windows were a reminder of the danger lurking outside. The sound of the wind howling as the trees shook was an ominous reminder of the inbound colder weather. The house felt smaller somehow, less like a home and more like a prison. A feeling I thought I'd left behind at the cabin in Middlehitch, at the school in Cardend. It was never going to feel safe, not until something was done in the Woods to turn things around.

I sat in front of the fire, pulled the grating away to throw a couple more logs on. I prodded at them with the poker then used the bellows until a flame leapt to life somewhere in the back. I lay on the ottoman closest to the fireplace and tried to ignore the sounds of the wind outside.

Ten years ago, I'd met someone who had also gone into the Woods, someone who had seen the Monoliths, had spoken to one of the creatures that resided within them. His name was Astor, a man who had somehow discovered a way to rid himself of his own ghost by killing it while it possessed someone else's body. I'd saved him from a facility, Elon, in Maine. Government trackers, ordinary citizens handed guns and given special papers to hunt Attached people, would take them to these facilities to have them studied and experimented on.

In the Woods, the creature I'd spoken to had given me no hope of being able to change the circumstances of The Great Corruption, as it had called The Merging. I'd only gone in hoping to find some way to free Brody from the clutches of the wolves and had stumbled out feeling dwarfed by the understanding I was the minutest fractal in a complex pattern unfolding. I understood nothing, only that survival was important, and I'd struggled ever since.

Astor, though…

Astor had apparently spoken to another creature in the Woods and this one had given him a vague, prophetic statement: "It all starts in the center."

Parting ways with Astor at Elon was the last I'd seen of him. He'd told me if we were ever to meet again, it would be in the Woods. For years, I thought about the possibility of running across him. I thought about all the questions I would ask if I saw him again, questions that had driven me ill in the wee hours of the night thinking too hard about them. I would ask him if he was ever haunted by the ghost he thought he'd killed. If he saw his ghost, perverse and vengeful like I saw Brody now. How did he cope? Did he care?

And hearing he'd come to Onyx River was the closest I'd come to having that conversation. But he wasn't here. I'd missed him again.

A creak on the stairs made me tense. I glanced over my shoulder. Gjon stood on the bottom step looking in my direction. "Hey," he called softly.

"Hi," I said, my voice barely having enough strength to carry across the room. I was tired, my heart sick with thought.

"I'd ask what you're doing awake," he said, crossing the hall to join me in the living room, "but I think I have an idea."

After the argument with everyone earlier, I could only imagine what Gjon had thought of my crazy plan to go into the Woods alone. He'd been silent through the whole thing. He must have felt alone then—betrayed. It was confirmed when he sat on the couch across from me and not with me on the ottoman. He needed to distance himself from me, after I'd told everyone I needed to part from them to try and save us, "try" being the operative term. There was no growing close to anyone in these times. We couldn't afford to, but we also couldn't help it. We were only human.

"I'm not sure anyone is sleeping tonight," I said, not wanting to confirm or deny his guess.

"You might be right. On my way here, I passed Richard and Ash's room. They were talking. I'm not sure what about but…" Our eyes met. He looked away quickly. "Never mind. It's no secret what they were talking about."

"Could have been a few different things," I answered. "Could be the Woods closing in. Could be the new monster Evie saw. Could be my plan to go into the Woods."

"Could be Richard sharing a dream of some musical he wanted to see on Broadway."

I let the tiniest of smiles light my face. "Sure."

We said nothing for a few minutes. The wind outside cut into the silence. It might as well have been someone sawing on metal or trying to push flat tires up a steep hill. Then we both tried to say something at the same time.

Gjon cleared his throat. "I'll go first."

I nodded.

"We've known each other for a time. We're still at the start of something. I've known your head was always in those Woods. You never talked about it. But I knew. There's something in there you have unfinished business with. No matter how close anyone gets to you, it can't break that connection." He shrugged. "Even though I'd hoped I could."

My chest stung with his words. "This is something that started before I met you, something I tried to run from for a long time. I wanted to be carried away from it. I wanted to forget. But I can't. It's taken me ten years to realize I can't."

He reached out to me and I hesitantly took his hand. It felt so good, so real and warm, so full of life. My mouth started moving. "I've asked myself, 'Why would you want to leave this place, these people behind?' And the only answer I have is there has to be a better way to live than we have been. There must be something I can do to make this better. Because I love you all, even if I tried not to get attached. I want what's best for you." I put my other hand over his. "Call it my fatal flaw. I was never part of any community before this. I was a loner. The thought of losing you, losing our group scares me more than wolves or the darkness."

Gjon took a deep breath, his brown eyes locked on me. "So, instead of us being taken away from you, you would rather leave first?"

"We're surrounded. Our options are limited. You have to admit you've wondered if there was ever a way to fix this? You have to have wondered what secrets are inside that could change this?"

"We've all wondered it, Liz. That's different than any of us wanting to go in alone without any idea of what to look for."

"I've been inside. I've seen things. I was told things by someone. I have to believe there's a shot at ending this."

"Anyone can make up a story, Liz. Anyone can lie."

I thought back on my limited conversation with Astor in the Elon facility. He had thought I knew something. Something to do with the Monoliths and the altars in the Woods. He'd had no reason to lie. As much as I knew Gjon was trying to protect me, I shook my head.

"Not this time."

He stood, the abruptness of it making me flinch. Standing over me, I could see the confusion in his face, like he wasn't sure what to do next.

"Go to bed," I told him. "I promise I'll still be here in the morning."

Gjon nodded and slowly made his way back across the hall to the stairs. I waited until I heard his footfalls fade into the house before turning my attention to the nearest window.

"Liz."

The urge to look was back again and more furious than the previous feeling. I had tried to ignore Brody for almost a decade, choosing to live with people and not in the past. For some reason he had given me this distance, not coming any closer. Last night, the vision I'd had made me wonder if it had been real, if he'd somehow come through my dreams to warn me he was restless now, the truce of giving each other space was over.

I stood from my seat on the ottoman and crossed to the window. I pulled back the curtain and was greeted with the backsides of the shutters. I had almost forgotten Gretchen had done that, permanently sealing us inside in case one of the new creatures decided to show itself or tried to break in. I could possibly see something from my room, but it wouldn't be close enough. I needed to see him again. I needed to talk with him.

If my plan was to go into those Woods, I didn't want to leave anything up to chance. If Brody still haunted me, I needed to know if he would follow me in. I needed to know if he would try to get me killed in there, or...if he would help me. I didn't expect the latter option.

I moved through the living room down the hall toward the kitchen. The door that led outside there was quiet and the clearing behind the house near the hunting shed would give me enough room to notice if there was anything prowling about. Pinpricks of fear raced across my arms and into my palms as I thought about how bad of an idea this was. I was flirting with getting myself killed right now, before I could even take the chance of going into the Woods. I had told Gjon I would be here in the morning. Was I going to break my promise?

The kitchen still smelled like crushed rosemary and roasted potatoes from dinner. I hadn't eaten much, having lost my appetite after the fight with Evie. My stomach growled now. I unlatched the heavy wooden door and listened for a moment. No sounds other than the wind. I pulled open the door and stepped into the dark.

It was warmer than I had expected: a revelation that filled me with panic. When the Woods moved in, they tended to warm the surrounding area. We hadn't noticed it in the summertime, so we'd had to keep visuals on where the trees moved. Now that the weather was cooling, it was more conspicuous when the Woods were close by. Even a few miles from us, their influence could be felt.

I scanned the backyard. There was one large oak tree between me and the hunting shed, its shadow spreading like a cloak across the frosted ground. I didn't see any movement inside of it. I closed the door behind me, and made myself close my eyes. I reached out with my mind.

Brody...

I forced myself to think back to the year before the Woods crossed over, to the night before he died. Holding him in my arms. Kissing him. His hands on my chest. On my hips. Between my legs. I thought about him holding me through the night in bed. About waking to see him smiling at me. I called to that version of the man I'd known and blocked out as much of the thing he'd become after the Woods as I could.

Brody...

The wind pulled at my hair. On the air there seemed to be a new chill caressing my cheeks.

Come back...

Something in my stomach dropped as I remembered the day I lost him. The gunshot tearing through his neck, blood flooding the sidewalk, his heavy body in my hands as I tried to call him back from death. The grief spilled forward, pricking at my eyes, thickening my throat. That sudden emptiness of thinking he was gone forever, knowing I had lost my closest friend, my closest love...

"I need you."

I said those words out loud. I felt my mouth and tongue create each one, though the wind was too loud for me to hear the actual words.

I opened my eyes.

A black entity stood in front of me, its arm reaching toward me.

I jerked back, tripping over an uneven board on the deck and landing on my back.

The thing was darker than the night, a void in the air that blocked my vision of the yard. While its shape was vaguely human, it didn't have a face. Even so, I knew what it was deep in my gut. It was him. It was my Brody.

Tears ran full bore now. I hadn't cried in a long time, not since losing Hank months before, and even then, it had been fleeting. This was every piece of sadness I'd locked in my body after years of strife and it came pouring out as I stared at that darkness. By killing him in Josh's body, I had done this to him. I had turned him into this...nothing.

Even as the darkness reached for me, I heard a scream rise from somewhere above me.

No. Not above me. Inside the house.

Stumbling over myself, I turned away from the nothing, tore open the door to the kitchen and slammed it shut behind me.

Sounds of commotion guided me through the house into the hall and toward the staircase leading to the second floor. Ash and Gretchen shouted. Feet pounded on the hall floor. I got to the top of the steps and saw a cluster of bodies standing outside of the room at the end of the hall. My heart drummed. Nettie's room.

"What the hell is happening?" I said, my voice strong again as I thundered toward the room. Ash and Richard started from where they were outside the room. Tears streamed down Richard's red face. I noticed an axe in Ash's limp hand. We locked eyes. He shook his head and stepped away from the door to the room so I could look in.

Evie sat on the floor sobbing. Gretchen held her, stroking her hair and hushing her. In the bed lay Nettie, her body still, almost the same shade of pale she always was.

Gjon stood over her, his hands on his hips, his breath hitched. He looked at me and then his eyes flicked to the side table. An empty prescription bottle sat next to a torn page beneath the soft glow of the lamp. I carefully stepped toward it, skirting around Evie and Gretchen to read the piece of paper. Nettie had torn a page out of a copy of Jane Eyre, the book lying on the bed next to her. She had scrawled in pen, "I love you all. But I need to be with Hank."

Everything in me wanted to scrunch the paper and throw it as hard as I could at the wall. With all the control I had, I set the paper back on the nightstand and turned my head toward Gretchen. "Get her out of here."

Gretchen nodded and carefully guided Evie from her crumpled position on the floor. Richard escorted them down the hall, back toward Evie's room, while Ash and Gjon gathered at my side. "I hate to be the one to say it," Ash said. "But I saw this coming."

"You don't have to say it out loud," Gjon answered.

Ash looked at me. "What should we do with her?"

Nettie stared at the ceiling. She almost looked serene. It was the first time I'd seen her like that in months.

"Nothing now. We'll bury her in the morning."

"Do you think she saw him?" Gjon asked. "You know. Like his ghost? Do you think he haunted her?"

The thought hadn't even occurred to me. I had assumed it didn't happen anymore, new ghosts weren't created, or if anyone died in the Woods, they were automatically bound to the place. I had also thought if there was anyone Hank would come back for, it would be Evie. But maybe he hadn't had a choice.

"Doesn't matter now," Ash said, curtailing my thoughts, saving me from having to answer.

I turned and left, numbly finding my way toward Evie's room. Gretchen and Evie lay on the bed, Gretchen's arms embracing Evie as she quietly cried. Richard sat on the bed on the opposite side, holding Evie's other hand. They turned their eyes to me as I entered.

"We'll have a funeral for her tomorrow. Bury her under the oak tree."

Gretchen and Richard nodded and I turned to go.

"I think she'd like that," Evie said, her voice ragged.

I nodded, swallowing hard. "Me, too."

FOURTEEN

Evie

It was cold and gray the next day, another reminder winter's claws were getting closer to digging in. I think I slept some during the night but wasn't sure. Gretchen volunteered to stay with me but I told her I wanted to be alone.

Tempest lay on the floor near the door all night, her ears pointed and listening. I wondered if she was as disturbed as I was, imagining what Nettie's last moments had been like. I wondered if Nettie had waited for an apology from me, if that was the last thing she'd needed before she left. I don't think Nettie had ever truly felt as though she was a part of the group; she had been a part of my dad and he a part of her. It didn't make sense for one to exist without the other. Some kind of Romeo and Juliet shit I'd been taught by Gretchen that was unhealthy in a relationship.

Gretchen had instilled in me when in a relationship, each person should be able to exist entirely on one's own, be an entire entity with a purpose, a sense of being, a drive. Symbiosis, as she'd called it, wasn't vital to survival. If the person you loved died, you had to carry on without them. You had to adapt to life in their absence. Gretchen had lost her husband. His ghost hadn't come back for her. I think if he had, she would have probably hated it.

It felt weird, understanding both types of women, understanding Nettie's untethered floating since losing Dad and Gretchen's hard determinism since losing Darnell. Which one was I more like?

Since losing Dad, I had felt the pull of those Woods, not because I thought his ghost might have been somewhere in them, but because I wanted an answer. I wanted to understand something about this thing that dominated our lives now, the entity driving us this way and that, zig-zagging across New England like ants trying to find their way back home after the anthill had been obliterated.

I wanted to search. That gave me purpose. Not in the same way Gretchen found purpose though. So, maybe I was more like Liz than anyone else?

The funeral was held before noon. Ash dug a six-by-four hole by the oak tree on the edge of the property. He'd started early and had refused to let anyone else help. We kept it at the edge of the property because of the wolves. I thought about how deep we were burying her and how I didn't think they would be able to dig her up, but none of us was sure, and it was better to be safe than sorry.

After Nettie was set in her grave, we gathered by the hole and each tossed a clump of dirt in along with a small devotion or sentimental item. Richard insisted on planting sage over her in the spring, a show of cleansing as well as in tribute.

I didn't understand the inconsistency of funerals. My dad had tried to tell me about them a couple times before. You were supposed to gather together and say goodbye properly, remember the dead person, celebrate them, cherish your memories with them but collectively. We never had one for my mom. We didn't have one for Darnell, Katrina, Sully, or Alari either. We hadn't had anything for my dad. While something in the back of my mind screamed it was unfair that Nettie was getting what seemed like special treatment, I knew this was the first time we had ever had a body to bury. The first time we had a moment to say our thoughts and choose how to say goodbye on our terms. The others had been ripped away.

Liz seemed unsettled by the day in general. She kept looking around us, as though the Woods might unfold from the forest. But when it was her turn to say something, she knelt, grabbed a large fistful of dirt like everyone else had, and tossed in the book Nettie had been reading. It landed with a thump against Nettie's arm and the side of the hole. "You were our mother," she said, staring at the book. "I hope you've found peace." Then, the dirt cascaded over the rough textured cover and Nettie's skirt.

We stayed while Richard and Gjon buried her. Gretchen and Ash kept loaded rifles within arms' reach. The area reeked of fear and loss and soon, I found myself needing to escape, needing to feel sunshine and something warm in my hands. I thought about Tempest, locked in the house with the rest of the dogs. I wanted to hold her, to feel alive with her.

When the deed was finally done, we all splintered. Richard went to tend to the indoor garden, Gjon to the dogs, Gretchen to the woodshed to inventory ammunition, and Ash to check on the well pump, which had been acting sluggish. Liz asked if I wanted to help inventory food. I blankly accepted, not entirely sure what I would do on my own anyway.

The kitchen felt smaller today. The wooden beams, natural cabinets, and counter tops all seemed colder than a day ago. The dried herbs hanging from the rafters had rained a few leaves on the hardwood floor during the night, something Nettie would have swept first thing in the morning when she'd come down to start breakfast. Come to think of it, no one had made breakfast that morning. Another reason I felt so utterly empty.

THE WILD FALL

The pantry was next to the back door, a tall dark-stained oak cabinet with five shelves inside we'd filled to the brim over the last few months as we'd scavenged the town of Onyx River. Liz and Nettie would take stock of the supplies each month to make sure we weren't running low on anything in particular. Nettie created meal plans for the week, choosing to open only what she could afford to that would work with each dish. Nothing was ever wasted; nothing was ever left to molder.

Liz handed me a pad of paper and a pencil and started with the top shelf, counting through the baking supplies: flour, sugar, powdered milk, powdered eggs, baking soda and so forth. Sundays were always bread days. Nettie had made a rosemary olive oil loaf last week which had barely lasted through Tuesday. There was no yeast anymore, so each loaf had the same base, one she'd kept a basic formula for in her recipe tin. She'd tried to show me how to make it. I hadn't paid attention.

I had been such a selfish shit.

"Evie?"

I glanced up.

"Did you get that?"

"Sorry. What was it again?"

"We've got five cans of baking powder."

I diligently jotted it on the paper.

The rest of the cabinet went without interruption. Liz surmised we had enough food to last us through the end of the month. For six people and three dogs, that was better than either of us had anticipated. Now, we had to make it to the end of the month.

As Liz put the rest of the stock on to the bottom shelf, she stiffened, rearing her head back a little as though someone had spit in her face. The movement was so sudden, I took a cautionary step back, too. "What's up?"

She was staring intently at something on the floor. I didn't see anything.

"Did you drop something?"

Her gaze never faltered. "Get Ash."

I frowned. "Liz?"

She finally looked at me. The gravity in her eyes was nearly palpable. "Get him now."

I whirled on my heel and took off toward the front door. Outside, a brisk wind pinched at my neck and face as I thumped down the steps toward the sound of Ash's muttering and cursing. He was elbow-deep in a man-made hole off to the side of the house where the well pump was, the sound of clinking and clunking nearly masking his grumbles. He swung his head to me when I entered the fray. "What's up, Eve-il?"

"Liz needs you."

He sighed. "She'll have to wait a minute. I'm in the middle of—"

"No. She needs you now."

Liz

"The absolute fuck?"

Ash's exclamation brought Gretchen in from the backyard, who paused in the kitchen doorway staring at us and what we'd found. "Holy shit."

My skin felt twice as cold as it had minutes before when I'd felt the draft waft toward me from beneath the cabinet. With Ash's help, I'd managed to pull the tall shelf away from the wall and found a door behind it: lost, forgotten…hidden.

"Maybe it's a leftover door," Gretchen suggested. "You know, the kind that opens into a wall or something."

I reached forward and gripped the old-fashioned style latch and thumbed it. The door creaked as the air pushed it into the room toward us. Through the crack, I could tell there was a depth and cavity inside that stretched beyond the wall.

"Goddamn it," Gretchen muttered.

Ash shook his head. "Basements. Why does it always have to be basements?"

"It's not the basement," I said. "We've been in the basement of this house. Its wall ends at the kitchen door. This is an entirely different room down here."

Gretchen yanked open a kitchen drawer and pulled out a rolling pin. She rested it against the palm of her other hand and said, "Alright, let's see." She looked over at Evie. "Grab some headlamps."

Evie vanished into the hall.

"Wait a minute, wait a minute." Ash held a hand out. "We should tell Richard and Gjon. Otherwise, it'll be like that time we went into the train station when you—"

I walked into the dark space.

"—Well, never-fucking-mind, then," he muttered.

Coldness seeped into me from both sides, goosebumps rising on my arms beneath my flannel. I blindly groped at the walls with my hand, searching for a light switch but found only cobwebs and dirt.

"Here," Evie said behind me as something poked into my shoulder.

I reached back and grabbed the headlamp from her. Its pale light swung through the dark space. The walls were covered by what looked like old wallpaper, crinkled and yellowed with age. A shelf full of old canning jars was tucked a couple feet above me, directly over a set of wooden stairs dropping farther into pitch black.

"Someone get me a weapon," I asked. A few moments later, the handle of my knife tapped me on my arm. I carefully took hold of it, my grip warm around it. Now, I was ready.

"It goes down," I called back over my shoulder.

"We're right behind you," Gretchen said, her voice so close to my ear it nearly startled me.

I put my boot on the first step and it squealed under my weight, but held. The rest of the way, I held my breath unintentionally and the sounds of each creaking step echoed in what felt like a cavernous space around me. One set of footsteps followed, then another behind me. I wasn't sure if Ash had decided to stay in the kitchen as a form of reticence or to go get Gjon and Richard, but the feeling of not knowing if he was at my back sent a bolt of panic through my gut.

"It smells funky," Evie whispered from behind me.

"Shh," Gretchen chided.

I finally reached the bottom step, my boots flexing the soft wood beneath me on the landing. There was a brick wall directly ahead of me. I swung my headlamp to the right. The room had a low ceiling, coated in ancient cobwebs and dangling with the white bodies of hundreds of dead spiders. The floor was cement, cracked in several places, which pitched at odd angles. An old washer-dryer combo was shoved off to the side, coated in a thick layer of grime, the shelves above stacked with empty bottles of detergent, dingy rags, and smeared jars.

I left the safety of the staircase behind and plunged deeper into the blackness. The brick wall had been the chimney. I circled around it, listening as Gretchen and Evie scuttled after me over the uneven concrete.

There was an old well in the corner, filled in, but no less spooky for it; an old wooden cupboard filled with forgotten canned goods with dates ranging back over twenty years; an antique-looking furnace no longer connected to anything sat against the far right corner like a giant mechanical skeleton, and a long oil tank skirting along the rest of the wall. With each step, the cold only seemed to grow deeper until I felt my teeth chattering and clenched my jaw to stop them.

As we wrapped around the chimney back toward the stairs, my light was swallowed by an even deeper darkness: an open doorway.

Gretchen bumped into me as I stopped. Her warmth at my back only made the subterranean chill before me much more prominent.

Evie rounded her and came to a stop beside me. "Whoa," she murmured.

"Where do you think it goes?" Gretchen whispered.

"I don't know," I answered. I didn't want to take my eyes off it.

"We're not going to do this right now, right?" Evie asked, her voice quavering. "We're going to wait until Ash, Richard, and Gjon are here, right?"

I nodded. The tunnel carved a crack in the safety this house once held. I had figured now we knew about monsters besides the wolves lurking in the dark and the Woods closing in, we could at least still barricade ourselves in here and be safe. This made me question that. Had the owners of this house left with everyone else when the military had come in to get them? Where did this tunnel go?

FIFTEEN

Liz

Dinner was silent. No one wanted to eat in the kitchen, now they knew the second basement existed and Nettie's absence created extra tension there.

We'd shoved the shelf back into place out of an abundance of caution. I didn't want anyone investigating it without the others. It may have been an old section of the basement they'd closed off previously. After all, the house had once been a hunting lodge, a family farm... Something about the darkness irked me though. It felt unfathomable. It felt like it led somewhere forgotten.

Ash had shot and butchered another turkey and pan-fried it in a skillet with a bit of salt and pepper. We ate it with the last of our broccoli and some onion. It was too much salt but I said nothing. I didn't want to start any conversation. I knew it would devolve into talking about the tunnel, or Nettie, or the Woods.

Everyone separated after the meal and I was about three steps on the stairs toward my bedroom before Gjon caught my hand. "Hey."

I turned back to him. "What?"

"Can we talk?" As if he noticed my eagerness to be alone slithering out of my mouth like a snake, he added, "Please?"

We stood in the entranceway in the dark. Rain lashed at the door nearby, wind making a chorus of the trees outside.

"I was thinking about our conversation last night."

I sighed. "A lot has happened since then."

"Yeah." He stared at the ground. I stared at him. Everything about this conversation: the discomfort of it, his posture, his expression, the squirrelly feeling in my stomach of anticipation for what would come out of his mouth next… The déjà vu surrounded me. I hadn't felt this way about anyone since Brody.

"I wanted you to know no matter what you choose, I'm behind you."

It took me a moment to remember where I was, a moment to remember what we were talking about. "You are?"

"It's your choice, Liz. And I care about you enough to want you to be at peace with things. If I lose you, I lose you. But I'm better for having known you."

Each word felt like a goodbye. The finality of it grounded me, my shock taking root and threatening to pull me into the earth with every new breath I took.

He put his hands on my arms and stepped into me. "You are a force of nature, Liz."

I touched his elbows, let the warmth of his skin feed my own cold figure as I drowned in the wake of his words. He was letting me go. This is what I wanted, wasn't it?

Gjon kissed my cheek and walked past me to his room. Moments later, I heard his door close.

Not knowing what else to do, I spent the night sitting in the chair next to the front door, watching the shadows and the moonlight trickle in, listening to the sound of the wind.

Gjon and Brody weren't the same person. Brody would have fought tooth and nail to keep me from doing something like this. Gjon cared too much to stop me from doing what I knew I needed to do. Had I wanted him to try and stop me?

Maybe.

"Hey."

Gentle fingertips nudged my arm.

I opened my eyes to sun, to a bedroom I'd never slept in but somehow knew. Stained hardwood floors, a four-post king-sized bed with a comforter the color of storm clouds. Green walls. Glass doors led out onto a porch overlooking an autumnal backyard.

And I followed the fingers to the hand, the arm, to the face.

Funny. I couldn't see his face. But I knew it was him all the same.

Brody.

He smiled. "You're sleeping away the whole day."

I lay back on the bed, my lips breaking into a wide grin. "You could have woken me sooner."

"Well, not to sound like a serial killer or anything, but maybe I like watching you sleep."

"That did sound like a serial killer."

He laughed. His dry, husky chuckle I hadn't heard in what felt like forever. "Shake a leg, Lizzy. We've got the whole day ahead of—"

A board creaked.

I bolted, the chair nearly collapsing under me.

The hair on my arms stood on end, goosebumps prickling. It took too long for me to register where I was, too long for me to think about what could have made that sound before it all crashed on me.

THE WILD FALL

The rain had stopped. On the porch outside, something scuttled along the floorboards.

I grabbed for the first weapon I could find: a broom standing against the wall by the coat rack, and peered out the sidelight windows next to the front door.

At first, I could only see part of whatever the intruder was, crouched on the deck with only its head and front arms visible behind one of the white chairs. After blinking, I realized there was no chair there.

Its limbs were crooked, as though making two perfect right angles, the elbows inverted almost like a canid on the front, knees buckled and broken on the back. The body was too long, like a log between both sets of limbs, the skin as white as the paint on the railing behind them. Its head seemed human, its limbs ended in hands and feet though it wore no clothes, the skin lumpy and blanched and spotted with dark bruise-like welts.

When it turned in my direction, my stomach dropped into my feet. Whatever human face it once had was now pulled back over its skull, black eyes crookedly surveying the deck from where its ear should have been. When it moved, there was a steady sound of bone on bone, like knuckles rubbing against one another, talons scritch-scratching over the wood like a mouse.

I wanted to look away but I couldn't, eyes glued to the monstrosity currently edging across our deck like a giant white spider. I needed to warn the others upstairs. I needed to get a better weapon. I needed to do something other than stand here. I couldn't though. I didn't want to move. I didn't want it to know I was here.

And though I remained silent and unmoving, the thing cocked its head in my direction and took one loping step toward the door, its body swaying beneath it before a back leg followed. Then another step. Another.

I pulled away from the window. Wood splintered in the floorboards outside the front door. A deep crackling inhale had me listening for an exhale. When it didn't come, I realized it was scenting the air; it was hunting.

A woof at the top of the stairs made me swing my head in that direction.

Evie stood there, her eyes rounded. My kukri was in her hand. Tempest stood behind her, a low rumble rippling from her throat.

Even as I reached out my hand for it, I realized too late the sounds on the other side of the door had stopped.

BANG!

I fell away from the door as the entire frame juddered. Wood splintered and squealed under the intense pressure.

Tempest launched down the stairs, her barks sharp and angry.

Outside, the thing screeched: a sound brought me back to a certain time and place. The cells under the Monolith in the Woods. The thing trapped inside. I'd never heard anything like it since. Until now.

Evie scampered down the stairs and grabbed Tempest's collar. "It's going to break through!" she screamed.

The creature's howl intensified.

"Get everyone up!"

My order was punctuated by lights clicking on upstairs. Ash was the first to appear, his hulking frame hefting his favored ax. Even in his boxers, he looked intimidating. "What the fuck is going on?"

Evie tugged at Tempest, trying to get her away from the door. "It's trying to get inside!"

The dog wasn't having it, her whole body pulling to get at the invading creature.

I threw my back at the door to help barricade it in time for another THUMP. "I want everyone dressed. Gather weapons. We're going into the cellar."

"The fuck you want us to do?" Ash exclaimed.

The door exploded with noise as the thing slammed into it again. The doorknob spun wildly. The deadbolt was the only thing holding the wood in place. It wasn't going to last much longer.

"Get everyone into the cellar!" I screamed.

Within seconds, the entire house was bustling. Richard wrestled Otto to the bottom of the steps. The dog whimpered as they got closer to the front door, the high-pitched sound sending my head spinning. Gjon bumbled down with Sanz and handed her leash off to Gretchen before he came to my side. He pushed his weight against the door in combination with mine. "A wolf? It's a wolf?"

I shook my head.

Fear prickled in his eyes along with a look I knew all too well. We couldn't fight this thing. We weren't going to stop it from getting inside.

Everyone hustled down the hallway and made for the kitchen.

"Get that cabinet moved! It's going to come through at any moment!" Gretchen ordered from the doorway. The steady shudder of wood on wood filled the air.

The door cracked behind me. A sliver of something sunk into my ear and I instinctively fell to the floor. Gjon pressed his back into the wood, his feet planted against the floor to provide as much leverage as possible. He reached for me.

I felt my ear and winced. A long splinter stuck out from the flesh behind my lobe.

"We've got it!" Richard shouted from the kitchen. "Run!"

"Go!" Gjon bucked his head in the direction of the basement.

I grabbed his hand and pulled him along with me. Our feet slapped against the hardwood floor. We were only a few steps away from the kitchen entrance when the front door gave way.

Tethered to Gjon, I yanked him along toward the black mouth where Ash stood waiting, his eyes speared with desperation. Claws tore at the floor in the hall, closer and closer.

We slipped into the darkness of the basement entry. "Close it!"

Ash and Gjon dragged the cabinet back, grunting with teeth gritting as the wood scraped over the kitchen floor.

Pale white fingers shot through the crack between the cabinet and the doorway and the scent of blood sparkled in the air. Ash screamed.

Pulling both of them back, I kicked the basement door shut.

In the dark, the panting and groaning was practically drowned out by the furious scraping on the other side of the cabinet. A flashlight clicked on moments later. Whose: I didn't know. The light bounced around the small stairwell before resting on Ash who lay propped on the top step holding his bicep. Rivulets of dark blood dripped from a gaping, ragged slice. "Fuck me!" he growled.

Gretchen appeared in the light next holding our small plastic bag of first aid supplies. "Shut up and let me help."

"We should get away from the door, away from where it can smell us," Gjon said in the darkness somewhere to my right.

Everyone descended the stairs into the icy cold basement. Clothed in only our essentials, we huddled together on the far side of the room near the old furnace for warmth. Richard propped the flashlight up so Gretchen could clean Ash's wound.

Gjon and I stood at the outer rim of our collective, our eyes locked on the basement steps. The scratching and banging above continued. My heart thumped so hard I could feel it in my temples, the acrid taste of adrenaline at the back of my mouth.

Gjon was tense at my side, his breaths quiet and steady.

Was this it? Was this the end? A sudden compulsion to grab onto Gjon's hand enveloped me and it took more will than I imagined to stifle it. Fear was like a cloud in my head. I didn't want this… I didn't want this…

The dogs whined and even as Richard shushed them and petted them, he swore under his breath. "Fuck, fuck, fuck…"

"Not helping," Ash said, seething through his teeth as Gretchen put another bandage on his cut.

"This needs stitches," she whispered.

"Do the best you can," I said.

Moments passed and the noise at the top of the stairs dissipated. The ceiling above groaned with the frantic movements of the creature as it scuttled about.

I let myself take a breath and tore my eyes from the door for a moment to look at Gjon. "We need to find something to reinforce the door."

He hummed.

I turned to Gretchen. "I need to borrow that light, Gretch."

She sighed before handing it over.

Gjon and I edged away from our group into the desolate space and let the flashlight roam across the walls. Besides old apple crates and coal barrows, there was nothing we could use to barricade the door and we didn't have any tools or materials to nail the door closed.

"Shit."

Gjon exhaled. "We need to get through until morning. Evie told us those things don't like light."

"We'll have to spend hours here. It's below freezing."

"We have no other options."

I swung the flashlight over to our group. Richard hugged Otto, both of them shaking all over. Ash leaned against the stone wall while Gretchen wrapped the wound. Sanz lay at her feet, her fur dust-coated already. Evie—

I blinked. She wasn't there. Neither was Tempest.

"Evie?" My voice was louder than it should have been.

Everyone looked around.

"She was right here a moment ago," Gretchen said.

BANG!

The door above shuddered. The thing was back.

A growing distrust gnawed at me as I swung the light toward the tunnel we'd discovered yesterday. The spiderwebs that had crisscrossed the doorway had been swiped out and footsteps lingered in the dust.

"Are you fucking kidding me?" Ash grunted.

"I'm sure she's just trying to find an exit," Gretchen said under her breath.

I launched myself into the dark tunnel. "Evie!"

The space was claustrophobic compared to the basement. The walls smelled like decay and earth, the beams above and around me moldered in places and split in others. The tunnel didn't seem structurally sound. Probably why they sealed off the basement in the first place; to keep everyone safe.

"Liz," Gjon said behind me. He hadn't entered the tunnel. "Bring the light back. We can't stay here in the dark."

I turned back and pushed the torch into his hand. "Stay here. I'll find her."

With manic scratching at the door overhead and the panicked breaths of my friends behind me, I threw myself into the darkness in search of Evie.

SIXTEEN

Liz

My arms out to either side of me, I guided my fingers along the rocky walls of the mystery tunnel. The light from our group's only flashlight faded as I turned the first corner.

"Evie?" I asked the darkness in front of me.

My voice bounced back at me. I felt like I was in one of those cardboard box tunnels my dad used to make when I was a kid. He'd set them up to stretch through our home from the living room into the dining room, much to the chagrin of my mom. My sister and I would crawl through them, giggling as our dad shook them from the outside.

I tried to clasp onto the comforting memory as I heard nothing back and continued on.

The odors of must and mold clogged my head the further in I walked. Anger tightened the muscles in my shoulders. Why had she left without saying anything to anyone?

It only took me a few more steps before I realized. She probably felt guilty: she may have led whatever this thing was to our front door. After all, we'd had no run-ins with any of these things in the years leading up to this, but we had also always been careful. We never ventured out after dark. We never made any noises that would attract the wolves or other survivors. We didn't take risks. And if we were unlucky enough to find ourselves in those situations, we never messed around.

Last night, Evie had been reckless. But she'd also told us about the danger before it blindsided us. If it hadn't been her now, it could have been someone else later.

I needed to find her.

I walked for ten minutes, following the tunnel's meandering walls with my fingers until it took a ninety-degree turn to the left. Where did this go? I had first thought maybe it connected with an old, buried coal chute or perhaps another storage room we didn't know about beneath the hunting shack. But we'd gone much farther than the hunting shack now. It almost seemed like we were heading back toward town…

Claws on rock.

I stopped moving. With how close everything was to me, I wasn't sure if it had come from behind me or ahead. Had that thing found its way into the basement? Or was it Tempest leading the way for Evie ahead of me?

The sound came again, followed by the repetitive sound of shoes in dirt.

"Evie!" I yelled, my voice bouncing around and vanishing into the dark.

A few seconds later: "Liz?"

"Wait for me!" I walked faster. "I'm coming to you."

"I was trying to find a way out."

Tempest gave a low woof.

I hesitated before saying, "It's okay."

I negotiated around another corner. A flashlight beam speared the darkness about ten yards down the tunnel from me. Tempest scampered to greet me and I gave her a small rub between the ears.

The closer I got to Evie, the more I heard her fluttering breaths. "I didn't mean for this to happen," she moaned. "I didn't want this."

The same words I'd thought to myself earlier. I put my hands on her shoulders.

"I know. But we have no idea where this leads. We need to get back to the others. We can't leave them—"

"—But there's something ahead," she said, her tone hopeful. "I heard something. And that smell? Can you smell it?"

I inhaled. It was faint, but it was there: woodsmoke.

I looked over my shoulder back toward the way I'd come . "We shouldn't…" I started.

"But what if?" Evie said. "What if there's someone else here?"

I grabbed her shoulder harder. "We need to get back to the others. If that thing finds a way into the basement—"

I couldn't bring myself to finish and I didn't need to. Evie stared through me, her fear heightened, her body trembling. "Let's go," she said after another moment.

We started back along the tunnel. I let her keep the light and stay in the lead while I took the rear. Tempest's shadow bobbed alongside our stretched and pulled shapes on the narrow walls.

After a few minutes, I stopped. It took Evie another few moments to realize I wasn't following. She spun around. "What?"

"Quiet."

I looked behind us. Evie's flashlight illuminated only a small portion of the dark tunnel but nothing seemed out of place. There were moments while we were walking when I could have sworn I heard another set of footfalls on top of our own. But the walls were close, the echoes sharp, and every sound felt like it came from right behind or in front of you.

Forcing myself to take a deep breath, I turned back around. "It's nothing. Let's keep going."

We did.

I was exhausted, my head pounding. The spot behind my ear where I'd been hit burned and throbbed with every step I took. We were in no shape to be investigating whatever the source of that smell was even though my cop brain from back in the day needled me to find out.

There.

Another sound.

A shuffle of boot against stone.

I turned.

Something slammed into my face. I buckled, slumping into the wall. The light from Evie's flashlight danced in my vision, splitting into multiple fractals that zigged and zagged and spun.

Evie cried out.

Tempest snarled.

The world dropped into complete darkness.

Evie

They melted out of the darkness as if they were made of it. Before I could even turn around, Liz was down. I couldn't even get to her before there was a bag being thrown over my head. The cinch pulled tight around my neck and even as I swung blindly trying to catch something or someone off balance, I knew it was useless.

Someone pushed my back and I stumbled across the uneven floor, tripping over Liz's prone figure. Once I was on the ground, it was no use.

Tempest snarled and barked. Cloth tore.

Someone screamed and swore. Moments later, I heard them kick her. She whined.

"Leave my dog alone!" I screamed.

Two hands bound my wrists together behind my back. The feeling of them made my skin crawl. No one had touched me like this since when I was a child, when the men had come and taken me from Mom's house. The entire experience unfolded like a paper crane in my mind:

the feeling of the gruff hands pulling my body out of my bed, the smell of liquor and cigarette smoke on the man's breath as he hurried to the stairs with me, the sound of Mom as she screamed and swore at him, the sound of the knife cleaving into her back…

I writhed and roared, my lungs on fire. "Get off me! Get the fuck off me!"

Someone swore again behind me. "Mmm! My fucking knee."

"Jesus, I've got to do everything…"

Hauled off the floor by my arms, I was thrown over someone's shoulder, the bones digging into my chest painfully. Warm splotches of light filtered like grains through the tiny holes in the sack. I couldn't tell where Liz was, where Tempest was.

"You got the dog?" someone murmured.

"I got her."

Tempest whined.

"Let's get 'em back to the Church."

Liz

"This is one of my favorite places," Brody said as he reached out and pushed a small branch out of the way. "It's kind of lost, I think. No one else knows it's here. Except for you now."

I pinched the end of the branch between two fingers and took it from him as he resumed along the meandering path. Brambles and red thorns grew in large coils, twisted and gnarled. A burr snagged on my jacket sleeve, but I pushed on, bringing the spiky orbs with me. Wind rushed in my ears. The evergreens were alive with it, their shush gentle and lulling. I wanted to stand there with them and let myself be gently nudged back and forth.

A bite of salt hit the tip of my tongue as I opened my mouth to ask how much farther.

"Not much," he said.

The brambles turned to tall yellow grass and soon enough, we passed through the legion of trees and out into the open.

I stared.

Ahead of us, a small grove of apple trees rested, the grass grown tall between them, the branches overgrown and crowded. Green-and-red-mottled fruit hung heavy from almost every tree. The base of each tree was littered with deer-chewed remnants.

Wow. My mouth shaped the word but I didn't hear myself say it.

He put his arm around me. "Isn't it something?"

"It doesn't belong to anyone?"

"Not that I can tell. It's just wild now."

We stepped farther in, our boots crich-crunching through the dry grass until we got to the nearest tree. We each reached up and picked an apple from the closest bunch. He tossed his. "Worms. Suppose it's too good to be true."

I checked mine over. "This one seems fine." I took a bite. The sourness punched me, made my lips purse. I handed it to him and he followed suit.

"How did you find this place?" I asked him once I'd finished chewing.

"My mom. She had a thing for orchards. And this used to belong to the giant farm down the road, the one that's abandoned?"

"It's a shame: all this getting left here with no one to pick them."

"Just the way of the woods, I guess."

I'd heard the statement before, but not from him. I wasn't sure where. A sudden unease hit me. I couldn't remember where I knew that from.

"Come on." He took my hand. "I'll show you—"

My eyes snapped open. Seconds later, pain flooded my senses.

My vision was filled with murky olive-colored spots that swam and gave off a shimmering rainbow effect like oil under light. I flipped over until my cheek smooshed into the cold rock below me and felt the contents of my stomach rocket through my throat. Convulsing the remainder of food out of my stomach, I barely had time to register a rough hand on my brow and someone saying my name.

Instinct lit through me. I flung myself into a sitting position.

"Easy, easy," the voice said.

I spun my vision toward them and through the colored spots, I recognized Gretchen.

"We were in the tunnel." My mouth was sour and every word was hard to push out. "Evie. Where's Evie?"

"I'm here."

I tried to look past Gretchen and saw a barely human shape against the shadows. The longer I looked, the more shapes I saw. Everyone was there.

"How did I get back to the basement?"

"We're not in the basement, Liz," Gretchen whispered.

It took longer than it should have for the words to register and by the time they did, the shuffle of footfalls echoed loudly outside of the room we were in. Moments later, a rectangle of white light cut at my eyes and illuminated the iron bars between us and it.

A cage? No. A prison cell.

"What is this?"

A figure stepped through the door. Tall and sporting a mess of dark curls, the woman looked like she may have once been a model, an American Gladiator, or perhaps both. Her sharp chin and long limbs made her look like she was made from iron rods, a crude frame somehow given life and puppeteered by someone unseen.

Flanked by two men dressed in olive fatigues, she opened the cell door and pointed to me. "That one."

"Who the fuck are you people?" I said as the men started in for me. One grabbed my arm and when I tried to kick his leg out from under him, my own legs gave out. I was in worse shape than I thought.

She didn't answer, only nodded at the second one to grab my other arm. "Quickly now."

I turned to look back at my friends but only caught sight of Gretchen's worried stare. She hadn't even moved. These people were dangerous. It meant someone had tried something before and things didn't go well for them.

The cell door banged shut behind me. Gladiator took the lead, stalking through the open door into a narrow, cement-lined hallway. Muddy yellow drop lights hung every few feet, casting alien circles of light in the near pitch black. Every time we passed beneath one, I took stock of whatever I could. Colors still danced in my vision, though the throbbing had lessened some.

Pipes ran the length of the hall, the sounds of running water coursing through them. Were we still underground? This place seemed more outfitted and better built than the tunnel system Evie and I had been in. I wasn't sure how much time had passed since then. From the stench of that cell, it had been long enough for people to soil themselves.

Another beam of light. The guy next to me had a beard longer than Ash's with streaks of white through it. He seemed young despite that, his posture hunched and the skin around his eyes sallow. His long fingernails dug into the flesh of my forearm with every step we took. His pace was slightly behind his associate's. He was having trouble keeping in step. Balance a bit shaky, maybe? I'd have to remember that for later.

Light gushed over us again. The other man was heavier set, though not by much. His hooked nose and hair that stood straight up reminded me of one of those birds people used to keep as pets, the ones that sang. It was another moment before I remembered: a cockatoo. Tattoos of scaled serpents slithered around his forearms and his biceps into the rolled-up sleeves of his jumpsuit.

The next light didn't come for a long time. When it did, it subtly tinged the air with its jade glow. Tubular green light strips snaked along the floors. The smell here was different: as if we'd gone farther into the earth, back into the meandering tunnels from before.

Gladiator opened a black metal door, the thing sticking before she shouldered it through. The large room had a low dirt ceiling, roots and spiderwebs lingering around the old log framework above. Dozens of candles emanated a warm fluttering light across the stone walls.

People were huddled around wooden benches, their heads bowed low while they scraped at their bowls of food. A few stared at my arrival before quickly averting their gazes. Fear was a mist in here, clinging to every person around me. I wondered briefly how many of them were here against their will, wherever here was.

At the head of the room was an enormous stone well. Three people were gathered around a tall rusted red pump with tools, speaking in hushed tones.

Gladiator stepped to the nearest one and whispered in his ear.

He turned around.

The man before me wore a rumpled black suit. His curly black hair was grayed at the temples but was cut neatly, his salt-and-pepper beard trimmed to perfection. Clear-framed glasses rimmed his studious brown eyes. It took longer than I wanted to recognize him, longer than it should have. I'd imagined us meeting time and time again and in every instance, he somehow looked the same as he had then.

He smiled, his teeth eerily perfect. "It's good to see you, Elizabeth."

"Astor," I said, the name dripping from my mouth like rotten food. "What the hell is this place?"

Instead of answering, he looked at both of the men holding me and said, "Kray. Moseley: let her go."

They obliged and I somehow kept my balance. The walk had given me enough time to take stock of my injuries. The right side of my face throbbed and I was subtly aware of the fact my eye wouldn't open as much as the left one.

"I apologize for the use of force. There was some miscommunication. I had said 'invite them;' not 'kidnap them.' Varsha likes to take matters into her own hands sometimes." He eyed Gladiator.

She glared but said nothing back.

"Answer my question," I said.

"This is the Church of the Night Forest under the town formerly known as Onyx River," he answered.

"'Under?'"

"The Woods are taking over our world, conforming it, and changing it." Astor clasped his hands together. "People were forced to either join government-run communities where individual needs are subject to being neglected, where racism, transphobia and bigotry run rampant or to carve out a small pocket of the world gone wild for themselves. So, the Church was born."

I glanced at the room around me, at the people who were all now staring in my direction. "They built this?"

"Some of it was already here. Onyx River used to be a mining town. Some of the cave systems existed for over a century before the townspeople started adapting them for their purposes. And every house in town has an access point in the basement. That way, no one is trapped. They can return to the surface as much as they please."

I flashed back to the drawing in the house on the edge of town Richard and I saw, the one where the person was in the basement... The way Otto growled when we stood at the basement door ready to open it.

"We've been living on the edge of town for three months and we've seen no one this whole time..." I said.

The pump behind Astor squeaked and he turned to the gushing of water as it spurted from the pump. There were collective sighs of relief from the others behind him. Astor clapped a man on the shoulder and beckoned Snake Tattoo for a nearby glass. Filling it from the pump, he held it out to me.

I stared at him, even as my throat tickled reflexively with the thought of drinking some. My body cried for food, for rest, for anything. Still, I stared.

"Haven't changed, I see," Astor chuckled, taking a sip of the water.

"You've got my group locked in a cell in the dark, pissing in their pants, and you expect me to take something from you?"

Astor's smile thinned. "Suppose that was silly of me, wasn't it?" He downed the rest of the water. "They are excess baggage anyway. It's you I've been waiting for."

I swallowed. "I'd be lying if I said I hadn't been looking for you, too. Seems like that was a mistake."

"Not a mistake, no." Astor gestured to the others to clear a nearby wooden bench, sat, and patted the seat next to him.

Reluctantly, I joined him there. I didn't like how everyone's eyes were trained on me but most importantly, I was beginning to suspect if I didn't start complying, my locked-up friends might not make it to see another sunrise. He'd called them "excess baggage."

"I stayed on the outer fringes, Elizabeth. Knew exactly where you were, how many you were with…who was missing."

The words brought goosebumps to my skin. My body stiffened with every revelation that came from his mouth.

"I figured you needed time, needed space… Especially after what you did to Brody." He leaned in and I smelled cigar smoke on his breath, rich and pungent. "I don't blame you for doing it. He was only going to get worse and worse."

The memory of murdering my friend, shooting him in my former fiancé's body cleaved through me like a knife through butter. The strange pain grew in my stomach until I forced myself to bury it, bury their faces.

I hadn't forgotten about Astor's strange ability to see Brody when we'd helped him escape from the facility in Maine. In all the time I'd spent with Brody's ghost since he'd returned, no one had been able to see him but me. But Astor could. More importantly, he could because he had also once been attached to his own ghost—a ghost he'd murdered similarly to how I'd dispatched Brody.

"You shouldn't be sad. After all, it wasn't him anymore. You should be proud of what you did. You took back your life." Astor took my hand and when I tried to slither mine out, he gripped it harder. "You made the right call."

I shook my head. "I only made it worse. He's not gone. Brody didn't die."

"No," Astor's hand slid away. "He did. That thing you keep seeing: the shadow? That's something else."

I frowned. "How do you know?"

"Because it happened to my ghost, too. It's harmless. Wretched. But harmless. And the more I ignored it, the more it shriveled until it faded away like dust."

Before he could get another word out, a door opened across the room from us. A teenager stepped through, skinny as a rail wearing a long-sleeved button-down shirt that billowed off their frame with every step. Black mascara and shimmering teal eyeshadow framed their eyes.

Astor cleared his throat. "Adora."

The teen turned in our direction, eyes pinpointing me. "Is this her?" they said as they got closer.

Astor stood. "It is."

Something akin to a smile warmed Adora's thin lips. "Finally. All the preparation is over."

I stared at the teen. "What are you talking about?"

Adora cocked their head. "She doesn't know?"

Astor shook his head and started corralling Adora back in the direction they came from, speaking to them in hushed tones. I tried to hear what they were saying but the sound of water coming from the well overpowered their voices.

Adora turned toward Astor. "We've waited long enough!" they spat.

The voices around us deadened into silence.

Adora sighed and closed their eyes. "He's waited long enough. Do what you have to do but do it fast. I want us ready by sundown."

They stalked off back through the door they came from, the rusty hinges squealing shut behind them.

"What the fuck is happening?" I asked Astor as he returned to me. "Ready for what? What are you people planning?"

Astor didn't answer, instead choosing to direct his attention back at Kray and Moseley. "Take her back. We have to prepare for the ceremony."

"Hey!" I leapt from the bench, nearly stumbling over my feet. "Don't ignore me."

He did, walking away from me toward the door Adora had vanished through.

I made to follow. Instead, the one with the snake tattoos stopped me short, his elbow busting into my gut from out of nowhere. I slammed into the ground heaving as I tried to regain my breath. I rolled over in time to see Astor swarm back into my vision, brandishing a pistol aimed at the goon.

"Touch her like that again, Kray, and we'll leave your body for the wolves and the soulless," he warned, his tone filled with danger.

Even Moseley seemed to cower next to his fellow guard.

Kray raised his hands in defeat, a slight shudder in his breath.

I heaved as oxygen finally rushed into my stomach. My coughs sounded hollow and my stomach punched with every one.

THE WILD FALL

Astor turned to Varsha. "Rif, get her back to her cell—unharmed. Make sure they get food, water."

Varsha flinched. "Don't call me that," she snapped under her breath.

Astor looked as if he'd been slapped. "Sorry. *Varsha.*"

She pulled me from the ground without much force. We walked back to the cell.

SEVENTEEN

Liz

The door opened to the prison. In the rectangle of light that swung in, I recognized each of my friends' faces: Ash, Gretchen, Richard, Evie, and Gjon.

"Get back from the door," Varsha barked as she neared. They skittered toward the back of the small square like mice. With a clunk of the door unlocking, the gladiator threw me in and slammed the cell door. When she left this time, she didn't close the hall door. No doubt, she wouldn't be gone for long.

I let myself collapse in Richard's arms as he stumbled forward to catch me. "Liz," he said gently. "Are you alright?"

Before I could answer, Ash jumped in. "What did you find out? Who are these motherfuckers?"

I filled them in on what I knew, keeping the fact I knew Astor a secret. I had never told them about being Attached, about saving Astor ten years ago from the center in Maine. I wasn't sure how they'd react. What I did mention was Astor had been watching us for some time, waiting to make his move.

"And the kid said 'I want us ready by sundown?'" Gretchen asked.

"Yes. They clearly have something planned but I have no idea what."

"Probably fucking cannibals," Ash grumbled. "Church of the fucking Night Forest bullshit. Why else would they have taken the dogs? They've probably got them boiling for stew right now."

Evie whimpered. "No! They can't!"

"Let's not get ahead of ourselves," Gjon interrupted. "They could be planning anything."

"Why else would they be keeping us in a fucking prison cell wading through our own shit?" Ash shouted, slamming his hand against the wall behind him. He seethed and held his arm closer. "Fucking hell!"

"Let me look at it," Richard beckoned, bringing Ash over toward the cell bars and yanking his arm into the light. The scrape from the monster was swollen, the skin around it tinged an angry red. "It's infected. We need to clean this, otherwise—"

"Otherwise, what?" Ash yelled. "Let the fuckers get sick when they try to eat me. At least I won't go down their throats without a fight."

"Shut up!" Gretchen hissed at him. "We need a plan. And we need to know how to get out of here without leaving anyone behind."

I glanced toward the open door hesitantly. "We shouldn't be discussing this now. There could be someone outside listening."

As the words left my mouth, Varsha returned with two men in tow, each carrying a box. After she unlocked the cell and warned us to step away from the bars, the men came in and set the boxes down. Once the cell was locked again, Varsha turned on a lantern nearby, flooding the room with a wan light. "In an hour, I'll be back to take each one of you to the showers. Astor wants you presentable for the Mother Adora." She stalked out of the room with the two men and shut the door behind her.

"Adora? Didn't you say that was the teen's name?" Gjon asked.

"It was. And they were probably fifteen…maybe sixteen?" I shook my head. "Mother? I don't get it."

"Food in the boxes," Richard announced, pulling out Tupperware filled with cooked rice and vegetables.

"Clothes, too," Evie said. "Guess that makes sense what with the showers and all."

"I knew it," Ash growled, closing his eyes. His face was pale and slick with sweat. "Sex cult."

"Well, which is it then: cannibals or sex?" Richard muttered, opening a container and dipping a spoon into the broth inside. "Open up."

Ash accepted the spoonful of broth and swallowed hard. After a moment, he said, "Probably both."

"Everybody should eat something," Gretchen ordered. "We'll need to have our wits about us when they take us to the showers. That might be our only chance to find a way out of here."

Evie handed me a package of crackers. I settled against the back wall. The chill from the earth seeped through my thin shirt. I closed my eyes. I tried to focus on the crunch of the crackers in my teeth, the salt as it melted against my tongue.

Someone sat beside me and I knew from his smell it was Gjon before I opened my eyes. He held out a cup of water to me and I took a small sip before handing it back.

"How are you feeling?" he asked. "You were out for hours. Woke once but I'm not sure you remember that."

"No. My head feels heavy."

"Ought to. The right side of your head is bruised."

I brought a hand to it and my skin flared with agony beneath my fingers.

"You were talking in your sleep some," he added.

I closed my eyes again. "I don't remember that either."

It was a lie. I didn't want to think about Brody. I didn't need the distraction right now.

Gjon chewed his food but didn't say anything more. Having him next to me was all I needed. I ate more crackers and tried to slow the pounding in my head.

The hour passed quicker than I wanted. Varsha returned with Kray and Moseley in tow. While she grabbed the empty box and utensils, she pointed to Ash and said, "Him first."

Kray went in for the grab.

Ash cuffed him in the face, which only brought on Moseley's rebuttal of a return punch to the jaw.

Kray recovered in time to stop Richard from coming to Ash's aid.

The two guards heaved Ash to his feet and muscled him out of the cell and into the hall.

Varsha shook her head as she closed the cell on us. "Don't fight us. No one needs to suffer any more than they already have." She walked out.

Gjon rose and scuttled over to Richard who was still in the place where Kray had pushed him. When Richard looked up, I saw the gleam of tears in his eyes.

Evie

First, they took Ash. Then, Gretchen. Richard. Liz. Gjon.

I was the last to go.

Unlike the others, who all had extra escorts, the woman Liz had called Varsha came alone. "Let's go, Chitti."

The halls outside felt like the tunnels of a burrowing animal. I wondered how long these people had lived like this, sheltered beneath the earth, hiding from what the world had become on the surface. Had they ever seen the Woods up close? Did they know about the thing that attacked us back at the house?

"What does Chitti mean?" I asked blankly.

"It's a pet name. Nothing special," Varsha said, her head held high.

"You're not from here, are you?"

Our shadows bounced beneath the bleary drop lights.

Varsha stared at me. "Why do you care?"

"Why not?" I wasn't sure why I bothered to ask. I didn't care. Maybe it would be useful information to the group when I got back.

"I was born in Jaipur."

"What brought you here?"

"My family. A dumb opportunity I thought would change my luck." Varsha shook her head. "Not my luck. His luck. In short: nothing. And then, this."

"Was he your dad?"

"I was—" Varsha halted in the middle of the tunnel, her eyes wide with some realization.

"I was what?"

"Nothing." She nudged me along. "Let's go."

The tunnel eventually branched off into a large room. The floor and walls were lined with wet stone tiles. Pillar candles flickered about the room, giving off an erratic golden glow and barely lighting the darkest corners.

Several other women stood against the farthest wall under shower heads spewing water. They didn't react to me or Varsha as we entered.

We approached an empty place toward the back.

"Strip. Clean yourself."

I stared at the others. "In front of them?"

"This isn't the time or place for modesty," Varsha said. "The Mother Adora has asked to speak with you first."

The news stunned me. "Why me?"

She squinted. "Why not?" She nodded toward the showers.

The only people who had seen me naked in the last several years were the other women in our group; one of whom was now gone. These other people barely registered I was there, a couple turning heads but quickly returning to their own cleansing.

Pinning my fears to the back of my head, I peeled off each layer of dirty clothes and stood under a lukewarm torrent of water, scrubbing the dirt from my skin. So much dirt. My fingernails were caked in it. My hair was greasy and stuck beneath my fingers as I let the water run over me.

The old bar soap smelled artificial and minty, no doubt an old bar from the picked-over hygiene section of a grocery store or gas station. I used so much of it all that remained by the end was a soft green brick, the maker's label worn away, the edges rounded.

After the shower, Varsha pointed me to a bench where I dressed in the clothes from the box she'd brought to us earlier. Everything fit loosely, hanging off my shoulders. The pants only stayed on because of a cinch tie at the waist. Then we left the showers and meandered into another long, dim hallway squiggling this way and that.

The tunnel system amazed me: a series of them interconnecting and branching toward who knew where. Did they all have it memorized? I supposed they did. They'd lived down here for probably the whole ten years since the Woods started claiming the land. As dark and cramped and permeated by the stench of earth as it was, this was their home.

The channel inclined and we eventually reached a dead end where a wooden door with a stained-glass window awaited us. Varsha knocked on the door and someone inside said, "Come." Varsha gave me a nod and set off back down the hall from where we'd traveled.

The stained glass glowed from the light within. The pattern portrayed a large purple rock, offset by facets of blue to give it a reflective surface. The sky around it was laced with shards of orange and yellow while below the rock, the scene seemed to break into a mass of tangled bits of green and brown. Was there an opening below? Yes. Some kind of a cavern dipped into the bowels of the earth and likely continued past where the glass stopped its portrayal.

The door opened and in the light, the silhouette of a teenage boy appeared. "Are you going to stand out there all day?"

Day. I had no concept what time of day it even was. It was perpetually night down here. A sudden desperate craving for sunlight simmered in my consciousness, a longing I forced back as I shook my head.

The door opened wider and I stepped in.

The chamber was small, like most of the other rooms in this underground community. An old pine bed frame set with a too-small mattress and adorned in a plush green comforter was squeezed into one corner. Next to it was a paint-chipped vanity with a missing leg where various colorful scarves and handkerchiefs lay draped over pencils and stacks of composition notebooks. A rechargeable lantern hung from a hook lodged in the center of the braced-dirt ceiling while a smattering of flickering candles cast dim light around the perimeter of the room.

The boy was my age, or at least, he appeared to be. A mess of curly brown hair atop his head gave way to severe cheekbones and a pointed chin. Thick brows punctuated his narrow eyes and straight slender nose. He wore the same loose clothing I did, the same loose clothing everyone else did here. But there was something different in his posture, in the way he drew back from me after closing the door, how he gathered himself on the lone Windsor chair in the room, legs crossed and stare direct. It reminded me of a movie I'd watched as a kid of a queen taking up residence on her throne.

"It's been some time since I've seen another so young," he said. His voice was wistful and stained by sorrow. "I hadn't expected it when they brought you all back here."

I frowned. I was here at his whim, it seemed. And we were only allowed to clean ourselves and have food because of him, too. "Who are you?" I asked.

"I'm Adora," he said. "And you?"

"Your prisoner, apparently."

"A precaution, dear. That's all. You wandered into our home, not the other way around. We don't know you. We have to be careful."

I didn't trust the words but also couldn't discount them. The tunnels underground were theirs. They likely hadn't seen people in what? A decade?

"Where are our dogs? What did you do to them?" The words caught in my throat.

"They've been fed, washed. It's been a long time since people here have had pets, let alone had interactions with animals. They're being treated well, I assure you."

The tension in my shoulders eased some.

He regarded me questioningly. "What are you doing all the way out here, girl?"

I didn't answer. His gaze felt like being examined under a microscope.

Adora continued. "I like to imagine most parents want the best for their children, it's in their nature to protect them. That's why we imprisoned you. We had to be sure. But, why would someone risk your life by having you fend for yourself all the way out here and not live in a protected government-run community?"

"Because that's a load of bullshit," I said, unable to stop myself. "GRCs aren't any more protected than anywhere else out here. If the Woods broke through a barrier wall and took over half a city block, people would be trapped. It would be chaos."

"You're probably right." He raised his eyebrows. "But the access to medical attention, food, community… Surely, that's not easy to come by out here."

I set my jaw. "We make it work."

Adora stood. "Tell me then: how many have you lost since your group decided to eke out a living off the grid?"

"What does it matter?" I bit back. "You're not going to let us go anyway. Who survived and who died is pointless."

"You misunderstand. None of us are free anymore. We haven't been since the Merging happened. We're all biding our time waiting for the inevitable."

"Is that what you are doing out here: 'biding your time?' Isn't this a version of what we've been doing?" I asked.

"Yes and no. We have sanctuary: a home protected from the creatures outside, a town self-reliant on wind and solar to power our electricity and our well. We have a community here underground. We have a doctor. We have stability. And we choose this life apart from the rest of humanity because we are different."

"Different?" I frowned. "How?"

Adora meandered over to the vanity and sat on the stool in front of it, the whole thing pitching forward before he cemented a foot in front to stop it. "Have you ever lost anyone?" he asked.

My throat thickened. Dad's face blasted through my mind before I could keep it. My fingernails dug into my palms as I tried to paint over his image with thoughts of hiking, Tempest...anything.

"You have," he said, his voice breaking slightly. "What did they mean to you? How did their loss impact you?"

I bit my lip, forcing myself to contain the fresh sadness the question caused. "Sometimes, I think of my dad and forget to breathe. And I ask myself 'What's the point?' before I make myself take the next breath."

Adora stared at the ground. "Do you wish he would come back to you?"

"All the time." I wiped my eyes with the sleeve of my shirt. "But he doesn't. I'm one of the few who didn't get someone back from the other side and I don't understand why."

He sighed. "It's a blessing, dear. That he didn't come back." He reached out for one of the handkerchiefs on the vanity and held it in his fingers. It was violet, painted with small flowers. "I wore this the day I left them. It was pretty, though it brought out the circles under my eyes, the bluish undertones of my skin."

I wiped my eyes and frowned. "Left who?"

Adora twisted the kerchief in his hands slowly. "It was an awful day. Sleeting, I remember the sky being almost green. I didn't have a lot of time left but I chose to spend it with them at home. Better than being hooked up to a million different kinds of machines in a hospital bed. But it happened all the same. I couldn't catch my breath. And I fell down the stairs, hit the motorized chair on the way. Sam said he found me—"

Adora stopped talking and I noticed the kerchief was taut in his hands, both pulling at either side.

"Sam?"

"My son. My youngest son."

The words sunk in like a blade. It all made sense: the strange body language, the talking down to me, the way he chose his words… It wasn't him in there…

"You're… You're a…"

"An Inhabited? That's what the GRCs call us, isn't it?" Adora shook his—no, *her* head, because it was, indeed, a *her* in there. "I never meant for it to go this way. When the Merging happened and I appeared to Sam for the first time, I thought I'd been given a second chance, another opportunity to take care of my family. Mark was swamped in medical bills, my oldest son, Rob, was into drugs and didn't talk to his father or brother anymore, and Sam…" Adora turned, a small smile lighting on her lips. "He was so happy to see me. I thought I could help them through him…"

"And you possessed him?"

The inflection of blame was there and Adora stood up as soon as she heard it, the stool clattering onto the ground next to the vanity. "It was a mistake. Sam tripped and fell in the cellar while doing the laundry for his dad. He cut his knee. I saw it and motherly instinct took over. I ran to him and tried to help…"

Adora froze with her hands at her mouth. "I was inside before I knew what had even happened."

"And Sam?"

"It was a flicker. A moment where I felt our spirits collide and he was ripped away into the blackness of the forest." Adora let out a shaky sigh. "I lost him."

My heart pounded with the revelation. "It was an accident."

"Does that make it any less horrible?" Adora scoffed. "Does that make me any less of a monster for letting my own son be sacrificed to the Woods?"

I looked away. Against the opposite wall of the bedroom was a chest with a knitted yellow blanket folded on top. I stared at it and thought about what would have happened if Dad had come back. Would he still have been the same? Would he have eventually made the same mistake Adora had made?

"That was his baby blanket," Adora said, moving by me to take it in her hands. "He used to take it with him everywhere: to preschool, to our campground, to the zoo even." She opened the chest. Inside was a variety of colorful plastic toys, comic books, an old game system, and stacks of crayon drawn pictures. "There's always the faintest smell of him, of how he used to smell I mean, when I open this chest. Some of the others get it. They have their own stacks and collections."

The words raised goosebumps on my arms. "What others?"

Adora turned to me. "You didn't think I was the only one, did you?"

EIGHTEEN

Liz

Evie had been gone longer than everyone else.

Too long.

I stood at the cell door listening for the sounds of footfalls in the hallway, every heartbeat getting progressively heavier than the last. There was nothing. Silence reigned.

"We need to get out of here," I said. "We need to find her."

"We've tried already," Gretchen answered from somewhere behind me. "These bars are solid. Unless they open the doors, there's no chance."

I turned to face the group. Everyone appeared slightly more alive than when I'd awoken earlier. Everyone was awake, the clothes were big but clean, they'd even left a lantern behind outside so we had light. They'd patched Ash's arm and returned him to the cell barely conscious, stating they'd given him something for the pain, likely codeine, judging by how in-and-out he'd been since. He lay on the ground using Richard's lap for a pillow.

"What if we cause a distraction? We pretend something's wrong with Ash? They'll have to come and check, won't they?" Richard asked.

THE WILD FALL

I glanced at him. "Not necessarily, but I'm not ready to give up on that idea yet."

"Evie might be fine," Gjon said under his breath. "The worst thing we can do is jump to conclusions and do something reckless before we're ready."

I forced myself to exhale. "We need to create a contingency plan. We need to have something up our sleeves in case the moment strikes. We may only get a moment with these people."

"If we're not all leaving together, then what's the point?" Richard murmured.

"Richard is right," Gretchen said. "We can't run around in these tunnels with no sense of direction trying to find a way out or trying to look for Evie. We'll end up right back where we started: here."

I left the bars and joined the group where they were settled, crouching to meet them at eye level. "I don't think these people are here because they want to be. From what I gathered, it sounds like Astor has been luring groups here to Onyx River for some time, enough time to build a reputation this place is something it's not."

"You think they're prisoners like we are?" Richard asked.

I nodded. "They've been made to stay here and become part of this community. Maybe they've been lied to? Maybe they've been told they'll earn their freedom if they keep doing as they're ordered? Whatever the lies or deceptions were, maybe we can get them to help us out of here."

"And if they're too afraid to help?" Richard asked.

"Then we'll have to figure something else out," I said.

The shuffling of footsteps from outside made us all tense. Moseley and Kray appeared in the doorway toting a makeshift stretcher between them with Varsha close behind. The two goons had AK-47s strapped to their persons.

"Everyone up," Varsha commanded. "Keep your hands where we can see them."

"He's sleeping," Richard said, staring at Ash. "Not sure I could rouse him if I tried."

"That's what these two are here for." Varsha tipped her head to Moseley and Kray.

The rest of us stood, our hands lifted beside our heads.

Varsha unlocked the cell door. "Single file into the hall. You first." She pointed at me.

I stepped out beyond the bars and into the cold, craggy hall where another man with a crowbar waited. He wouldn't look at me when I tried to make eye contact but waved his hand to follow him.

I listened to my friends plod after me as we descended through the narrow, blearily lit tunnel system. Far behind me, Kray and Moseley's grunts echoed as they struggled to heft Ash onto the stretcher.

When I thought we were returning to the room where I'd met Astor, our guide pitched us a different way, following a skinnier tunnel up, up—toward the surface? I wasn't sure. I didn't know how far underground we were. I could only hope we were being brought somewhere closer to a possible escape. At the same time, Evie was somewhere in this place by herself. I couldn't leave without her.

We ascended steps sculpted into the earth, the tangles of tiny roots catching on the toes of our boots. Tangerine light emanated from a slanted doorway ahead, a light I associated with sunlight. But when we reached the room, I realized it was the flickering of hundreds of candles.

Six pews crowded into the tall area leaving a narrow walkway to an ornate wooden pulpit. A hand-sewn banner hung on the wall behind it depicting a faceted rock surrounded by trees. Beneath it was patched with varying dark squares of fabric. Roots and other vegetation had been added with fabric markers to give the appearance it was underground.

"Sex cult," Richard muttered somewhere behind me.

"Sit!" Varsha barked, her voice echoing in the cavernous space. I shimmied to the end of the first bench, Gretchen behind me. We both sat. The warmth from Gretchen's body bolstered me as shivers racked my body. It was colder here closer to the surface, I suspected.

Gjon and Richard slid into the pew opposite us while Kray and Moseley finished hefting Ash into the room via the stretcher. They set him on the floor behind us, both panting and groaning from the effort of carrying him.

My eyes searched the room. They had entrenched old stained-glass windows into the earth on either side of us, though no light shone through them to display their splendor. There weren't any doors in or out of the room other than the one we'd come through. I squinted as I stared at the banner at the head of the room. It was a familiar sight: a stone Monolith like the one I had seen in the Woods almost ten years ago. Did these people know what it was; what it meant?

"You have five minutes to pray alone," Varsha said.

I turned to look over my shoulder. She was retreating, back out the door we'd come through.

"Pray for what?" I asked.

She raised an eyebrow. "Absolution. Clarity. Insight. A chocolate cake. A new bike. Pray for whatever the fuck you want." She left.

Kray and Moseley remained, Kray aiming his AK-47 at me. "Pray to the Woods. Pray to the Monolith," he whispered.

Evie

"I need you to understand," Adora said, closing the lid to her son's trunk of belongings. "All you need to do is look at everything that's happened in the last ten years and realize we are simple subjects here for a more divine purpose."

"Subjects?" I repeated. "What does that even mean?"

Adora waved at me to sit on her bed and I did. I was tired and my mind scrambled trying to take in everything she'd said so far.

"Humanity dominated this planet for centuries. We're a conceited, single-minded species, intent on furthering our own agendas without much care for who or what gets harmed while we do it. Hundreds of ants run over by a single car tire, air poisoned from one day's work at a factory, oceans spoiled by refineries and deep-sea drilling… Is it not fair the planet should want revenge? To take back what once belonged to it?"

I frowned. "You're an environmentalist?"

"No," Adora said, mouth a straight line. "I'm a practitioner of truth. I take the signs the Merging has given us and interpret them as a plea for renewal. Much like the meteor that killed dinosaurs billions of years ago, it is time for humans to relinquish their hold on this world. It's time for the Woods to rule."

"So, why don't you get on with it and kill yourself?" I spat.

Adora closed her eyes and giggled. "Of course. Hand me a knife and I'll stab myself in the throat right now, if you'd like."

My eyes darted around the room. There was nothing I could use as a weapon.

"That solution, though it would help marginally, is like throwing a cup of water at a house fire. It would be a waste. My strength is in education: I used to teach girls and boys your age, prepare them for life. That's what I've continued to do for the last ten years. The children of this town were so confused and so anguished by everything that happened. But they didn't have to be."

"Children?"

The horror rushed back to me swiftly. In my head, I was looking over the class photo from the church up above, the endless sea of funeral programs from teenagers who had died before they should have. They had come back to their parents when the Merging happened…

"The students killed in the bus accident," I said to myself.

"Brilliant kids who all died in vain. Who all should have stayed dead."

"They didn't know what they were doing, did they?" I asked. "When they possessed their parents, their friends?"

Adora returned to her vanity, grabbed her kerchief and tied it around the top of her head. "No. But they understand now. Once you let go of the idea your survival is imperative, that the world needs you, you take the first steps to understanding what your true fate can be."

"Oh, I see." I nodded slowly. "You convince them to kill themselves so you don't have to."

Adora cocked her head as she stared through the mirror at me. "Harsh and not entirely right. My efforts are more pragmatic."

"What you're doing is disgusting. Sorry if no one dared to throw it back in your face before," I said, jumping to my feet. I didn't want to be in this room anymore. I needed to get back to Liz and the group and let them know what was going on.

"How sad," Adora said, standing. "To think you are the first to lecture ethics with me."

The words stunned me. I wasn't sure how to respond.

Adora stepped toward me, and I unconsciously fell onto the bed. With her standing over me, I thought I could almost see the echoes of Adora in her actual human form: a tall, stoic mother who probably ruled her family with an iron fist. The kind of woman who dictated policy, who remained measured in the face of adversity, probably even as she was dying.

"When the prophet, Astor, came to us, he showed us what was wrong. He told us what he'd seen in the Woods, what they needed from us. And it all makes sense."

"P-prophet?" I sputtered.

"A man shown the error of his ways. A man who paid for them. He showed us the truth of the Night Forest." The sincerity in her voice chilled me.

I fought to control my panic as I said, "And what's that? Suicide?"

"Morality is a social paradigm," Adora said, slowly leaning over me. "The Woods are beyond that. They're wild, unforgiving… They never tire. They only consume."

"Get away from me…" I said.

Adora planted a hand next to me on the bed, then another as she fully leaned over my prone body. "You can't fight something that isn't fighting you. It's just *being*."

"Get away from me!"

A knock at the door pulled Adora back into an upright stance seconds before the door opened.

Varsha stood in the frame, taking in the scene.

"Yes?" Adora turned to meet her underling's gaze.

"They're in the nave," Varsha said. She stared at me. "What were you—"

"Take this one back to the cell. She won't benefit from worship like the others," Adora said, returning to her vanity and collecting one of the composition journals from the top of it. When Varsha hesitated, Adora cocked her head. "Quickly. We haven't got all day."

Varsha frowned as she stalked forward and helped me from the bed.

Trembling, I let myself be moved, be maneuvered to leave that awful room if only to get away from that horrible woman. Worse was Adora's words stuck to my mind like glue. Worship. What the hell did she have in store for Liz and the others? I closed my eyes momentarily as tears of anger slipped from them. Were we ever going to get out of here alive?

NINETEEN

Liz

We sat for the five minutes, occasionally casting glances at one another while the two men with guns looked on. We didn't speak, knowing if we did we'd be reprimanded. The whole time, my mind fired off idea after idea, trying to figure out how we could escape. Every thought came back with a similar expectation of failure, of getting some or all of us killed.

The sound of shuffling drew our attention toward the doorway. After a few moments, a line of people filed in, each wearing the same kinds of clothes we had on, each with their eyes directed at their feet, each holding wooden masks depicting skulls over their faces…

I heard Gretchen inhale sharply beside me and I reached over to grab her hand.

Surprise was similarly painted across Richard's and Gjon's faces across from us.

Three more people filled the pew next to Gretchen and the rest of the seats next to Richard before others started filling seats ahead of us. I stared at the masks in the lambent flickers of the candles around

THE WILD FALL

us. Each one appeared different, mottled by black and gray shades in strange places aside from the holes where the eyes and nose could come through. The mouths were painted on, the shadows of teeth against a shiny black gullet making my skin prickle.

I didn't recognize any of the body types or people who walked past. Thoughts of Evie and her absence only stoked the fire of fear that had ignited within me earlier. Where the hell was she? What had they done to her?

I noticed Varsha was among the parishioners as she walked through. Her mask was painted in a startling red, the black and gray creating a realistic three-dimensional appearance of a skeletal face. The eyes appeared particularly tormented. She sat at the edge of the front pew in our row.

I sneaked a careful glance over my shoulder. Kray and Moseley had donned their own masks where they stood, still with hands on weapons.

Everyone here was a prisoner. I was convinced.

Through the dark doorway appeared Astor, the only one at the mass not wearing a skeleton mask, though he stared at the ground like the rest of them as he made his way down the aisle. He took the end of the pew opposite Varsha. He glanced over his shoulder in my direction and I made sure the look I returned was filled with venom.

The last set of footsteps to come through the door belonged to the one Astor had called Adora, who the others had called "The Mother, Adora." A piece of multi-colored fabric with varying patterns cloaked their face and slid noisily across the floor behind them. A flowery handkerchief was tied around their messy brown hair, their face painted in pale powders and pastel shades. They practically glided from the door to the pulpit.

Standing behind it, Adora gazed out at their flock. "Pray to the Woods…"

In unison, everyone around us responded: "Pray to the Monolith."

Adora leaned over their podium. "The time is nearly here, friends. Tonight, we will greet the darkness, embrace the only purpose that matters anymore."

No one said a thing.

The words made my throat begin to close. I felt claustrophobic in this sea of people, more people than I'd been around in over ten years.

It was Gretchen's turn to squeeze my hand now. I saw her out of the corner of my eye watching me.

"This has been the longest night, children," Adora said, as they came out from behind the pulpit and gestured to the worshipers. "It's been cruel: our time together has been fraught with confusion, with remembrances of a time long gone, of a time when we embraced normalcy with our beloved ones. And as we endured these hardships together, we learned we had to keep stepping forward. We had to keep striving for a new purpose, a new goal. We needed to find meaning in this new world."

I glanced at the backs of the heads of the people in front of me who weren't reacting bodily to anything Adora said. I wanted to see their eyes, wanted to know what they were thinking about every word coming out of their mouth. Were they as filled with fear as we were? Had they been broken by listening to them for so long? By being trapped underground for so long? I needed to know how much of this bullshit they believed.

"At last, we found it. At last, we were gifted with the prophet, the one who showed us what we were and what we could become." Adora stared ardently at the first row of pews. "Astor came to us and brought us hope."

I frowned.

"Astor spent time in the Woods. He met with the creatures within. He told me what was at stake, what we had to do…" Adora took a deep breath. "That we needed to relinquish our hold on this once beautiful planet, let its ghost take over."

This time, people reacted. They nodded. They audibly cheered. I could even see the glimmer of tears in the faint candlelight in their eyes.

Gretchen's nails dug into my hand and I was sure mine did the same to hers. We locked eyes for a moment.

Adora moved and it brought my gaze back to them as they returned to the pulpit. "Let us pray." They started humming.

Everyone in the room joined in. The sound was familiar, a song from before. It had been so long since I'd heard it that I struggled to think of who had sung it, the nostalgia surrounding it pulling me back to a time and place I hadn't thought of in years.

I was in the back of my mom's wood-paneled station wagon picking at a blister on my hand. My sister was crying: in my memories, she was always crying. My mom had turned up the music on the radio as we drove away from our summer home forever, the one we always used to go to with my dad before he died. The radio had been playing "House of The Rising Sun."

Hearing the ominous throaty hum of the tune right now sent my nerves sizzling.

Every person in the pews was rocking back and forth with the rhythm of the song, as if it flowed through them like water.

Adora produced a glass bottle from beneath the pulpit. Uncorking it, they took a swallow of the liquid inside, tipping their head back once they'd finished and shaking their head. They held out the bottle.

Astor stood, taking the bottle from their hand and then passed it to the next person in his row. The man pulled his mask back from his face and took his own swig from the bottle. As he passed the bottle to the next person, I realized a second bottle had appeared from somewhere and had been passed to Varsha, who took a healthy drink before sending it down her pew to the following parishioner.

As the bottles made it to the last people in their respective rows, Adora danced, their body gyrating in hypnotic swings of their hips and shoulders. They raised their arms over their head, fingers stretched to the ceiling and hummed louder. "Feel it!" they shouted. "Feel it pass from your lips all the way to your heart. You know it's destiny."

Astor and Varsha collected the bottles from the rows and started to the next one.

Within moments, Adora lowered to the floor, their arms swaying back and forth over their head the whole way down. Their gaze was locked on their fingers as they spun them and twirled them in the air.

"God, I always hated communion," Gretchen muttered. "You know this shit is drugged."

"We need to get the hell out of here," I said into her ear and looked over my shoulder again.

Moseley and Kray were still at the back of the room with their guns, watching everything happen. There was no getting by them.

I tried to make eye contact with Richard and Gjon across the way. Gjon's eyes were filled with panic; Richard's were locked on Ash who was unconscious and prone at the feet of the two soldiers in the back.

The people in the first row began to shudder and sunk onto their knees, their hands reaching for some invisible thing above them; some were threaded together in prayer. A woman in the front row clutched something close to her. I squinted to see: a teddy bear.

Row two finished. Varsha dropped to the ground before the bottle could be returned to her, her head lolling as she held herself up pitifully with an arm.

Astor took the second bottle and continued the process alone, sending it to one row and the other bottle down the opposite. They were drinking in the row in front of us.

Through everything, the feverish hum of the song grew and grew, the tones varying as people succumbed to the drink. I watched Adora: waiting for tell-tale signs of struggle, of death. But they remained kneeling where they was, singing loudly and weaving their fingers through the air as though they were drunk or high.

"This isn't killing them," I said to Gretchen. "But this is our chance."

"How?" she hissed. "These two behind us will shoot us."

As the bottle passed between two of the people in the row before us, I heard shuffling from the floor behind us followed by Ash's voice: "What the fuck?"

I looked in time to see Moseley shove the gun into his face while Kray took a cautionary step back.

Richard leapt from his spot in the pew. "No!"

Astor was quick to respond, hustling to the back of the room and pointing at Moseley. "Not here! Not now!"

Moseley swelled and stepped over Ash into Astor's space. "What does it matter?"

Astor snatched Moseley by the throat, his other hand forcing the AK-47 toward Moseley's feet. "I said 'Not here.'"

"What's happening?" Ash said from the floor. "Where's everybody? Rich? Gretchen?"

"I'm here, Ash!" Richard called to him.

Astor let go of Moseley's throat with a thrust, pushing the guard back off his center of balance. The guard tripped over Ash and fell backward against the door frame, gasping for air.

Returning to the row in front of us, Astor seized the bottle as it came back toward him and held it out toward Kray. "One drink. First, him," he nodded toward Ash. "Then, your partner. Then you."

Kray clutched at the bottle feebly and squatted to pour it into Ash's mouth.

"Don't!" Richard shouted. "Don't drink it!"

"That's enough," Astor said, seizing the second bottle and forcing it into the hand of the person at the head of Richard and Gjon's row. "Relax. Drink. It'll all make sense when you wake."

Kray passed the bottle to Moseley, who seized it and pitched it back to take a quick pull. He forced it back into Kray's hand and got back to his feet. Kray took a swig from the bottle and handed it back to the waiting Astor who placed it into the hands of the first person in our row.

I watched the man take a drink, licking his lips as he passed it on.

"Drink," Astor said.

I looked to see him standing at the head of Richard's and Gjon's row.

The bottle was in Richard's hand. Tears rimmed his eyes. He said something but the singing around me cut out the sound of it.

"Liz," Gretchen said as the bottle in our row came to rest in her hand.

Kray pointed his weapon at Richard, even as he shook his head.

"Pour it out," I whispered to Gretchen.

As I said the words, Astor turned in our direction and spied the bottle in Gretchen's hands. "Sister. Take a drink."

"We're not doing this," Gretchen said, her voice firm and measured.

Astor sighed. "Kray, give me your weapon."

Kray handed it over as he succumbed to the drink and sank to the ground. Astor aimed the gun toward Ash. "You're all expendable. It's easier if you do this one little thing… Make it easier for me." He turned to Richard. "Go on."

Richard stared at me. The fear in his eyes sent shudders across my skin as he tipped the bottle back and took a drink. Hope shriveled inside me.

Astor turned back to Gretchen. "Now you."

Gretchen trembled. We still clutched each other's hands.

I turned my attention to Astor. "Please don't do this."

Astor looked at Ash. "You could have more time together. Seems like an awful lot to sacrifice for your pride, Elizabeth."

For moments, I forgot how to breathe.

Gretchen looked at me. There was no emotion in her eyes, no tears, no fear as there had been with Richard; only acceptance. She tipped back the bottle and drank.

As Astor gave a satisfied nod and started to turn back around, Richard hurled himself over the other parishioners at Astor.

He knocked Astor into the end of my pew, the gun falling beneath him.

Scampering for traction, I launched over the back of my pew. When I turned back for Gretchen, she pointed at the door. "Go!"

I didn't hesitate. I jumped over the bodies of Ash and Moseley, reaching the door at the same time as Gjon. He pushed me into the dark hallway first and we clomped across the earthen steps. The sounds of scuffling, shouting, and the horrible dirge faded the farther we ran in the tunnels.

Everything hurt as I ran. My side panged and my face tingled as I forced myself along the uneven path. Gjon's breath was cold against the back of my neck.

We reached the first intersection and continued forward after deciding the other way seemed to only descend.

"We need to find weapons," I puffed, trying to take in air at the same time.

"Keep going," Gjon urged.

We cut to the right at another convergence, our boots sliding on the dirt. Far behind, I heard the sound of footfalls. I hadn't heard a gunshot. Was Astor chasing us?

Another passageway split off and we took it, finding a door. I yanked it open and though it stuck at first, it finally gave. We crowded into the small room and closed the door as silently as we could behind us.

Gjon pushed his back against the door and I crouched beside him. His heartbeat hammered so hard, I could feel it through my arm.

Our chests heaved. We both tried to quiet our breathing.

Far off, Astor shouted my name. A thread of terror uncoiled in me.

"Shh," Gjon whispered, though I never would have said a thing.

We stayed put where we were, listening. The dirt floor stuck to my clammy hands as I braced myself against it. The smell of Gjon's sweat mixed with the stench of soil. I focused my eyes on something against the wall, a flat board of some kind though I didn't look at it as much as I stared through it. I was trying to concentrate on something, anything to fight the fear climbing in my chest.

The more I stared, the more I realized what I was looking at. They were plaques, looking vaguely stone-like in color though the words on them appeared to be painted on. Names. Dates. Things like "beloved daughter" or "cherished father." I stiffened in place.

They were grave markers.

What were they doing in this weird little storage room?

Gjon started moving and I shifted to allow him to crack the door open and listen. There was no noise nearby, only the hum of Adora's dirge echoing from their chapel, the sound of water rushing through pipes overhead. Nothing else.

He tapped my shoulder and waved.

I shook my head. "We can't leave without Evie."

"Where do we look?" Gjon asked. "This place must have dozens of rooms, dozens of hallways. And we still have no map."

"She's probably back in the cell block," I guessed. "After all, everyone else was in the chapel with us. There were no guards to keep watch over her. They'd have to have put her somewhere she'd be secure."

"It's risky. We still don't have a weapon."

I scanned the storage room. It was filled with moldy cardboard boxes and dust-caked plastic bins. We carefully unfolded the soggy flaps on the boxes and peered inside. Old clothes, picture albums, stuffed animals, books, long-dead cell phones and tablets, blankets and children's toys. Nothing that could be used as a weapon.

"Why do they have all this stuff here?" Gjon asked as I opened a photo album and flipped through it. "Why not leave it above where it didn't take up space?"

Most of the photos in the album showed a child, a young girl and her parents in an urban setting, most likely South East Asia judging by the architecture and clothing. As I continued, the girl got older. Her cheekbones grew more defined, her hair a longer, wilder mess of curls. I recognized her. It was Varsha, our guard.

The scenery changed to a more familiar town: Onyx River. Varsha appeared to be in her late teens now, accompanied in photos by her aging parents. One such picture had her feeding cake at a birthday party to an older man I'd recognized from previous pictures as her father.

I glanced at the caption and frowned. "Gjon…"

He stepped over. "What's wrong?"

"Look here: that name in the caption is 'Arif,' right?"

"Yeah."

"I heard Astor call Varsha 'Rif' earlier…"

Gjon's brows knitted. "You think she's Inhabited."

"I think they're all Inhabited, except for Astor. He's puppeteered this whole thing in his favor. He's killing them off because he thinks all the ghosts are corrupted." I set the photo album back in the box. "We need to get out of here. We need to find Evie first."

I went for the door and felt hesitance in Gjon's movements as he joined me. When I looked at him, I read the confusion in his face and realized I'd said something wrong.

"How do you know what he thinks about the ghosts? Do you know him, Liz?"

I swallowed and forced myself to take a stale breath. "I did. Ten years ago. He's been searching for me and he found me. It's my fault we're here."

I didn't wait for him to answer before I stepped out into the hall and not a moment later, I heard his following footsteps and the door close behind us.

The singing had stopped. I could only imagine how out of it Richard, Gretchen, and Ash were along with everyone else in the chapel. I didn't know how long they'd be this way. I didn't know how long of a window we had before we came across Astor in one of these crooked hallways.

We backtracked through the hall from where we came. Once the path to the chapel appeared, I retraced my memory of where we'd been steered from the lock-up. The entire time, I listened for the slightest noises, wondering if we'd come face to face with Astor around the next bend of a tunnel.

Taking a turn, we came to a dead-end with a door made of metal. I exhaled. This was the room I'd been dragged to once I'd awoken here. I'd taken us the wrong way.

"Come on," I said, turning around.

"Why didn't you tell us?" Gjon whispered.

"I didn't know what to think, okay?"

"Bullshit."

I turned around quickly. "We don't have time for this."

"I'm calling you out, Liz," he said, shaking his head. "We might not get out of here alive anyway. I want to know what this is about."

I reached for his hand, my thumbs rubbing his knuckles. "I promise I will tell you once we're out of here. But we have to hustle."

After a moment, he nodded and we resumed our trek through the tunnels. The last intersection made me realize I'd gone right instead of left. We clambered down the left-side tunnel.

I was sick of the greenish lights, of the cold, damp air. I wanted to get out of there. I wanted to see daylight.

Finally, a doorway revealed itself ahead of us and I ran to it, shouldering it open to the cells with heady anticipation.

In the wan lantern light inside, I recognized Evie's figure standing against the back wall of the cell. She leapt to life the moment I came through the door. "Liz, Gjon! What's going on? Where's everyone else?"

"We don't have time," I said, searching for the keys that normally hung on the rack next to the door. "Damn it! Where are they?"

"Varsha took them. Said she was late, she needed to get to the worship service."

I grabbed the door bars and shook them. "Fuck!"

Gjon put his hand on my shoulder. "There's nothing we can do."

"The fuck there isn't," I coughed, stifling the break in my voice.

"He's right," Evie said, reaching through the bars and grabbing my hands.

I took a step closer, looking into her big brown eyes, her face that looked so much like Hank's. The remembrance brought fresh tears to my eyes.

"You need to go. You need to get—"

"Well," a voice said from the doorway.

I turned.

Astor stood with the AK-47 hooked around his shoulder, pointing it at us. "I didn't think you'd leave her behind, Elizabeth. Not when you couldn't leave Josh behind at the institute ten years ago. You're soft. All I had to do was wait."

I gritted my teeth. "If these people knew who you were, that all you care about is purging them..."

"That's enough," he said. "Let's go."

I planted my feet. "No."

"No? No, what?" Astor smiled. "You've got nowhere else to go. You have no room to negotiate, no room to breathe. If you had listened to me and stayed in the chapel, you could have prevented this."

I frowned. "Prevented what?"

He pulled the trigger.

Gunfire exploded.

I cowered against the cell door, my head on fire with the blasts of sound, fear pulsing through my body.

In seconds, it was over. Evie was screaming and sobbing. Astor was smiling like he wasn't sure he knew what he'd done.

Gjon lay on the ground, clutching his abdomen. Blood splurged out from beneath his hands, racing down his body.

"NO!" I screamed. "No, no, no, no!" I dropped beside him and pushed my hands onto his.

Gjon's face twisted horribly as he cried out.

"I told you: you could have prevented this," Astor said, his tone apathetic.

"Get a doctor! Do something!" I yelled.

Astor stepped backward out of the cell block and closed the door behind him. Seconds later, it locked.

TWENTY

Liz

Holes.
They were everywhere.
Blood oozed from some, streamed from others.
Every second felt like an hour.
I yanked the huge shirt over my head. I tore at it with my fingers, with my teeth. My face throbbed with the effort until it gave way. I pressed the cloth into Gjon's stomach and watched it saturate with blood.

"Water, Evie! I need water!"

Seconds later, her small hand thrust through the bars close to me with a half empty bottle. I opened it and poured it over the hole on his chest. It refilled, the tendrils of red slipping along his pasty skin.

"Liz," he croaked. His hand clamped around one of mine.

"Save your strength," I said, not wanting to look at his face. This wasn't happening again. I wasn't going to let this happen again.

"You're s…" he slurred, his breaths shallow. "You're sleeping.…"

My mind stung with familiarity. I'd heard that recently, hadn't I? I didn't let it slow me. I poured water over a bullet hole in his thigh. He didn't react, even as it filled with blood moments later. I tore another scrap from the shirt and pressed it into the bullet hole.

"You're sleeping the day away."

The memory injected through me, the familiar voice, the tone… I stared into Gjon's face, searched his eyes. My fingers intertwined with his. "What did you say?"

"That date… The date I had with the girl before…" Gjon groaned and squeezed his eyes closed.

"Gjon," I said, the name losing permanence in my brain. "Is it still you?"

He snapped his eyes open. "But I remember her face… I was dreaming about her a moment ago. She looked just like you."

"Gjon, I need you to hold on, hold on." Even with the words coming out, my mind was struck by hopelessness. I couldn't force myself to move, to look away. I'm not sure I even blinked.

He squirmed. His skin was as gray as the cement on the walls of the room. "And the orchard? That was you, too."

It couldn't be. I held my breath. "You… It was a dream. How do you know—"

"Come on." He closed his eyes. "I'll show you."

His body settled. As the moments passed, his warmth faded.

"Gjon?" I touched his cheek. Blood smeared his skin. "Gjon…"

The squelching heartbeat I'd felt beneath my fingers only moments before was silent.

Evie

We were alone with Gjon's body for hours.

I think I fell asleep, exhausted from crying, exhausted from once again losing someone close to us in the last few days. All I know is that I opened my eyes to the sight of Liz sitting with her back to my cell. Gjon was cradled in her lap. She'd closed his eyes.

I straightened, clearing the sleepers from my eyes, and asked how long we'd been here.

Liz shrugged, not looking at me. "I don't know."

"What are they going to do with the others?"

"Not sure. Probably kill them, too." Her voice had lost all emotion.

I scooched closer to her and reached for her through the bars, putting a hand on her shoulder. "It wasn't your fault. I know what you're thinking."

She didn't move.

"It wasn't your fault Dad died. It wasn't your fault Nettie died. It wasn't your fault we ended up here. No matter what: it's not your fault."

Liz inhaled. "That's the problem, Evie. If we hadn't followed my idea of coming to Onyx River, none of this would have happened."

"There is nowhere else we could have gone where a version of this wouldn't have eventually happened," I said.

"Not like this," she said, finally turning around. Liz's bruised face was puckered with anger, her lip trembling. "Your dad might have lived to see you turn eighteen. Twenty-one. Thirty."

"Or I might have died before him."

"I came here because I was trying to find Astor."

The words made me go rigid. "I thought you didn't know him."

"I did. He was the reason I wanted to go into the Woods. Something he said all those years ago when I met him, something unbelievably stupid…" Her voice fell to a whisper. "I was chasing a dream that I could change things. I thought there were answers out there that suspended disbelief. Hell, if ghosts can come back, if soul-eating creatures can roam the world, why can't there be a way to stop it? But that was looking at it like a fairytale. Like there needs to be a reason. Sometimes, there isn't one."

THE WILD FALL

Her words hung in the air, each one leaving their mark on me as I pulled my hand back through the bars and laid it in my lap with the other. I wasn't sure what to say. Worse, my thoughts were spiraling with the thought of Dad, about his sacrifice for the group being meaningless.

Noise from outside the cell door sent my nerves alight before the door opened. Varsha appeared, her eyes falling on Liz and Gjon. Shock radiated from them. She aimed her gun at Liz. "Come on. I'll take you to the showers. Clean you up. Get you a new shirt."

Liz chuckled.

A small part of me shriveled at the noise.

Varsha frowned. "You're laughing?"

"It doesn't fucking matter anymore," Liz said. "Whether I'm clean or dirty. Whether I want to do something or don't. We're all about to die anyway."

"Pessimistic viewpoint," Varsha said, stooping to look her in the eye. "We're doing this voluntarily, you know. We have to let the Woods take the earth, let humans die out."

"Is that what this is about? Worshiping the Woods?" Liz practically spat the words. "I don't think so. You can't live with yourself, knowing you stole your daughter's body, knowing you craved the feeling of warmth, and touch, and taste. You are doing it because you can't live with the guilt."

I stared at Varsha, the gravity of Liz's words hitting me. When Adora had mentioned the others in this place were Inhabited, I hadn't stopped to think of what that meant. I hadn't stopped to think of how that had happened to each and every person underground. But it clicked now. Things I'd heard from my group over the years, the things they'd said in conversations when they didn't think I could hear them. And the thing Adora had said only hours ago made my insides squirm.

"Ghosts come back hungry…"

Varsha stood back and aimed the gun at me, keeping her eyes on Liz the whole time. "I said, 'Get up.'"

Liz sighed before she carefully laid Gjon's head on the cement floor and got to her feet.

I stared at Gjon's lifeless body. I didn't want to be alone with it. The thought of it coming back to life shot through me. I caught Liz's gaze momentarily and felt shame for letting her see it.

They left the room, Varsha glancing back at me before she vanished around the corner of the doorway. She hadn't locked it.

Moments later, I knew why.

Adora stepped through the opening with two of her followers behind her carrying a stretcher similar to the one they'd used to transport Ash back to the cell after his shower. They wore masks over their faces, while Adora had on the makeup I'd seen her in earlier, though it was smudged and missing in places.

After one glance at Gjon, she waved her disciples forward. They set the stretcher down and cautiously hefted his body onto it. One unfolded a blanket, one of those dollar-store velour ones in navy blue. They draped it over him before hefting the stretcher in their arms and toting it out the door.

Adora remained.

I glared at her.

"You can hate me. I'm sorry that your friend received such a violent end. I hate that you had to watch it happen."

"You didn't exactly try to prevent it either," I bit back. "Like you're not trying to prevent your little mass suicide."

Adora sighed. "What we are doing is different. We're not trying to off ourselves in the quickest way possible. We're not doing it for grandiosity or as a show. This is a pact we've made. We each have our reasons for wanting this hell to be over."

THE WILD FALL

I turned away from her and sat cross-legged on one of the blankets on the floor. "Reasons you've been fed by someone who you shouldn't trust."

"Astor helped clarify our needs. He stands to gain nothing from this. And he could have easily left us to rot here."

I stared at the wall, looking at the lines in the rocks. I didn't want to listen to her anymore, not when I knew she was going to keep justifying every awful thing she'd done.

"It's not my duty to change your mind. I only hope you will so you won't leave this world hard-hearted like I did the first time."

I heard her footfalls as she left and closed the door behind her.

The tears started falling again.

I was going to die and there was nothing I could do to save myself.

Liz

My brain tumbled like a stone as I stood under the torrent of water.

I replayed Gjon's last words. I replayed our last kiss. I replayed the conversation we had in the house, when he was going to let me leave to go into the Woods. I thought about times we ate together with everyone else and sometimes caught each other staring.

After every unstoppable thought, I'd squeeze my eyes shut and scrape at the blood on my hands and my body.

How had he known about my dreams? How had he known about Brody's orchard in this non-existent future where everything was impossibly perfect? How had he known exactly what Brody had said?

Every time I faked myself out about the possibility it had been Brody all along, I made myself stop and think about how it couldn't have possibly been. I'd seen Brody's shadow lurking in the darkness outside our various residences for nearly ten years. I knew that had been him against all odds, killing him had turned him into that horrible thing.

It still didn't explain what had happened in the cell.

And then, it clicked. I'd probably been talking in my sleep. Especially after being knocked out in the tunnels and dragged here, I'd been out for a long time. I didn't know what I'd done, what I'd said. He must have listened to me, mumbling away.

As it poured over me like a warm dawn on frost, my entire chest tightened. My arms became locked in place. My whole body expelled the sob as if trying to rid something horrible with it. I practically gagged as it forced me to my knees. The second came slightly easier, then the next, and the next, and the next. On hands and knees, I cried, my fingers clutching at the shower drain below me.

Thoughts I hadn't had in years welled to the surface of my mind. Was this hell? An existence where I was somehow doomed to watch the people I cared about die over and over? Was I the catalyst for every single bad thing that would happen to them?

I was sure of it.

Until I died, all I did was cause others pain.

In an instant, my fear and my sorrow gave way to doubt.

I had done this to my friends. I needed to find a way to get them out.

I forced myself onto my feet and stared at the door leading back out into the hallway. Again, I couldn't keep my mind from playing Gjon's words over again.

You're sleeping the day away.

What if the thing that had once been Brody could help? What if I could call him like I had at the house? Like I had when I needed him all those years ago?

The shower room door opened.

Varsha entered, carrying a stack of new clothes. These were closer to the ones I'd worn before I'd been forced to change: hiking pants, long-sleeve shirt with a vest…

Varsha was also dressed differently: in jeans and a plaid shirt.

I realized their meaning: Adora wanted everyone to leave the world as themselves.

Varsha set them on the bench. "It's time." She walked to the wall opposite me and turned a lever. All at once, the water stopped. The dripping from the shower head pattered on the cement at my feet.

"Time to die?" I asked, though my tone was firm.

Varsha blinked. "Time to see what comes next."

TWENTY-ONE

Liz

I walked at gunpoint, directed by Varsha for every left and right to take. With each and every divergence, I realized we never had a chance of finding our way out of here. There were too many tunnels, too many routes we could have accidentally taken. We'd have been hopelessly lost.

The air temperature grew colder the farther we walked until we reached a set of stairs leading to a trapdoor. Varsha pushed it open and we emerged into a finished basement. Another set of stairs led us into a home I vaguely recognized: it was one of the ones on the main street in town, one of the ones we'd raided when we first arrived to check out Onyx River.

Outside one of the front room windows, a blue haze broke the darkness, a blue I thought I'd never see again. It was the blue of dusk after sunset before night descends.

We opened the front door and stepped out into the cold shell of approaching winter. Candlelight drew my eyes to a spot down the road. People walked ahead of us, parishioners from the underground church still donned in their gloomy masks. Some carried lit candles, others carried placards over their heads I recognized.

The placards from the storage room. The grave markers of the dead.

I searched the silhouettes for Gretchen, Richard, and Ash but couldn't make out anything definite in the dwindling light. The tip of Varsha's gun poked into my shoulder blade followed by her voice: "Keep going."

We trundled toward a tall imposing structure, a chapel standing before the village center where the shops were. A structure with white siding, a bell tower that sat silent even as people flocked toward it. No one went inside. Instead, they skirted around the side of the building, over the uneven ground toward the yard behind. I stopped in my tracks.

The Woods had moved in even more since we'd been underground. The blackened trees stood within fifty feet of the building, their darkness terrifyingly thick. As I cast my eye along the horizon, I noticed the darkness extended through town, the trees cutting through the shops on the main avenue. Brick storefronts had crumbled. The road where we'd normally have walked to get to our home at the old bed and breakfast was cut off by a tangle of limbs and brambles.

Even before we reached the chapel, I could hear the sound of a bonfire raging, crackling and roaring, and see evidence of its light dancing across the grass behind the building.

Passing through the shadow of the bell tower, I stared wide-eyed at the gathering. Thirty, maybe even forty people were gathered in rings around the fire, still holding their candles and their grave markers. On the opposite side of the fire, dogs barked. I gasped. Tempest bucked and snarled as she pulled against a leash. Otto and Sanz whimpered and strained against their handlers who every so often would yank them back. Seeing the dogs tugged at a chord in my chest. Gjon would have been relieved they were still alive.

Varsha came around to my right and nudged me toward the left of the group closer to the chapel. As people parted and I stepped through them, I noticed my friends. Gretchen, Richard, and Ash all stood among the others, hands tied in front of them. Ash was at least awake now, his eyes darting to me as I came into view.

"Shit," he said under his breath as I joined them. Varsha grabbed a small nylon rope from one of the others and started tying my hands together.

"Where's Evie?" Gretchen asked under her breath.

"Last time I saw her was in the cell block," I answered.

Varsha pulled the rope tight and I squeaked as it pinched my skin.

"And Gjon?" Ash asked.

My mouth cracked open. "He..." The memory of everything that happened came washing over me at lightning pace. My stomach sloshed. I couldn't say it. I couldn't even think it.

"No..." Richard said.

Ash shook his head, his body trembling. "No. Not Gjon. These fuckers didn't..."

Gretchen's jaw was like iron. She reached over and grabbed my hands. I held onto them, for her strength, for the love of my friend.

"Quiet," Varsha commanded, stepping away but keeping the gun level with us.

I released Gretchen and tested the rope. It was solid. There was no wiggling out of this.

The general noise around us quieted and three figures stepped forward through the masses: Adora, who clutched some kind of material in their hands—a sweater, maybe?

Evie stepped beside them, fear pinching her face.

I took a step forward and Varsha jabbed the gun at my side. "Stay!"

Behind Evie came Astor. My entire body seized, hot anger spilling through me as I watched him take his place on Adora's other side.

THE WILD FALL

He took their hand and kissed it before handing them something. My heart thudded harder as I recognized the gleam of a knife in the firelight. Then, he retreated back into the crowd. I watched as he stepped back to the edge of the throng, coming within a few feet of me. Our eyes locked. Every speck of hatred I had for him was in my returned look.

He merely waved in response and turned his attention back toward Adora.

"Friends," they called over the fire. "Dear friends. Don't be afraid. A day we've feared and longed for is finally here. We're going to be with them again. We're going to meet the souls of our beloved at the gates to paradise, look them in the eyes, and tell them how much we love them. All will be forgiven."

Adora held the knife aloft. "First, we have to cross the bridge. We have to get ourselves there."

I watched as they slowly slid the blade across the flesh of their forearm. A clean line of blood appeared and dribbled down their white flesh.

Shuddering, they grabbed hold of Evie's bound hands and drew the knife across her skin.

Evie whimpered.

Gretchen jerked forward next to me and I grabbed her arm. "Don't."

Tempest barked frenziedly from the other side of the fire.

The blood of Evie's wound stained her jacket as she recoiled it against her body.

Adora passed the knife to the person on the other side of Evie.

The woman cut herself across her upper arm quickly and all while biting her lip. She passed the knife on.

Gretchen leaned against me. "That won't kill them."

"It's enough to draw attention," I said, glancing toward the Woods. Ash's eyes were locked there as well. "The wolves will smell that."

"Not only the wolves," Richard added.

The Woods stood silent. I knew what came with the revealing of blood, with the darkness. With the recognition of Adora's intent, a new sickness gripped me. They were too cowardly to do the deed themselves. They were inviting a bloodbath to happen.

"We need a plan," I said under my breath. "When shit happens."

"Duck and run," Ash said. "It's all we can do."

"The chapel?" Richard muttered.

"Someone needs to get Evie," Gretchen added.

"I will." I wasn't going to leave her behind. She was here because of me.

Adora was talking and I had missed what they'd said. Moments later though, they began to sing. Others joined in as they cut themselves, raising their arms over their heads. Blood dripped across their skin, dotting along their heads, causing dark rivulets across their clothing.

This was my only chance. I had to try and make contact with Brody now.

I closed my eyes and let my thoughts drift into the past, into the memories of things I had fought not to remember for years.

My lips formed the words. "Brody, I need you. I *need* you."

Evie

Clutching my hand close to me, I stared over at Adora as she sang at the top of her lungs, as her crazy flock started singing along with her.

Fear fluttered in my chest. I felt lightheaded and weak, guided purely by instinct.

Tempest barked for me. I hadn't seen her in days. Now that I saw her, heard her…I needed her. I didn't want to die.

More and more people joined the horrible dirge. I watched as the knife reached familiar faces off to my right, faces I hadn't seen in what felt like forever. Varsha grabbed Liz whose eyes were closed. She was talking to herself, her words too fast to match the beat of the song the others were lilting. Was she praying? Had seeing Gjon die broken her?

Varsha sliced Liz, who barely reacted, before moving on to Gretchen.

Gretchen fought back, the knife at her throat only seconds later. She let Varsha cut her arm, her teeth clenching as her skin was split open.

We were fucked.

A howl erupted from the dark Woods, a sound that curdled my blood.

Everyone stopped singing. Sparks of fear lit in people's eyes for the first time since they'd gathered at the bonfire. Had Adora told them their fate was to be torn apart by monsters? Had they been told their souls would be ripped from the bodies of the people they'd loved?

I stared at Adora. She alone was still singing. When she looked back at me, she smiled.

A new kind of fury hit me from somewhere deep within.

"Keep going!" Adora cried to her followers. "The end is nearly here!"

I braced myself before a scream exploded from the bottom of my stomach. I raised my right leg and kicked Adora in the back as hard as I possibly could,.

Adora stumbled forward into the bonfire.

Her shrieking pierced the darkness at the same time as another scream from the opposite side of the flames. Through the watery smoke, I recognized a woman being yanked off her feet by something huge, a blur of blackness slamming her against the grass and dragging her off.

Soon, everyone was shouting and running.

Scrambling to my feet, I watched as Adora writhed on the ground, wreathed by orange fire as it clung to the frail frame of her teenage son. No one rushed forward to help. No one cared. All that mattered was themselves.

Someone knocked me over, the earth pummeling me. The man who ran into me scrabbled across the ground, digging the toes of his boots in and clawing with his fingers until he could get up. Seconds later, he was snapped in the jaws of a giant dark monster, its talons shearing at his legs as it gnawed on his chest and head.

I flipped over in time to see the sole of someone's boot seconds before it connected with my head. Tumbling across the ground, I lay there, grass and sky teetering, colors washing around in my vision. Fur touched my hands and face. Whimpers in my ear. My Tempest. She'd found me.

Darkness swallowed my consciousness.

Liz

I opened my eyes to carnage.

Adora was on fire, squirming on the ground and screaming.

People scattered.

Wolves darted in and out of the darkness, picking off whoever they could catch, bodies practically dissolving as their claws cleaved through them like clay.

Gretchen grabbed me as people rushed all around us. "The chapel!" she yelled. "Get to the chapel!"

"Evie!" I shouted back.

"Richard's got her!" She nodded her head in Evie's direction.

I searched the crowds until I spotted Richard about twenty feet away. He darted between people, stopping short of a woman as she was tackled by a wolf. She reached for him before being dragged back and pinned. The wolf closed its jaws around her face.

"We've gotta move!" Gretchen heaved at my arms. Pounding our feet against the ground, we raced for the chapel. Others were headed that way. The only refuge. The only salvation.

Gunfire exploded ahead of us. Screaming, people ran back toward the bonfire and the waiting wolves. On the hill next to the church stood a lone figure, armed with a shotgun: Astor. He was never going to let anyone get out of here alive.

Anguished shrieks echoed into the sky from all around us. Women and men cried and hugged one another and were ripped to pieces.

"Where? Where do we go?" Gretchen yelled over the noise.

"Richard!"

Ash's voice sliced through the mania. He was only a few feet away from us on his knees, his face twisted in horror.

Closer to the fire, a wolf stood on top of Richard's body, tmaw buried in his chest. It yanked at a string of gore from inside him.

My legs felt like jelly. My stomach gyrated.

"No!" Gretchen screamed beside me.

Behind Richard, I saw Evie collapsed on the ground. Tempest guarded her, hackles raised, snarling and barking at anyone or anything that got close.

"Ash!" I yelled, yanking Gretchen with me as I ran to him. "Take her! Get out of here. Run!"

Tears streamed down his cheeks. "Where are you going?"

"I need to get Evie!" I ran toward her.

"Liz! Don't!" he shouted behind me.

"Run, Ash! Run!" Gretchen cried.

I focused on Evie's body, tried to shut out the carnage around me. The gunshots, the whimpering, the sound of teeth crunching through flesh and bone, the inhuman wails of people having their souls torn out of them…

I jumped over someone's body, nearly tripping on another. I gave the wolf a wide berth before crashing on my knees next to Evie and Tempest. Tempest snapped at me and I threw out my hands on instinct. Seconds later, she calmed and licked my fingers.

The side of Evie's head was bleeding. I cupped her cheeks in my hands. "Evie? Wake up!"

She didn't stir.

I looked at the spot where I'd last seen Gretchen and Ash. They were gone.

Barking across the way brought my attention to two figures disappearing around the other side of the chapel, two dogs at their heels.

Feet away, Adora's dead eyes stared at me blankly, part of their face and body charred. One glance to my right showed me five or six other bodies, their limbs rigid, skin silvery with death and facial orifices yawning open in emptiness. To my right, Richard: his head thankfully turned away but…I couldn't look away. The creature on top of him was devouring his left arm, gnawing at his elbow where the bone clacked between its teeth and crunched like rocks being rubbed together.

I drew in a deep, fluttering breath.

Please don't let her die here like this.

I tried to heave Evie into my arms, but my legs gave out. We dropped to the grass again.

Tempest whined and paced anxiously.

Don't let this be it.

The sounds around me faded, the light from the bonfire almost dimming. I realized there was someone standing over me, over us: a dark empty figure, a vacuum bleeding cold into the space before me.

It was him.

"Brody."

He reached out for me and I did the same.

I fell into blackness.

Air rushed around me, buffeting my hair, my arms and legs. I hung, suspended, my weight gone as though I were a bird. From here, I could see my actions as though looking through a telescope and watching the movements of someone doing something far, far away.

THE WILD FALL

I knelt and lifted Evie into my arms without difficulty. With Tempest bounding ahead of me, we ran over the grass, sights set on the darkness of the overbearing forest. I could still feel the shock of each step distantly in my knees.

Snarling, howling, squealing, the snap and roar of fire... It all blended together around me, muffled as if my ears were filled with cotton. I heaved Evie across the barrier, through the tangle of weeds, the goliath trees overshadowing us as I brought her farther and farther into their domain, away from the chaos at the chapel.

I don't know how long we ran. It was an endless cascade of vegetation, uneven earth, and darkness... My breath swelled erratically with each step, my throat growing more and more ragged as we raced.

Complete blackness closed in, swallowing my sight. I was only aware of the slight coolness of leaves on my skin, the dead weight of my body as I slumped across the earth, and the slightly metallic taste of blood tinging my mouth. I let myself go.

TWENTY-TWO

Evie

Awareness ebbed into my pounding head. It was muggy, like being inside a bag left in a hot car. I struggled, trying to interpret what I was feeling, why it didn't make sense. Was this sand underneath my fingers? Finally, I opened my eyes.

Yellow filled the gaps between the black treetops, like the gold of a sunrise before it appears over the horizon. But the trees were wrong. Not the evergreens of the New England woods I grew up with, not the snow-topped pines or helicopter-seeded cedars from my childhood. Intersecting rows of branches topped each other above. Motes of something floated in the air between us.

I got to my hands and knees. My stomach revolted and I flipped over to puke on the ground. I blinked. The ground. It was like sand. Grains stuck to my fingers as I struggled to get up. The landscape was interspersed with tendrils of sparkling sand, blackened fronds, and the gnarled trunks of hundreds if not thousands of strange, lichen-coated trees.

I was in the Woods.

Whimpering nearby made me swing my head around. Tempest lay nearby, her eyes watching me meekly. My heart leapt with relief as I scooched toward her. She started to rise and it was only then I noticed the leash on her collar grow taut. I followed it to the hand grasping it, to the wretched clothing and the face at its head: Astor.

I froze.

"Didn't think you were ever going to wake," he said under his breath. "We've been here nearly a full day. Lucky we didn't get picked off by any wolves or the soulless."

"Why are we here? What's going on?"

Astor shrugged. "That, you'll have to ask your savior once she wakes." He pointed.

Liz lay on her back in a bed of fern-like bushes nearby, unconscious. I got to my feet, my shoes scraping against the grains as I ran to her side. I shook her arm. "Liz?"

Her face twitched.

I touched her forehead. It was ice cold—a cold I wasn't comfortable with.

I turned back to Astor. "We can't stay here. We're going to get seen."

"No shit," Astor replied, standing. He tossed Tempest's leash to me and I barely caught it. "You take the lead. I'll carry her."

I grimaced at the thought of Astor even touching Liz after what he'd done to Gjon but bit back any retort. Now wasn't the time to let my vitriol loose. I bent and grabbed hold of Tempest, nuzzling her neck. "Where do we go?"

"Forward, I suppose," Astor said. With a grunt, he hefted Liz's prone form onto his shoulders from behind. "Until we find something that vaguely resembles a building to seek shelter inside."

"Why don't we go back to Onyx River?"

"There's nothing left," he said. "The Woods swallowed it all. The wolves took their souls. The soulless took the rest."

My cheeks burned at the statement. "What about Gretchen? Richard? Ash?"

"What about them? They were nothing special. Probably fertilizer for the ground like the rest of those abysmal people."

Anger burned in my chest. "You fucker…"

He stared straight through me. "You see what I've got on my belt?"

For the first time, I looked. A gun poked out over the top of his pants at his hip.

"Don't push me," he said. "I'll kill the dog first. Slowly."

Spurred on by the threat, I stood quickly. "Let's go, Tempest."

We set off into the Woods.

We walked for only an hour before we found the first building: an old gas station. Pulling open the glass doors and hearing the resounding ding of the bell inside, I felt a small part of me unclench. I held open the door for Astor as he squeezed through with Liz.

The station was small, like all the ones I'd been in since the Merging. A single counter backed by an array of cigarette cartons stood to our left while the rest of the shop was lined with three short aisles of various aged roadside snacks and knickknacks.

"Help clear the counter," Astor said.

I took my arm to it, swiping the old moldering chocolates, penny cup, and lottery ticket displays to make room. Astor backed to the counter and dropped Liz carefully onto its surface. He groaned, arching his back. When he noticed me staring, he waved to the back of the store. "See if you can find some water."

I took Tempest with me and we skirted an aisle toward some old fridges. It took a bit of elbow grease to get the doors to pop open. Most of the drinks inside were black, the only thing to tell them apart being the old labels. I found water in the third fridge and pulled as many bottles out as I could. I brought them to the front of the gas station and set them on one of the nearby shelves.

Astor grabbed one, twisted the top, and took three or four long chugs from it, draining it.

I glanced around until I noticed a collection of plastic-sealed paper bowls. I tore it open, pulled a stack of two or three bowls out and filled them with water. Tempest lapped it as I set it on the floor.

I sat cross-legged next to her and drank. The water was warm but felt incredible. The thudding in my head lessened the more I had. When the bottle was empty, I glanced back at Astor, who had started to gather cans from some of the nearby shelves.

"What is it?" I asked.

His head appeared from behind a shelf. "What's what?"

"You're obsession with Liz?"

Astor ducked back out of sight. "It's not an obsession. It's a bond we share."

I frowned. "What kind of bond?"

"Well," he grunted, "for starters, I'm sure she never told you back when the Merging first happened, she was Attached."

I shook my head. "No way. She couldn't have been. We'd have noticed."

"Precisely; she would have given herself away if she'd been Attached when she met you after our little adventure in Elon. But she was Attached before. Like me, she found a way to get rid of her ghost before he became a problem."

I stared at the empty water bottle in my hand. It didn't make sense yet...

In the years I'd spent with Liz, there had always seemed to be something she was running from, a shadow that loomed over her shoulder that she never wanted to acknowledge. There were times I'd gotten up in the middle of the night and had seen her standing at the window to the cabin staring out into the darkness as though she recognized someone or something out there.

It hit me then: the dark shape I'd encountered in the cabin, the thing I'd seen depart with the darkness that morning months ago. Had it been there for her? Was that Liz's ghost?

Worse was a memory from when she'd saved me even longer ago, back when I'd been kidnapped by my grandfather's ghost, by his obsessive girlfriend. When Liz came to save me, she'd said "We came to save you." I'd always thought she'd meant Dad. But she'd been as surprised to see him there as I was.

"The ghost was of a man she once knew, perhaps had a romantic entanglement with?" Astor came to the front and set a collection of cans near the water. "Either way, it didn't end well. The only way for her to kill him was for him to be possessing someone."

"So, when you say you two share a bond, do you mean you were also Attached?"

"Precisely. I was haunted, for lack of a better term, and once I recognized the ghost wanted nothing more than to make my existence a living hell, I tried to take out my frustrations on him with a tire iron in the back of a car shop. He'd inhabited the mechanic, some mangy ex-con trying to avoid being found by the army during the evacuations.

"Anyway, he didn't come back. Thought he would. And when I realized I had discovered how to make it stop, I knew I had to help others. I knew I had to help rid the world of this ghastly infestation one way or another."

"Who was it?" I asked. "Who came back for you?"

Astor rolled his eyes. "He didn't come back *for* me. Not sure he understood how he'd come back at all."

When I kept staring, he turned back and resumed his foraging. "He was a student of mine: Graham Toole. I used to teach classes in Myth and World Literature at the University of Southern Maine. We had an argument about something in class one day, some paper I thought he'd copied straight from a website. I got him removed from the class. Couple days later, he committed suicide. Turns out he spent a whole weekend composing that paper from scratch, hadn't even heard of the other person who had based their dissertation on the exact same point. How was I supposed to know?"

I swallowed. "And Graham killed himself because you got him expelled? That seems…"

"Excessive?" Astor sighed. He walked back over to the front and set more cans down, then sat with his back against the counter. "Kids pin their hopes and dreams on the expectations of their parents. I didn't know the kind of home-life Graham came from, didn't know his parents refused to feed him when he didn't get straight-A grades. Didn't know they'd beat him senseless once after he skipped school and missed an exam. Didn't know if he told them he'd been removed from my class, they'd have kicked him out of house and home."

I stared at the floor, at the dust and grime. "Fuck."

"Yes," he said. "Fuck."

"So, Graham hated you."

"Yes. And no." Astor pulled one knee to his chest and propped his hands on it. "Hated me because I potentially could have made his life a living hell. Didn't because the world went to hell in a hand basket anyway. He wasn't sure what chance he could have stood against this. At least that's what he said at first. Then, the guilt-tripping started. There's only so much a man can take.

"The only thing that matters though is Graham's death eventually brought me to the Woods, which brought me to the Monolith, and to the Others."

I blinked. "What Others?"

Liz

The restaurant was exactly like one I remembered from back home, a place I never would have gone to by myself. The kind of place that only took same-day reservations, that had velvet curtains in the windows, candlelight and black accents. A plush carpet in the entryway and a fireplace that was always blazing when you passed by on the street at night. People digging their forks into soft, filled pasta with creamy sauces; slices of dark, dense chocolate cake that made your mouth water…

I felt like a stranger. I felt like I didn't belong there.

And then, he arrived. He sat across from me and it was like everything was as it should be. His face was familiar and foreign at the same time; there were times he looked like Gjon, times he sounded like Brody, times out of the corner of my eye when I saw Josh's smile…

A date. This was our first date.

I never went on a date like this with any of them.

As the unfamiliarity intensified, I was pulled into consciousness.

My eyes opened

The world was fuzzy, confusing… It felt like I was a million miles away.

It felt like there was someone watching me closely but I couldn't see them.

Like there was someone standing right behind me.

"Liz?"

The voice was from nearby. Evie. She crossed to me, her hand resting on my arm. "You've been out for a long time. I wasn't sure you were going to…"

More movement, this time from beneath me. Another person popped into view, stood and stared at me with cold black eyes. Everything inside of me withered under that gaze.

"Astor," I said, wanting to spit the name from my tongue.

"You can't get rid of me , Elizabeth," he said, handing me a water bottle.

I took it from him, my movements still slow. Why did it feel like I was stuck in syrup? After a few agonizingly long moments of twisting the bottle cap off, I guzzled the water, draining the whole thing. My vision brightened, my joints throbbed but didn't feel stuck, my head like I'd taken it out of whatever oven it had been inside.

"Where are we?" I asked. Old aisles of packaged chips and soda lined the store, Powerball and lottery tickets lay scattered across the floor. The entire place smelled of mildew, soil, and dust.

"In the Woods," Astor said. "Wasn't sure how much you'd remember from your race to escape last night."

The memories came to me in bits and pieces: the bonfire, watching Richard die, seeing the dark shape emerge and reach out toward me...

A tickle on the back of my neck. I froze. I could swear there was someone there, someone so close to me it made the hairs on my neck stand at attention.

Astor cleared his throat.

I raised my eyes to him, keeping them slightly narrowed. "And you followed?" I prompted.

"Naturally. After all, isn't this the place you've desired to be for years? The place you've been wanting to ask me about all this time?"

"You know it is." I swung my legs around on the counter and got down to the floor.

"We'll find our answers together then." He touched his hand to the holster of a gun in his waistband. "First, we need to know where we're going."

I crossed my arms. "We're not going anywhere with you."

He pulled the gun from his waistband and aimed it at Evie. "I insist."

Evie closed her eyes and took a short steady breath.

Tempest growled.

"Fuck you," I muttered.

Astor nodded. "Second thing we need is a bag for our supplies. Since you're awake, I suggest you look for something. I'll keep an eye on Evie and the dog."

Cursing him in my head, I walked toward the back of the store, combing the shelves for some kind of container or bag we might be able to use. The entire time, I couldn't get over an oppressiveness, as if something hovered over me with every step. I didn't remember this feeling from the last time I found myself in these Woods.

As I inspected the back of one of the shelves, the memory of the shadow reaching out for me splashed forward in my head, newer, more real, the feeling of iciness crackling into my fingers from its touch…

"Easy."

The voice was in my ear. I spun around, practically falling on my ass. There was no one there, no one behind me.

"You okay, Liz?" Evie called from the front of the store.

Taking a shaky breath, I forced myself to exhale. "Y-yeah." I got back on my feet.

"I'm here."

Again, in my ear. The more I thought about it, the more it felt like a buzzing inside my skull.

"I know you can hear me."

What is this? I thought. *Who are you?*

"You know. You've known this whole time."

A pang started somewhere deep in my chest under my left rib. I winced. *You're not real. You can't be.*

"Lizzy. It's me."

But… I stared at my hands. *You died. I killed you. You possessed Josh and I killed you for it.*

"Yes, you killed a different part of me."

I turned you into that... dark shape and you've been watching me ever since.

"I kept my distance. It was clear you didn't want me there. But I couldn't leave. I couldn't tear myself away."

Tears slipped down my cheeks, painting my face in hot streams. I put a hand to my mouth and stifled an exhale, which should have been a sob, which should have been a scream.

You're inside me?

"You needed me. I came."

I touched my arm. My own skin felt like snow. *Can you feel this?*

"Yes."

"Have you found anything yet?" Astor called. "We need to get going."

I took a breath, getting my voice under control. "Give me a few more minutes."

Astor grumbled.

I need to kill him, I thought-spoke. *We need to kill him before he hurts Evie. Can you possess him?*

"No."

Why not?

"Because I can't leave you."

I swallowed. *What?*

"If I leave you, the Woods will take you. They will claim your soul."

Flashes of remembrances blipped into my head: the memory of being suspended over the Woods, over their sharp and dark treetops, something clinging to me like a hook in my skin. This was different: it didn't feel as though someone was holding onto a small part of me, more like I was embraced by a cloud of tiny things, almost enveloped.

"If you're going to kill him, we're going to have to do it together."

Astor has something I need to know first, something I've been searching for for years...

"Whatever he has, it isn't going to be worth shit by the time he's done with you. Don't underestimate him."

I nodded, even if Brody already knew I didn't have a choice.

"Now, find something to carry your supplies in."

In the back office, I found someone's old messenger bag. I emptied it of papers and filled it to the brim with canned goods and water. It was over ten pounds and Astor decided I should carry it, figuring I was less of a threat if I was literally weighted down.

We exited the gas station and cautiously meandered out to the front of it. The remnants of a paved road lay in a broken and brittle mess, stretching in and around trees that had punched through it from the invading woodland. A nearby sign, rusted and misshapen, said "Gregory—Two Miles."

"We should follow the road," I said. "There's no guarantee the town of Gregory isn't in the same shape as Onyx River, but we can hope."

"No," Astor said. "We're not trying to find our way out. Our answers lie farther inside. The answers I need for why the sacrifice didn't work are in there."

I followed his eyes to the brush, to the tangle of vines and fronds. I imagined the wolf we'd seen after running through the field, the one who had taken Hank, and a bristle of rage swept through me. Almost as soon as it did, coolness blanketed me, my cheeks tingling.

"Don't," Brody's voice soothed.

"How will we know where to go?" Evie chimed in.

Astor pointed to the soil. "We follow the crumbling path that brought us here. It runs to the Processors, which in turn, runs to the Centers."

The name clicked in my brain.

Go to the Center. That's where it starts.

THE WILD FALL

Astor had said those words to me ten years ago and they had cycled through my brain on repeat ever since. Clearly, he'd learned more about whatever mysterious miracle we needed to end the Woods' reign, and it lay at the Center.

Despite my want to find answers, too, I knew Evie shouldn't have been a part of this trek and she was my responsibility to keep safe. "You want us to go deeper into the Woods when we have no protection from what might be hiding out there?"

"Trudging along that asphalt path might lead us to wolves, the soulless, or worse. Even if it sounds like civilization could be around the next bend doesn't mean it will be." Astor turned toward the Woods behind the gas station. "There has to be a way to stop this and I'm not going back to the outside until I have some answers." He nudged Evie with the gun. "Let's go."

Evie and I locked eyes for a moment. I nodded in the direction Astor wanted her to go and said, "Go on."

"Come on, Tempest," she said, taking the lead.

"You next," he said, waving me on with the gun.

The next several hours were spent slogging along the weed-clogged path, navigating the deformed trees in the near darkness. When I'd been here months ago looking for Hank, I thought it had changed. Now, I knew it had. The vibrancy I'd once seen here—greenery, the haunted kind of beauty of its flora, how the trees had made an almost strange kind of architecture before—was now dilapidated. The trees felt older, dried and blackened. The plant life on the forest floor was also shrunken. As we passed through the dessication of each plant, mini hurricanes bristled in our wake and leaves, branches, and burrs fell to the ground.

I kept my eyes trained on Evie and Tempest in front of me, my ears listening to the surrounding wilderness. If something did come out for us, it would be quick. With the heavy pack weighing me, I wasn't sure I could act with the speed I wanted.

Behind me, Astor talked to himself, saying things like, "This isn't right" and "What's going on?" While I was tempted to turn and ask him, I didn't want to give him the satisfaction of still being curious, of showing I needed his knowledge.

The trees dwindled and the yellow-orange sky opened more in front of us. Clouds churned above though they didn't darken or obscure the ochre glow in the slightest. The ground turned from soil to sand and our heels sunk in as we continued making our way.

Then, a lookout point opened in the trees before us and we found ourselves at a ledge. Evie and Tempest stood at its tip, the wind billowing their hair and fur. I approached her and put a hand on her shoulder.

She jerked a moment before looking back at me. "Your hand is so cold."

I let it drop to my side and stared out over the valley below.

Emptiness was its most defining feature. A plain of undulating sand, the husks of long-dead trees with naked branches puncturing spots here and there. Once-proud structures gathered to create something vaguely urban. Each one crumbled, the structures bleeding their bricks and stones out into the open roads. Windows leered, black and unoccupied. Everything was blasted with windswept ginger sand.

In the distance, at the end of a path framed by enormous humanoid sculptures, was a building whose familiarity punctured me.

Years ago, I remembered seeing a sandcastle-like construction that echoed with the sounds of torture. Flame billowed in its hundreds of tiny windows and screams rippled into the sky from its innards. Whatever disgusting shade of life had once held court there now seemed to have been snuffed out.

When I looked over at Astor, who had stopped next to me, his face had slid into incredulity.

I couldn't help myself. "Not what you remembered?"

He studied the landscape. "No."

"Where is this 'processing' place you were talking about?" Evie asked.

Astor pointed to the sandcastle building. "There."

"And what the hell was this?" she probed farther. "It looks like a town."

When he didn't answer, I said, "It may have been."

Astor nodded to a trail meandering down the cliff side. "This is our way. Let's go."

TWENTY-THREE

Evie

The climb down seemed to take forever and only a minute. It was hard not to take my eyes off the remains of the city below us. I'd seen numerous towns left abandoned in the wake of the Woods taking over, in the wake of the army coming in and evacuating civilians. We'd raided countless grocery stores, homes, gas stations, storage facilities. None of that compared to this.

There was an indescribable wrongness about how empty this place was. Worse was the expectation from Astor that it wasn't supposed to be like this, like he'd been waiting for something that ultimately was missing when we crossed through the trees and found this place. I didn't know what we should have seen, couldn't fathom what kinds of things had used to live here.

Worse was the niggling little feeling in the back of my head that we weren't alone. We hadn't seen any wolves or soulless since we'd entered the Woods. I'd imagined this place being home to hundreds of them if not thousands, so many they would eventually pour over into our homes in a thriving, undulating horde. Their absence left me worried they were hiding in plain sight, ready to jump out and take us when we least expected it.

Shuffling through the desert, we made our way toward the town. A strong wind blew walls of sand at us. Tempest whined as I took my handkerchief off and covered her eyes. I gripped her collar to guide her and pulled my own shirt over my mouth and nose to protect them. I shielded my eyes with my arm.

The great structures looked as if they'd been made of porous rocks and clay. The walls appeared fibrous and almost transparent as we neared. Apart from the whistling wind, the only other sounds were the crumbling of stones as they tumbled from roofs and window ledges above.

Once we were within the main avenue of buildings, the wind was cut and we were able to move without the need for protection.

"How high are some of these?" I asked, staring at the nearest building. It reminded me of a picture I'd once seen of a skyscraper. This one looked like it could fall apart by touching it with a finger.

No one answered me, not that I'd expected them to.

I glanced at Liz.

She'd been different ever since waking in the gas station. But she'd been different since Gjon had died, too. And her hatred for Astor seemed to lift off her in chilly waves. I knew the moment she could, she was going to kill him and there was nothing I could do to help her. I'd have to get out of the way and let her do what she needed to do. Then, maybe we could get the hell out of here together.

"Don't look," Liz said.

I looked. It took a few moments, but when I finally saw, I stared in dumb fascination.

Piles of sand-coated bones littered the fronts of the buildings as if dumped there. The fragile silhouettes of fingers and ribcages stood out against the rotting facades. Dented skulls with teeth missing and eye holes that seemed much too large could be picked out amongst the mass of speckled white.

I'd seen dead bodies before. Everyone had tried to shield me from them, how the earth decays the human form, putrefies it and eventually, makes it a part of the environment around it. The problem is: there were so many, it became impossible not to see them. As time went on and nature had its way with them, they became less and less common. These days, if we came across anyone, they were reduced to bones and tattered clothes. Even so, they were always together.

These piles of bones were all disconnected: heads removed from spines, fingers from hands, legs and arms from torsos… And there were dozens of piles lining our path through town.

"What the hell?" Liz muttered.

Tempest got closer to me, her eyes darting along the road. If she was whining, I couldn't hear her over the jumble of thoughts in my own head.

Astor's only response was to walk faster.

We cleared the town within twenty minutes, continuing to follow the brittle stone path toward the processing building. As the structures dwindled, they gave way to sculptures of towering beings, carved into black rock that gleamed and shimmered in spite of the sand blasting its surfaces. The perhaps once-sharp-hewn features of their faces were eroded, their forms not appearing impressive as they may have once been, but instead cloaked in secrecy.

"You mentioned the Others back at the gas station," I said, turning toward Astor. "Was this them?"

He cleared his throat. "I only ever got to talk with one. But from what I observed: yes."

"They were in charge here," Liz added. "At least I think they were."

"You knew?" I asked blankly. "You knew about this stuff?"

"I came here once a long time ago," she said. "I came here trying to save someone. I ended up in a Monolith, deep underground. I talked to one of them."

I watched a statue as we walked by. It must have been thirty stories tall, its face obscured by whirling sand. "What did they say?"

"Not much. It spoke in riddles, talked about The Great Corruption, how there was no way to stop what was happening to our world—"

"That's not true," Astor cut her off. "There's a way. At least, I was told there was a way."

"You convincing those people to kill themselves back there was your way?" Liz hissed.

Astor stopped. "Yes. I'm a monster. But if that had worked, if that had been what we had to sacrifice so our world could thrive again, you wouldn't be pointing the finger. You'd be basking in the glory of surviving like everyone else."

"Except you didn't plan on me surviving," she said, continuing on.

The statue line continued for nearly a mile. The processing building appeared through the gloom like the monstrosity it was: a dripping, semi-solid-looking piece of architecture with the shape of a hollowed-out human skeleton, solidified mud clinging to its every rut and furrow. A tower jutted out of its right side at a forty-five-degree angle, the top of which had broken off and fallen to the sand below. It lay in an obliterated mess at the base of the building as we approached it.

As soon as we were out of the shelter from the statues, the wind snapped at us, razoring our skin with fiery grains of sand in every gust. We ran for the shelter of the doorway at the front of the building and once past the entry, huffed in the stale air, catching our breaths.

The darkness inside loomed, pockmarked with pinholes of light from the windows on either side of us. Sand sprinkled across the rock on the outside, almost seething in its anger.

Tempest rumbled at the darkness.

"We need a light," I said.

Astor nodded to Liz. "Open the bag. I grabbed some road flares from the gas station."

Liz flipped open the top of the messenger bag and searched until she came across the pack. She handed it to him. "They're ten years old. They probably won't work."

"Only one way to find out," he said, pulling one out and popping the cap off. Holding it away from him and toward the ground, he struck the flare against the cap once, twice, three times…

We watched as he tried over and over to light it. Finally, he tossed it. "Give me another."

Liz obliged.

This time, on the first strike, it ignited with a flash, the red spark sizzling as it bloomed light over the craggy walls around us.

"We've got about thirty minutes, give or take," Astor said. "Let's see what we can find."

A wide, low-ceilinged room spread out in front of us with a hall that ascended and curled as it did so. As we walked, I couldn't help but watch our sputtering shadows as they slanted along the walls.

The hallway was lined with dark insets, doorways that had once opened into rooms, but were now all bricked-over. Rusted, broken chains hung from the walls; the links snapped. I leaned to touch one and it dissolved beneath my fingertips. "What the hell did they chain here?"

No one answered. When I looked at Astor, he ignored me. The red light cast harsh shadows over his face as he kept walking.

Toward the middle of the hall, the bricked-up doorways stopped and revealed stone bars that closed off each small room from us.

"The Processor is a prison?" I asked.

This time, Astor nodded.

"A prison for what?"

"For the ghosts in purgatory," Liz said. "Otherwise, they would escape."

Her voice didn't sound like her own then. It was hard for me to imagine this other person Liz had been before she fell in with us, this haunted woman who had kept these secrets all these years from us. I felt like I didn't know her anymore.

Astor turned toward her. "This isn't purgatory; this is…everything."

She frowned. "What do you mean?"

"It's hard to imagine anyone could hold onto their tired principles of faith after the Woods appeared. If anything, it should have forced people to think in different ways."

She glared at him. "You expected people to drop their belief in God? Allah? Buddha? Centuries-old religions people have clung to in times of war and strife? Not much of a mythology professor, are you…"

"In the end, I'm glad they didn't because it was easier to convince them to kill themselves for the sake of their gods," he said in a lackadaisical tone that made my head swim. "But to imagine after seeing this place that there exists a heaven and hell separate from this? No. It's all here. And everything that dies, every earthly soul gets brought here: to these buildings."

My knees shook. "Everyone?"

He blinked. "Everyone."

My skin was numb. Before I knew what I was doing, before I had the sense to figure out what was rising in my throat, Astor walked away. Liz's cold hand touched me on my shoulder and she crouched to look me in the eyes. "He's lying. He's trying to make you crack."

I bit down hard, trying to keep the sob from working its way up my throat and out of my mouth. "He can't be here, right?" I whispered, the words coming fast. "Dad can't be here. He'd have come back to me. He would have."

Liz looked over her shoulder at Astor who was holding the flare to the bars of one of the rooms to look inside. "Astor is here with an agenda and it doesn't include either one of us making it out of here alive with him once he has his answers. He's the type that will hurt you because he can." She took my hands in hers. "He's lying."

I forced myself to nod, even as a tear slid to the end of my nose.

"Come on," she said, turning back around. "Stay close to me."

Breathing deeply, I followed. Tempest stayed beside me, her claws clicking on the stone floor as we walked farther into the prison for souls.

Liz

"Why'd you lie to her?"

Brody's question nearly stopped me in my tracks. *Because he's being cruel. And she doesn't need to think about Hank being trapped in a place like this.*

What Astor had said was like medication slowly dripping into an IV in my arm, deadening my thoughts. It meant anyone who died in the last ten years was here, any soul sacrificed to the Woods had ended up lost in this realm. I closed my eyes for a moment as faces I hadn't thought about in years scrolled through my mind's eye.

Jake.
Elden.
Lennox.
Carmen.
Josh.
Hank.
Nettie.
Richard.
Gjon…

"Hey. I need you to focus," Brody said.

You've known the whole time, haven't you? I thought.

"Not the whole time," he said. *"I learned. I saw…"*

Saw what?

"Carmen."

The word skewered me. Brody had seen his wife's ghost. I wanted to know: where? How had she been when he saw her? Was she in a place like this?

"I can't answer your questions."

Right. I'm sorry.

"Keep up with them."

Evie and Tempest had edged out in front of me but not too much. She was staying close like I'd asked her to and that was enough for now.

Astor led us to the walkway, gradually sloping to the right and ascending.

"What are we looking for here?" I asked him.

"Something that will explain what happened to them," Astor answered. "There has to be an explanation for why the Others vanished."

"They didn't vanish," Evie said, making us both turn toward her. "You saw. They're *dead*."

The words were harsh and I know, delivered with the intent to get a rise out of Astor. She was going to get us killed if she didn't watch it.

"They ruled this land for centuries," Astor answered, his tone dripping with irritation. "I have a hard time believing in ten years, everything they've built has withered to pieces."

"None of this was planned," I said, trying to divert his fury away from Evie. "They had no intention of letting the Woods merge with our realm. When I was here ten years ago, the Monolith I was in crumbled and was destroyed. Which is why the one I talked to called it The Great Corruption."

Astor turned away from me and kept walking. "I heard that name as well. But they had a plan. They told me what it would take to get things back on track."

"Why you?" It took me a moment to realize I'd asked the question. It hadn't been me. It had been Brody using me. I cleared my throat.

"Desperation? Fear? Survival instinct?" He shrugged. "Maybe I was the only one they could get to listen?"

"And they told you you had to kill a bunch of people?" I nodded to myself. "That's rich. Considering the great losses of life that already happened, you'd think they had all the souls they needed."

"It wasn't just souls," Astor growled. "They had to be willing souls. They had to sacrifice themselves for the cause. At least, that's what I thought. Now… I'm not so sure."

We passed by a set of openings that looked out on the city we'd left and the statue-lined road. We'd only gone up one level but it already felt like we were a dizzying height off the ground. Gusts of wind whipped at the outside of the structure, and I felt the sharp sting of it as it slashed through the tiny windows at us.

The cells on this floor appeared shallower than others, the rooms more confined. We passed by one that had a stone chair inside with chains wrapped around it. They lay empty across the ground, the bars pried apart. The faint white scratches of claws on the stone floor sent a chill through me. I had seen cells like these beneath the Monolith, cells occupied by things that resembled the soulless. Was that what they had trapped here? Were they trying to keep those things imprisoned here?

"What did this place do?" Evie asked behind me. "You called it a 'Processor.' How did they 'process'…people?"

"All kinds of souls ended up here. Clueless ones, wicked ones, innocent ones… The Processor was where they were brought to sort through them all."

"Brought?"

"The wolves…" he said. "They were the hounds of the Woods. Their sole purpose was to gather lost souls and bring them here. Pure souls were taken to Centers. Corrupted souls were sent to Monoliths."

THE WILD FALL

A snapshot of Brody tied to a stone pillar at a Monolith ruptured through my brain. I remembered the thing at the bottom of the Monolith said all the souls were corrupted, that they couldn't "spin" or be "recycled."

"What was the purpose of the Monoliths?" Evie asked.

"To purify."

I swallowed. Was every soul that escaped from the Woods corrupted? I asked Brody.

"*Yes.*"

Evie cleared her throat. "And what about the pure souls? What happened to them at a Center?"

"They were recycled," I answered before Astor could.

"Recycled?" Evie's voice broke. "Like what? Plastic bottles?"

"Yes," Astor said.

I opened my mouth to ask another question but was silenced by Astor putting a finger to his lips. We listened to the sounds of the zephyrs slicing at the building, the sand scraping over the rocks. Behind it all was a muffled sound, a stifled, urgent squeal..

We followed the sound to the cell at the end of the row.

Evie shrieked and backed into the wall next to a window.

Tempest yipped.

We stood face to face with a soulless.

Chained to a chair in the prison, the soulless was almost nothing more than a shell, a thing rasping in a corner, clutching to a whisper of life. The chains had chewed into its white figure so deep the skin around them had sagged to wrap around the links. With every exhale, a whistling moan emanated from its mouthless, anemic face.

Astor stared at it. I could almost see the cogs turning in his head, the red flickering light from the road flare waxing on its face.

Why do they have soulless imprisoned here? I asked Brody.

"*Because they were trying to clean up their mess.*"

I frowned. What did he mean? Instead of asking Brody for clarification, I turned my attention to Astor. "Why is there a soulless here?"

Astor glanced at me out of the corner of his eye. "What makes a soulless?"

"The wolves. When they take a soul from a still-living body."

"So, it stands to reason the wolves brought soulless back here under their masters' orders. To try and keep them from wreaking havoc. To stop the bloodshed."

The thing in the cell arced its head in our direction, its cry turning into a hiss.

"Why were they created at all? I don't understand."

Astor shook his head. "I don't think they were supposed to be."

I glanced over my shoulder at Evie. She cowered against the wall, covering her eyes with her hands. Tempest whined and pawed at her ankles.

I let the statement marinate in my head, turning it over and over.

"*You know what that means,*" Brody said.

I did, but I was afraid to say it. *The wolves created the soulless without being commanded.*

"*Which begs the question… Why?*"

Tempest lapped at Evie's hands and rubbed her muzzle along Evie's face.

Because they were hungry.

"*Not hungry: greedy.*"

I exhaled, shuddering.

"*Once the wolves got a taste of the world outside, they didn't want to go back to be handed scraps to fetch souls. They wanted all the souls they could get for themselves.*"

"My god…" I whispered, backing away from the cell.

Astor did the same. "This all but confirms my suspicion."

I held my hand out to Evie. "Come on. We're getting out of here."

The gun was out faster than I'd assumed he could pull it and aimed in my direction. "Where do you think you're going?" Astor snapped.

"You said it yourself: your suspicions are all but confirmed. You know what caused this. You've answered your questions. We need to leave before we get found by wolves, or soulless, or both now."

Astor cocked his head. "We didn't answer the most important question of all, Liz. How do we make this stop? How do we do what the Others couldn't?"

I threw my hands up. "Maybe we don't. Maybe this is how it's supposed to be."

The squealing in the cell got louder.

"I don't buy that," Astor growled. "They told me there was a way to stop it. There must be another way."

"They told you ten years ago when there might have been something to save!" I yelled. "There's nothing now!"

Evie leapt to her feet. "We're *not* nothing!"

We both glanced at her.

"This can't be how we die…" she continued, words fluttering.

The thing in the cell howled relentlessly, a maw tearing open on its featureless face, blood soaking the white as it screamed anew.

Overhead, scratches drew our heads back. The scrabbling grew louder as it crossed the ceiling in the direction of the slope.

"They're above us!" I exclaimed.

"Go, go!" Astor shouted.

Yanking Evie off the floor, we ran down the hall back the way we'd come. Tempest bolted out in front, her silver form blazing through the darkness and leading us back toward the first level.

A feral roar pierced the hall behind us and shot my heart into my throat.

Our boots scuffed on the rough rock as we rounded the corner into the first-floor hallway. The orange light from the doorway ahead beckoned us.

Around us, the red light from the flare fizzled and then went out.

"Shit!" Astor yelled behind me.

Opening the bag as I ran, I dug my hand in to search for a new road flare. As I grabbed one, Astor screamed.

I spun.

Astor was on the ground, his ankle snared by the long claws of a soulless. He blindly fired the gun as he tried to flip over. The first shot was wild, striking a wall off to the left. The second hit the thing in a leg and it howled as it let go.

I unslung the bag from my head and threw it to Evie, who barely caught it. "Run!" I commanded her. I popped the cap off the road flare and struck the ends, watching the sparks cascade each time as it failed to light.

Astor got to his feet and ran toward me. "Light it! Light it!"

It wasn't going. No matter how many strikes, it failed each time.

I looked in time to see the soulless in midair, leaping at me.

It crashed into me like a pile of rocks and we cascaded over the floor, my head bouncing against the stones like a ball. White sparks danced in my vision as I found myself pinned beneath enormous claws, my arms and torso locked by the surprising weight of the monster. Its red-soaked white face leered in my vision.

Gunshots exploded on my left. The side of the soulless's neck split open in two spots.

Screeching like metal on metal pierced my ears as the soulless cried and I closed my eyes against the awful sound.

Razors dug into the flesh of my arm and I screamed. When I opened my eyes again, I saw the claws buried in my forearm.

Red light flooded my vision, nearly white at its center.

THE WILD FALL

The monster roared and flung itself off of me. I felt the claws pop as they tore loose from my flesh. My entire arm was a mountain of pain.

An arm swung around me and lifted me off the ground. I ran, adrenaline driving my feet forward, the bloody light of a new flare like a tide behind us sweeping us toward safety.

We erupted out into the open, into the blistering wind. Astor's arm clung to me, pulling me along toward the side of the building until we were no longer in the path of the gusts. There was a tangle of black brambles there, old carts and boxes I practically fell into. The pain was blinding.

As my vision bled in and out, I saw Evie, the sparking road flare clutched in her hand, the bag hanging heavily from her shoulder. "What do we do?" she murmured.

Astor looked from me to her and then to something over my shoulder. "The Center is ahead. Help me get her into one of these carts."

I closed my eyes.

"I have you," Brody said, his voice enveloping me. *"Let me help."*

I caved and sank into the abyss of nothingness.

TWENTY-FOUR

Evie

The Processor was left behind. I walked and carried the bag of provisions. Astor pushed an old wooden wagon that seemed like it would imminently fall apart, the old nails rusted, the wood brittle and moldered. Liz rode inside it, dazed, in and out of it. Her right arm was a ragged mess of flesh, wrapped in the cloth of Astor's sweater. He wore only a t-shirt now, his muscles flexing as he forced the cart on, his brow beaded with perspiration.

Tempest sauntered beside me, whining.

The desert gradually blanched from its dusty monochrome into a colorless expanse. The black vines and hedges rose around us like an old vineyard, rows and rows of them cascading across the hills into the distance. The sand turned white but the occasional blast of it carried on the wind still nipped our skin.

A blue-green blur in the distance sharpened as we drew closer to it and grew in size. I realized whatever the blur was, it surpassed the dark storm clouds we were nearing, its hulking shape vanishing into the yellow sky beyond it, seemingly forever. Gradually, it revealed itself to be concave, the edges curving. Black pinpricks pockmarked the surface above the clouds. It was a building, larger than anything I'd ever seen before in my life.

Beneath the clouds, the building was shielded by the white striations of hundreds if not thousands of trees. Their branches cascaded into the black cumulus. It was almost as though the structure was made of trees and then turned to stone somewhere within the clouds.

"How is this possible?" I breathed.

Astor stopped pushing the cart. "If there's one thing I've learned about the Woods, it's that nothing in here makes any damned sense."

I stared at the contrast of white against blue-green, against yellow. This must have been what he was talking about: the Center. This was the place where souls were recycled. I'm not sure what I had expected. My brain had fathomed a factory, something industrial, something I could draw comparison to. But this… It was like some insane tower, the kind I may have dreamed about when I was younger, when everything was possible no matter how beautiful or scary it was.

Tempest's whining got louder.

"Can we take a break?" I asked.

Astor didn't acknowledge me.

"Hey, I asked if we could stop?"

"No. We're being followed."

I scanned the horizon behind us, panic tickling the back of my neck with his words. I couldn't see anything.

He glanced at me with annoyance. "Besides, we're almost there."

"I need water. Tempest needs it, too."

Astor opened his mouth but didn't make a sound. After a moment, he said, "Fine. But not for too long."

We stopped and drank. The winds had abated the closer we came to the Center, which only managed to punctuate the silence of this place even more.

Liz was awake, her pallor wan, eyes glassy. I tilted the water into her lips and she gulped it, coughing a little. "Why didn't you leave me behind?" she asked.

Astor chuckled. "Just because you want to give up, Elizabeth, doesn't mean I do. And I figure you deserve these answers as much as I do." He glanced at me out of the corner of his eye. "As we all do."

Liz closed her eyes and gritted her teeth.

"How is it?" I asked, staring at the blood-soaked sweater.

"Numb. Thankfully, numb."

I frowned. "That's bad, isn't it?"

"I'm not sure." Liz closed her eyes.

Of all the medical knowledge I'd tried to glean from Gjon, I was sure too much blood loss and feeling numb signified the person was dying. At the worst, they'd lose their limb. We didn't have anything that could cut through bone. I was terrified of the possibility we'd need to.

I focused on Astor for a moment, on the gun at his hip. All this time, he had pushed us to find out more about why the Woods were here, to find out more about why his scheme to kill everyone in the Church of the Night Forest didn't work as he'd planned it. At first, I'd thought he would use the gun without much care. After all, he'd killed Gjon on a whim. Why wouldn't he kill us and then press on to his precious Center alone?

As the time had passed and I'd watched him save Liz, carry her, push her all this way, I began to realize this was never about him. He'd brought Liz all this way because he needed her... I wasn't sure why yet.

"What are you going to do when you find out?" I asked him. "What's your next step?"

"Easy: I'll do whatever I have to satisfy the will of the Others, to make sure things go back to the way they were."

"You keep saying that," Liz garbled, sitting straighter. "You know even if you are able to get the Woods to retreat, to 'recycle the souls' or whatever your aim is…nothing will ever be the same. The whole world has been transformed by this. This is the new normal."

"I'm not naïve," he said. "But your thinking is also linear and narrow minded. I'm surprised. I thought you'd have understood more of this place having been here before."

"What does that even mean?" I interjected. I was tired of them talking around me, of no one acknowledging I was here, too. "Why don't you ever explain what you're saying? Didn't you use to be a professor?"

He shot me a look. "I did. Some people are teachable and others will never understand. I'm beginning to think you are both the latter."

Liz pushed herself from the wagon, her legs wobbling as she stepped out. A drop of blood left the ends of her fingers and spotted the white earth.

"Should you be getting up?" I asked her.

"I'm fine," she said, looking toward the tower. "Besides, he won't tell us because he plans to kill us. He doesn't want to give it away, right?"

Astor didn't say anything.

Leaving the cart behind, we continued toward the tower.

We walked for another hour before a doorway presented itself, a rectangular black maw in the face of a smooth edifice before the tangled white Woods. Smaller statues of the same figures we'd seen on our way to the Processor lined the steps in front of the door, each a frail figure with hollow eyes and limbs like brittle chalk, hiding amongst folds of loose cloaks. Some held canes in their knobby hands, others sat with crowns like colosseums atop their heads, the architecture fading into their faces and obscuring their features.

All ignored, all left barren along the earth.

We approached the door. The iciness seeping out made me sick to my stomach. For whatever reason, I knew there was emptiness inside; a vacuous space once inhabited and now left to ruin. I froze steps before the opening and couldn't make myself take another. I didn't want to go in. I didn't want to see another forgotten place. What's more: I knew this place more than any other was a place where energy had thrived. While I didn't understand the concept of recycling souls, I imagined it was the closest thing to hope in this demented place, that it was where life was reborn. What was the point of us going inside if all we were going to find was nothing?

Tempest nudged at my hand with her nose.

Astor and Liz glanced back at me from the door.

"Evie?" Liz said.

"I don't want to go inside."

Astor groaned. "We don't have time for this…"

"Shut the fuck up," Liz snarled at him. She walked back to me and reached out to take my right hand in her left. I let her.

"Hey," she whispered. "I need you to do something for me."

I stared past her at the blackened doorway.

"Look at me."

I did. The woman who I'd looked up to for the last ten years of my life was no longer the same as I'd imagined her. Beaten and bloodied, Liz somehow still had a warmth in her eyes, a care I'd known had always been reserved for me, maybe the daughter she'd never had. After everything we'd been through, after everything I'd put her through, she still chose me over the Woods.

"I want you to think about the day when I met you for the first time. Do you remember?"

I nodded. It was raining in my hometown of Cardend. Dad and I had gone to the laundromat. Liz was there, reading a magazine. I'd seen Dad go talk to her, watched his awkward apology with curiosity piquing in my head. She'd seemed so lonely. I'd walked over and invited her to go get pie at our favorite diner. And Dad, though he'd scolded me for talking to a stranger, repeated my invite.

"Remember when we came for you at the hydroelectric plant?"

THE WILD FALL

The plant had been dark and damp. I'd had a cold, my nose and ears stuffed up, my throat sore. I'd dropped my favorite stuffed animal when the men came and ripped me out of bed. In thin pajamas, cowering in a dark office… It was the scariest place I'd been in my life. Mom had been stabbed, Dad wasn't there… And Liz appeared, scooping me up and running with me.

"We?" I whispered.

"My ghost, Brody, helped me get you out. And he's going to do the same thing now."

My lip hung. "What? What do you mean? I thought—"

"I want you to remember how brave you were then and I need you to be that brave now," Liz said. "Because if anyone is getting out of here alive, it's going to be you. Do you understand?"

My throat tightened. I squeezed her fingers. "We're getting out of this together."

"Enough!" Astor barked from the doorway. "Let's go."

"Promise me, Evie," she whispered, her voice cracking.

I nodded, my gaze flickering to the door.

Liz turned and started for the entrance.

I followed, a new resolve tightening in my shoulders. I wasn't going to leave her behind no matter what.

Liz

"I'll carry the pain," Brody had said from the darkness. *"So you don't have to. I owe you that much."*

As I came out of unconsciousness that final time, it was with renewed senses. My arm felt like nothing, a dead weight at my side I had faint control over. When I looked at the wound, at the bloody fabric tied around it, my stomach went to my throat. And then that dissipated.

Brody groaned.

How are you doing this? I had asked.

"We're connected."

I didn't understand it. But I also wasn't going to question it anymore. To be able to move without pain was enough. And I was certain as we entered this Center, we were coming toward a conclusion with Astor that I needed to have my senses for. I let Brody hold the pain. It was a final sacrifice.

Through the blackened doorway was an expansive room with no ceiling. High above, I could see a tiny circle of yellow sky. The longer we stood in the room, the more the darkness adjusted, the easier it became to see what lay around us.

Columns and buttresses made from what appeared to be thousands of human bones encircled the room while a stone staircase corkscrewed around the perimeter of the space down into the ground. A strange bluish light emanated from below, enough light to illuminate only certain shadows and details around us.

Astor walked to the edge of the stairs and looked down. "This must be it."

I cautiously walked beside him and gazed in.

A glimmer of sapphire sparkled far below. It was faint, and seemed to respond to Astor's voice, its aqueous surface pulsating with his next words.

"I would bet this is where the souls are recycled."

"Why are there stairs leading into it?" Evie asked.

"Perhaps because souls make the conscious choice to recycle themselves? It was one of the things they told me when they were instructing me on how to spur on this process again. The sacrifice can't be an accident or caused by killing another."

"That's why you convinced those people to kill themselves," I said.

"It needed to be enough to jump-start the world," Astor said, his tone suggesting I should have understood this all along. "But for some reason, it didn't work. If it had, this would be…more alive. The light would have returned."

I thought about Adora and her followers: souls trapped in the bodies of those they'd haunted. Souls that had escaped the Woods, defied the Others, and exited the cycle.

The souls are corrupted. They can no longer spin.

The words came back to me then, whiplash streaking my brain. What the thing had said under the Monolith all those years ago finally made sense.

"Pure souls," I said under my breath.

"What?" Astor turned to me.

"Adora and her cult couldn't revive the cycle because they hadn't been pure souls. Only pure souls are needed to restart the cycle."

He shook his head, his eyes wide. "Of course. Why hadn't I seen that? Why didn't I…"

"So, a bunch of people have to choose to die? Is that what it means?" Evie murmured.

I turned to look at her.

Where I'd pictured sadness, there was instead anger igniting Evie's features. "That's insane! That's so stupid!"

Astor sat down on the ground and put his head in his hands. "I wasted so much time…"

"Asking people to surrender, asking people to sacrifice themselves for this is…evil," Evie spat.

Tempest rubbed against her, a low growl rumbling in the back of her throat.

I couldn't take my eyes off the blue below. Everything Evie said was true. It was insane. It was stupid. Why was this what was needed to remake the world? Why was this great a sacrifice asked to fix a mistake that wasn't even our fault?

Astor pulled the gun from his belt and trained it on Evie. "Right. No time to waste."

I moved between her and the gun quickly. "What the fuck do you think you're doing?"

"You said it. Pure souls. She's the purest one here."

"The hell you will!" I yelled. "She's one person. You said you needed a bunch of pure souls."

"I've got to start somewhere," he said. "I'll go back and convince others: the right ones this time."

I took a deep breath. "Then you'll have to kill me, too."

He shrugged. "Fine. I had hoped you were going to understand this plan, maybe understand a few dying for the sake of billions was a risk we needed to take. But, you've gone soft. The Liz I met ten years ago would have done whatever it took, I think."

"There's another way," Brody muttered. *"Tell him there's another way."*

What?

Astor steadied his aim.

"Don't shoot. There's another way!"

He cocked his head. "No. There isn't."

"Think about it," Brody added. *"What caused the imbalance? What makes a soulless?"*

I blinked. He was right.

"The wolves," I blurted. "They've stolen innocent human souls for ten years. How many do you think they've eaten? Even one single wolf?"

The confusion in Astor's eyes cleared. "Fuck."

A low howl rippled through the air outside the tower door.

"We've had some following us," I said. "You know it. They smelled my blood. All we need to do is lure them into the well."

"There will be only one way to tempt them," he said.

"I'll be the bait," I volunteered. "We need to get them here though."

Evie shook her head. "There has to be another way."

"We've got limited options. Besides," I said, glancing over my shoulder at her. "We've only got one shot at this. If it doesn't work, he's going to kill us both. He doesn't want to help carry my ass all the way across the desert again and he doesn't want to chaperone you. The man has bigger fish to fry." I looked back at him. "Isn't that right?"

Astor stared back and forth between me and the doorway to the Center. Gradually, he lowered the gun. "If this doesn't work, I'm not even going to warn you before I start shooting."

TWENTY-FIVE

Evie

We only had a few minutes before the wolves came into view. We knew if we climbed the stairs to the windows in the tower, we'd never be able to see their approach over the storm clouds covering the treetops. Plus, it might have been thirty or forty floors before we reached one.

Instead, we fled the tower and regrouped amongst the statues outside. I climbed to the top of the one sitting on its throne with the colosseum crown, positioning myself onto its skinny shoulders to see out over the white plain.

They came in a pack of three, their lithe black bodies skirting over the land like minnows. I relayed the distance to Astor and Liz below.

Tempest padded back and forth, watching me.

I climbed down.

"I think you should stay there," Liz said. "You'd be safer."

"I'm not sitting this out," I answered. "A wolf killed Dad. I'm going to do this for him."

"That's how you're going to get yourself killed, little girl," Astor said. He had gone to retrieve the wooden cart and was pulling it toward the door.

I leveled my gaze with Liz, trying to ignore his words. "For Dad."

She nodded. "For Hank."

We helped Astor push the cart through the enormous doorway. The blue light seemed to have gotten brighter with our activity. Or maybe it was the approach of the wolves. Maybe it sensed souls.

Positioning the cart, Astor looked at Liz. "Okay. Your turn."

Liz unwrapped the sweater from her arm. Bits of skin and hunks of flesh dangled from her. She held the sweater out to Astor. "Time to let the blood do the talking."

Liz

I walked to the door, blood oozing from my wounds. I dipped my fingers in it and painted the stone doorjambs.

Hey.

"Hmm?" Brody was slow to respond. I imagined him in my arms the day he died, the blood coming from his mouth, the distant look in his eyes.

I need to know something.

"What's that?"

Did you stay away because you cared? Or did you stay away because you thought I wouldn't forgive you?

"Lizzy..." His voice sounded hoarse.

I need to know, Brody.

"I never left."

The statement struck me like a pillow hitting my face. Surprise, but not hurt. *What?*

I've been here the whole time. I've been here since I jumped into you at Elon in Maine. A part of me has always stayed. The part of me you killed, the part of me that came back after and watched you was also me. But a different part; an uglier part. And that part stayed away because yes, I do care. Because I do love you. Because you shouldn't forgive me.

My vision blurred. My cheeks singed and a burn in the back of my throat almost made me forget to breathe.

My dreams…

"*I was part of them because I was part of you. Because we are merged.*"

And… Gjon?

"*Maybe he's part of your future.*"

The words tingled, and all over, I watched Gjon die in my arms again. I watched him tell me how much he cared for me by letting me go. I watched him from across the dinner table, laughing at some dumb joke as he poured me wine.

How? How can he be part of my future when he's gone?

I imagined Brody shaking his head as he said, "*He's not gone. All he needs is to be recycled.*"

"Liz!" Astor shouted from inside the doorway. "They're coming."

I wiped the tears from my face. "I don't understand," I whispered to myself.

"*You will.*"

Evie

I heard the first one before I saw it. It sniffed from outside the main entrance, its snorts loud. Then, I watched its head pass through the doorway, tongue dragging along the jamb to taste the blood Liz had wiped there.

Rage made me lightheaded. I was staring into the face of a thing that had killed so many, of a kind that took my dad from me before it was his time.

The face drawn in a snarl, its black lips curled, white shining off its golden eyes, slick fur bristling like grass along its backside and the tail, like a whip. Behind it, the other two followed, sauntering, their shoulders sharp and muscles lean.

I tensed, my grip on the rope tightening. I watched Liz in the cart and feeling drained from my face. Her eyes were glossy, her pallor white. She looked like she was barely awake. Her hands were on the rope but I wasn't sure she had the strength to hang on even if she wanted to.

"Almost…" Astor said under his breath next to me.

The wolf in the lead finally locked eyes on the cart and Liz.

It froze.

I inhaled through my nose and I stared at its eyes, even as its teeth bared and it stooped low. The others followed suit, one sidling to the left while the other took the right.

Astor braced his feet, leaning back. "Get ready."

The first wolf jumped, talons raking the air.

"Now!"

I gnashed my teeth together and yanked with everything I had.

The cart rolled off the edge toward the abyss. The wolf on the left jumped after the first.

My heart pounded as Liz fell, the rope swinging in a wide arc.

The lead wolf collided with the cart as it cascaded into the depths, cracking on the side wall of the well. Both were gone before I could blink.

Liz slammed against the backside of the well-wall, and the rope jumped with her weight as we held on.

The second wolf yipped as it snapped at her and missed, its form twisting and turning as it plummeted into the blue yonder below.

My whole body careened forward with the new weight and I strained to get it under control. Below, Liz groaned and held onto the loop tied around her waist and through her legs. I could only imagine how much it hurt.

"Fuck," Astor grunted, his eyes bugging.

The third wolf glared at us and loped around the edge of the well toward us.

"Fuck!" I yelled. "Fuck!"

"Let go!" Liz called from below.

The wolf sprang, its claws slicing into Astor's frame. He yelped as he was slammed against the wall next to me, his body bouncing off from it and stumbling over the brink of the well. The wolf held onto him as they dropped, his scream uncurling agony inside of me, before they promptly vanished against the ocean of blue.

I fell forward; the rope and Liz pulling me toward the edge, I braced myself. My boots caught on the stone lip and yanked me upright once more.

Liz dangled below, staring at me. "Let go, Evie!"

"No!"

"You can't hold me! You'll fall, too!"

"I can fall!" I yelled back without even thinking, the words rolling out of me like a churning sea. "I don't want you to die!"

My fingers burned. I closed my eyes. My neck and arms and legs labored with effort. *Don't let go*, I chanted to myself.

"It's not dying!"

I opened my eyes. "What?"

"I'm being recycled. I'm coming back."

My hands burned, the cut from the bonfire screaming with the agony of the rope's rough surface.

I cried: unhinged, abysmal, primal, and let go.

Liz

I fell into the blue.

Moments shattered the world in front of me, pulled existence like cotton candy swirling and ebbing in a haze.

Gjon's shoulder pushed against mine in the bleak cell. His smell as we embraced for what I thought might have been the last time. His voice as he told me about his dreams. The warmth of his arms around me as we nestled in a bed too small for both of us.

Richard's gentle voice as he strummed his guitar. The light from the morning sun as he walked the rows of green sprouts in the garden and watered them.

Nettie's rare smile. Her food, an expression of her love, and the happiness that fluttered in my stomach like moths whenever I finished one of her meals. A short white dress on her tiny figure.

Hank's scarred lip twitching at the prospect of danger. The light green of his eyes as he told me not to worry, as he put his hand in mine. The feeling of him lifting me over the fence… His wedding, dappled in sunlight.

Josh. His mischievous, gorgeous grin. The sound of his voice on the phone. His weight on me when we made love. His ring gliding onto my finger.

Brody. Our coffee breaks. Our heart-to-hearts. Our fights. Our apologies. I felt him in me, filling the grooves in my fingerprints, the hollows of my curves, the everything and the nothing I had become.

They were all there. Every one of them was a part of the blue, a part of the vortex as it churned and writhed and rode over me.

We walked on the beach.

We hiked through the weeds and the burrs to the apple orchard.

We talked in bed.

We sat across one another at dinner.

We cooked. We ate.

We married.

We caressed. We joined. We existed.

I was whole.

We were whole and alive.

TWENTY-SIX

Evie

Tempest's nose poked at my face, the cold wetness of it plucking me out of my sorrow.

There was a sound, a rumbling building from below. When I looked at the well, I was met with a light too bright to look at. I covered my eyes.

Forcing myself to my feet, I followed Tempest to the doorway and gazed out over the vast white landscape as it morphed before our eyes. Trees broke through the ground as vast cracks skittered along the surface to make room for them. The old statues fell apart, limbs crumbling with the trembling of the earth, the partitioning of old soil to greet new life.

Tempest barked as she backed away from the building. I turned, realizing the light had grown to fill the entire space inside, and now pierced through the dark clouds over the white Woods at its base.

Grabbing Tempest's collar, we took shelter under the doorway as the forest continued to grow and change around us, bursting with new greenery, with life.

TWENTY-SEVEN

Evie

The town of Gregory appeared out of the mist of a fading forest. It reminded me a lot of Onyx River. A covered bridge signaled the way into town, which crossed a small river. We walked an empty road lined with white-sided, green metal-roofed homes. Each one sat on a small hill with stairs clambering to a front porch.

Tempest padded at my side, her ears pricked, her eyes watching the neighborhood for any activity. I hefted the messenger bag over my shoulder, lighter now as we'd been on the road for the last couple days. There was almost nothing left and we had drank the rest of our water that morning. Being in a place with a running river was a comfort.

I didn't see the door open. It was out of my vision, a house we'd already passed.

"Evie!"

The voice turned me around, made me spring for the knife we'd found along the way, our only weapon.

Gretchen stood on the steps to the first house after the bridge, her hands covering her mouth. Sanz stood behind her and let out a baying woof, her rusty ears perked

Ash emerged from the door behind her, Otto nosing out between his legs. "Holy shit." He smiled.

Deliriousness doubled over me. I dropped the bag and ran to them.

Gretchen met on the steps, her arms clinging to me, her cries mixing with my own. Moments later, Ash's arms folded over both of us.

Tempest yipped and rubbed at the other dogs, her eyes bright and tongue lolling. They danced around each other, panting and barking and licking one another.

"I'm so glad you're here," I sobbed.

We all sat on the steps, still hugging. I didn't want them to let go. I didn't want to ever let go of them.

"Liz?" Gretchen whispered the question.

I shook my head. "She's okay now," I added, forcing myself to swallow the hard lump in my throat. "I think she's in a better place."

Gretchen's face pinched, fresh tears mixing with the others.

Ash took off his hat and closed his eyes, a single sob escaping his lips.

We retrieved the bag from where I'd left it and walked into the house. It reminded me so much of our home at the cabin in Middlehitch: the pastoral daylight-soaked entryway with a coat rack on the wall beneath the stairs, the kitchen in a room off to the left, a living area off to the right with cat-scratched couches and a cast-iron wood stove.

It was as if I was reliving a memory and somewhere inside of it, there was a presence, a thing that crackled with vibrancy, with energy, with love. Somehow, everything I had left behind was there like an ember glowing in the ashes. I sat on the couch and closed my eyes and thought of home. I thought of everything that had already been and was yet to come.

ACKNOWLEDGMENTS

Many thanks goes to the incredible number of people who have supported me in my endeavor to bring you The Wild Oblivion stories over the last couple years.

Rebecca Cuthbert: you are a wonderful editor, author, and friend and I appreciate the time you took to look at this book. You're the best.

To Wendy Dalrymple, Erica Robyn, Paul Preston, and Steve Talks Books for help with my cover reveal! This is a cover I'm proud of and you all treated its release with such kindness.

A special thank you to the authors who have blurbed my book [names to be added before publication]. I was intimidated to ask anyone to blurb a sequel and you were all so wonderful about it.

To my friends and writers in arms: Todd Keisling, Rob Ottone, Michael Tyree. I can't tell you how much I appreciate your friendship and support.

To my awesome partner in crime, Colin: you've listened to me go on about this universe for years now and I appreciate how you bounce back with ideas to get me out of corners, with comforting shoulder rubs, and delicious dinners to keep me going. You rock.

STAY TUNED

FOR

MORE STORIES

FROM

THE

WILD

OBLIVION

photo by Colin Borowske © 2023

Katherine Silva is a Maine horror author, a connoisseur of coffee, and victim of cat shenanigans. She is a two-time Maine Literary Award finalist for speculative fiction and a member of the Horror Writers of Maine, The Horror Writers Association, and New England Horror Writers Association. Katherine is also editor-in-chief of Strange Wilds Press. Her latest works are all novelettes within The Wild Oblivion universe and are now available wherever books are sold. A sequel to *THE WILD DARK* entitled, *THE WILD FALL*, is due out in August 2023.